Neal & Merry Book 6

MURDEROUS SECRETS

A brilliantly gripping crime mystery

JANICE FROST

First published 2018
Joffe Books, London
www.joffebooks.com

Please join our mailing list for free Kindle books and new releases.

www.joffebooks.com

ISBN 978-1-78931-255-3

To my lovely friend, Nikki Kennedy. Thank you for all your support over the years.

ACKNOWLEDGEMENTS

My thanks to Greg Algar for showing me around his micro-brewery at The Dambusters Inn, Scampton, Lincolnshre and for taking the time out of his busy schedule to answer all my rookie questions about the mysterious process of brewing beer.

My thanks also to Darren Bell of Lincoln Yurts for sharing with me his knowlege of running a glamping business.

CHAPTER ONE

Ava Merry was feeling distinctly underdressed. She had just arrived at PJ's flat, expecting to be greeted by a fellow 'land girl.' Instead, a vision of floaty 1940s loveliness appeared at the door holding a glass of fizz. PJ — real name Polly-Jane, though no one called her that — was Ava's friend and colleague. She had recently become a detective constable, working alongside Ava, who was a detective sergeant. She had also recently broken up with her fiancé.

"You're inappropriately dressed for bringing in the harvest or mucking out the pigsty," Ava pointed out.

"I know, I know. Sorry. I know we agreed we'd both dress as land girls . . ." PJ ushered Ava into her tiny flat. "But that get-up looked awful on me." She gave Ava the once-over. "Alright for you with your tiny waist. Dungarees make me look like a sack of potatoes tied in the middle."

Instead, PJ wore a knee-length periwinkle blue dress of some slinky, rayon material. It had shirring at the waist to flatter her size 14 curves. She had done a great job on her hair, too. Her naturally unruly mop, which she often straightened until it was sleek and glossy, was set with smooth curls. No way had she managed that on her own.

Ava thought of the hour she'd spent in front of a YouTube teach-yourself-vintage-hairstyles video to achieve her own poor imitation of victory rolls. Thankfully, a red-and-white-checked headscarf hid the messier bits. She gave a soft whistle. "You look like a 1940s pin-up girl. Veronica Lake or Rita Hayworth."

"Well, you look glam, too, even in bib 'n' braces. Then again, you'd look sexy in an old bin bag."

Ava laughed. PJ's self-confidence had taken a downturn since her fiancé, Steve, had ditched her in favour of travelling the world and embracing new experiences. He'd had a cancer scare and, after obtaining the all-clear, he'd decided that he needed to live each day to the utmost. His plans to travel the globe didn't include marriage and settling down with PJ.

Still, PJ was a naturally optimistic person, with a bubbly personality and a big heart. Ava was sure she'd bounce back, given a little time. The 1940s dance had been PJ's suggestion, and Ava had been happy to go along with it. She hoped a night of jiving and bopping to big band music would be just the thing to lift her friend's mood.

It was the sort of event that Jim Neal would shun, Ava thought, her mind straying to their serious, sometimes dour, DI. Neal was in Scotland attending the wedding of his younger sister, Maggie, to his best friend, Jock Dodds. Neal was best man. Ava had been invited. A sigh escaped her, unchecked.

"Wishing you were in Edinburgh?" PJ was a mind-reader when it came to emotions.

"No, I was just thinking how much Jim Neal would hate the prospect of spending an evening in a draughty old barn with a bunch of 1940s geeks."

"They're not geeks. It's a themed dance. But you're right. He'd hate it. Shame. I can totally see him rocking the glam RAF pilot look. You know, little leather bomber jacket with sheepskin lining? Aviator goggles?"

Ava rolled her eyes, but the image PJ had planted in her mind was not unappealing. "Alright, Betty Grable," she said. "How about lending me some of that red lippy you're wearing?"

"Sure. I'll just get it for you. Glass of wine while we wait for our ride?"

"Okay, thanks, Peej." Ava helped herself from a half-empty bottle of prosecco in the fridge.

This was only her second visit to PJ's new place. The first time had been when she helped PJ move in. It hadn't been a happy occasion. After Steve had had his life-changing experience, the house they had been buying together had to be sold. PJ couldn't have afforded the mortgage on her detective constable's salary.

Ava looked around. "You've done the place up nicely." The one-bedroomed rented flat had been empty when PJ moved in but, after coming to a financial arrangement with Steve, she had now brought most of the furniture and other household items from the house they'd shared.

"Yeah, well. Makes a difference when you get all your things arranged the way you want them. Trouble is, everything reminds me of bloody Steve." She handed Ava the lipstick. Suddenly, she covered her mouth. "Oh, Ava! I'm so sorry, I forgot to ask how Ollie's getting on!"

Ollie was the reason Ava had been unable to go to Maggie and Jock's wedding. The day before she was due to depart for Scotland, her seventeen-year-old brother, who lived with her, had been rushed to hospital with what turned out to be a burst appendix. There was no way she could leave him.

"It's okay. He's doing really well."

"And how are you coping with your mum's visit?"

Ava sighed deeply. "She only just arrived this morning, and already we're driving one another bonkers. She's pining for her latest man. But the worst thing is she keeps asking why I haven't met anyone yet. It broke her heart when I stopped seeing Joel, even though she never actually met him." Ava had a brief affair with an A&E doctor, Joel Agard, about a year and a half before. She'd liked him a lot, but not as much as he'd liked her, and they'd gone their separate ways. "Thank goodness she's leaving soon."

"Well, at least you're getting away from her for a few hours this evening." They chinked glasses.

A few minutes later, a horn outside alerted them to the arrival of their taxi.

Their driver, who immediately introduced himself as Arthur Spencer, was the chatty type. He was very interested in their costumes and the event he was driving them to. "The wife and I love dancing. Ballroom, mind you. Friends reckon we're better than some of them what's on *Strictly*."

PJ, a more sociable soul than Ava, chattered back. Ava suspected that before they reached their destination, PJ and the driver would discover that they were related in some way — third cousins twice removed at the very least. PJ was Stromford born and bred. She seemed to know or be related to half the county.

Now that her brother Ollie had moved in with her, Ava didn't go back home much. She figured it had to be weird to live somewhere all your life, like PJ, meeting people you went to school with in the street and knowing everybody's business. Sometimes PJ's local knowledge was useful for her job, though. No one else in the team was from these parts. Tom, the other detective sergeant, was from London, and Neal, of course, was Scottish.

"Right out in the sticks, isn't it?" Arthur commented.

Ava looked out the window. There wasn't much to see now that they'd left the bright lights of Stromford behind, just darkness and black shapes that were probably hedgerows and trees. PJ had told her the event was being held in a barn owned by the Stratford family. They'd bought the farmhouse and some of the land surrounding it to run a glamping business and brew beer. The dance had been organised by a local charity to raise money for a nearby hospice.

The city of Stromford was surrounded by countryside, much of it farmland. There was no need to travel far to feel a long way from anywhere. Ava lived only three miles south of the centre of Stromford, in a rented cottage on a quiet country lane that felt much more distant from the city than it actually was. It didn't suit her mother at all. She preferred bright lights and big cities to rural peace and quiet. Just as well. She'd probably visit more often if Stromford appealed to her.

"How far did you say this place was again?" she asked PJ, when she could get a word in.

"About twenty-four miles from Stromford. Should be there soon. We've been going for half an hour already."

"Another ten minutes, I reckon," the driver chirped. "How are you young ladies getting back later?"

"Taxi," PJ said. It was no surprise when Arthur volunteered his services. At least PJ would probably be drunk and fall asleep on the way back, Ava thought. She wouldn't have to listen to her and Arthur's banter.

Arthur missed the turn-off. The satnav had gone quiet some time before, baffled, no doubt, by the expanse of flat nothingness all around.

"I've gone too far," he said. "Too busy gassing. I brought a passenger out this way earlier today, funny enough. I don't often come this far out of town, never mind twice in one day. He wasn't the chatty type, mind. Bit of a toff, I reckon. Too good to talk to the likes of me."

Arthur executed a neat U-turn and backtracked a mile or so up the road. Then, without warning, he veered sharply to the left, tipping PJ sideways onto Ava, momentarily crushing her against the door.

"Sorry, ladies. Nearly missed the road again in the dark."

It was more of a track than a road. Five minutes of bumping over uneven ground. There go my victory rolls, Ava thought, feeling her hair loosening some more at every jolt.

"I can see some lights," PJ, said, sounding like an excited child. Ava saw them, too — straight ahead, twinkling through a small conifer plantation that screened the farm buildings from the track.

"We have arrived!" Arthur announced, swerving round a long bend. The track opened into a cobbled farmyard flanked by a stone-built farmhouse and a cluster of rustic outbuildings.

The barn was a short distance from the house, beyond another cluster of outbuildings. A succession of light-reflective arrows pointed the way. As they drew closer, the smooth strains of 'Moonlight Serenade' drifted through the frosty night air to greet them.

Arthur drove past rows of parked cars and then pulled up at a rough concrete ramp alongside the barn. PJ tipped him — rather extravagantly, to Ava's way of thinking. He promised to pick them up, whatever time of night — or morning — they called.

They looked at some of the guests milling around outside the barn entrance. "Loving the costumes," said PJ. An eclectic mix of military and civilian dress from the period was on show. Some costumes looked as though they had been hired, others had probably been scavenged from vintage clothes stalls or charity shops. To Ava's relief, she wasn't the only land girl. As they stood in the queue to show their tickets, an air raid warden in a tin hat and a woollen waistcoat winked at her and asked if she'd save him a dance. PJ grabbed Ava by the arm and propelled her towards the entrance.

"Cool," Ava said, taking in the vaulted ceiling, exposed brickwork, timber beams and twinkly lights.

"Big, isn't it?" PJ said.

"Vast," Ava agreed.

Tables were arranged around the barn's perimeter, leaving plenty of room in the centre for dancing. On a temporary stage, the band was now playing another Glenn Miller favourite: 'In the Mood.' A buffet was laid out on trestle tables topped with red, white and blue checked cloths. Ava spotted a stall selling hot dogs and burgers, but it was the bar that had caught her friend's attention. "Come on," PJ urged, "Let's get our first drink in."

The band seemed to have exhausted its Glenn Miller repertoire for now. It struck up a lively dance number, immediately drawing lots more people onto the floor. One or two couples, obviously practised at forties dance steps, were demonstrating how to do the jitterbug.

"They've certainly gone to town," Ava said. "It's for a good cause though, isn't it?"

"Yes. A hospice in Langby." Langby was a pretty market town in the Stromfordshire Wolds, and the nearest town to where they were now.

They had to push and shove their way to the bar through a throng of people. PJ ordered two lime daiquiris, "To ease us into the theme." Then, they chose a table with a good view of the dance floor.

Ava sipped her drink, feeling contented. For now, her sense of disappointment over missing the wedding had retreated. It wasn't long before she and PJ were up on the dance floor, learning the steps to the Jitterbug and the Lindy Hop as they went along. It was great fun. As the evening wore on and she started feeling a bit tipsy, Ava switched to tonic water. She wasn't on duty until Monday morning, but she was looking forward to a long run the following day and didn't want it hijacked by a hangover.

PJ, on the other hand, was well on the way to being drunk. "I haven't had this much fun in ages!" She collapsed into her seat after some energetic jiving. "Steve was a bit of a stay-at-home."

"Your sailor looked like he was having fun, too," Ava said. PJ's most recent dance partner was a young man dressed in an American navy uniform — just as if he'd stepped out of the musical *On the Town*.

"He's my cousin," PJ sighed. Her eyes roved around the dance floor. "Hey, check out Gregory Peck over there! He's really hot and, as far as I know, we're not related."

Ava grinned, recognising the PJ that she knew and loved. When a red-haired man in an RAF uniform asked PJ to dance, Ava decided to slip out of the barn to get some fresh air. She zigzagged across the dance floor, dodging couples slow-dancing to a trio of crooning female vocalists who had taken over from the band.

The air wasn't all that fresh directly outside the barn, for a group of smokers had congregated there. Ava gave them a wide berth.

A small group of young lads caught her attention. They were heading in the direction of some outbuildings beyond the farmhouse. Ava followed behind them. No harm in seeing what they were up to.

She watched as the smallest of them tried the door of one of the larger outbuildings. To her surprise, it was unlocked. All three went inside.

Some instinct stirred within Ava. It wasn't that she suspected something was wrong, but the unlocked door bothered her. The boys had left it ajar. She stole a look inside. One of the boys was shining his phone on a bottle of vodka that another had produced from inside his jacket. So that's what they were up to. They took turns to have a swig.

It was hard to be certain, but they looked to be around twelve years old — definitely too young to be consuming alcohol. Ava was reluctant to spoil their fun, but knew she should intervene.

She was about to step forward, when one of the lads said, "What's that?" She froze. "Shine a light over there, Ed."

Ed obliged. The beam of light from his phone illuminated a vehicle of some sort, old and khaki-coloured. "It's an old ambulance from the war," Ed said, angling his phone light at the familiar Red Cross symbol on the side of the vehicle.

"Cool," said one of his friends. The bottle was forgotten in their excitement.

"See if it's open, Kieran," Ed said. Kieran obeyed, stopping only to activate the torch on his own phone. Watching him, Ava felt an inexplicable quiver of unease.

Kieran pulled on the handle of the right-hand door to the ambulance. There was a moment's silence, followed by a slightly hysterical laugh.

"There's a dummy inside dressed up like a sort of gangster."

Ed and the other boy jostled to be next aboard to see what Kieran was talking about. Ava overheard snippets of their conversation.

"Kind of . . . realistic . . ."

"Gone a bit over the top with the blood . . ."

"Looks like a scene from that horror movie me and my brother saw last week . . ."

Her heart gave a sudden lurch. She felt an unwelcome sense of foreboding. Time to announce her presence. She crossed to the ambulance and mounted the step, startling the boys, but it couldn't be helped. The first thing she noticed was the familiar coppery scent of blood. "Right, you lot, out now!" she ordered. They didn't need telling twice.

The dead man, who was dressed as a wartime spiv, was lying on an old-fashioned, narrow wooden stretcher. His right arm hung rigid and lifeless over the side, the fingers of his hand almost brushing the floor. His throat had been cut — inexpertly. Blood from a ragged slash to his neck had pooled in the collar of his white shirt and was already beginning to dry. Rips and tears all over his blood-soaked jacket spoke of multiple other wounds. His wide-open eyes stared at the ceiling as if in astonishment.

Ava took a step closer. She felt for a pulse. Nothing.

After a moment or two, she turned away and stepped down from the vehicle, pulling the door shut behind her. She slid the bolt back into place.

The lads, gathered near the door of the ambulance, had fallen silent. Their grave faces told her they had finally grasped that what they had seen was no dummy.

CHAPTER TWO

"What's your name?" Ava demanded of the young man nearest her, the one whose name had not been revealed.

"M-Matt," he said, in a shaky voice.

"Right, Matt. I want you to run back to the barn and find one of the organisers. Look for someone wearing a yellow sash with the name of the charity written on it. Ask them to bring whoever's in charge over here, immediately. Don't tell them what's up. The fewer people who know about this the better. The last thing we want is a full-scale panic and everyone stampeding to the nearest exit."

"Who says you're in charge?" It was Ed.

Ava stuck her hand inside the cross-body bag she was wearing and pulled out her police ID. "I do. Or, rather, this does." That shut him up.

Matt ran off on his errand. Ava asked the two remaining boys if their parents were at the dance. They nodded. They were dressed identically in baggy trousers and white shirts with polka dot ties. Their hair was slicked back with gel. Even allowing for the clothes, they seemed oddly alike.

"Are you two related to each other?" Ava asked. It turned out they were non-identical twins. The other boy, Matt, was their cousin.

"Can we go?" one of them asked.

Ava had no power to keep them there. After making a note of their names, she said, with some reluctance, "Okay, you can go, but . . . I'd be grateful if you'd keep this to yourselves, at least until more police arrive."

They both nodded, solemnly. Ava suspected that the cat would be well and truly out of the bag the second they were out of sight. She needed to act fast. Where the hell was that official?

While she waited, she called it in.

Matt returned at last, accompanied by a man and a woman, who had clearly been well briefed despite Ava's instructions.

"Bea Stratford," the woman said, looking worried. "This is my husband, Aubrey. We own the farm." She pointed at Matt. "This excitable young man came to us spouting some nonsense about a dead body in the back of the ambulance." Matt stared down, guiltily.

"I'm afraid it's not nonsense," Ava said. "Thanks, Matt. You can go now." *Go forth and spread the word.* She showed her ID to Aubrey and Bea Stratford to convince them that she had some authority.

Aubrey took a step towards the ambulance. Ava blocked him. "I'm sorry, but I can't let you do that, Mr Stratford. I need to protect the integrity of the crime scene." It had already been compromised by the three boys — not to mention herself. No way was anyone else going in there.

"It's my vehicle," Aubrey said. "This is our land, our property." Ava half expected him to claim ownership of the body in the ambulance, too. It was interesting that neither of the Stratfords had asked for the identity of the murder victim. Perhaps they wouldn't believe the story was true as long as the doors remained closed.

"The police will be here soon," Ava informed them. "They'll need to cordon off this whole area. We need to bring the dance to an end as soon as possible. Ideally, we need to get contact details from everyone at the dance, including the organisers and any bar or catering staff." She frowned. It was a near impossible task without backup. People had been coming and going all evening. "Do you have a guest list for this evening's event?"

Aubrey and Bea exchanged looks. "Yes," Bea said, bringing music to Ava's ears. "The tickets were numbered. I wrote the names of people who bought tickets next to the numbers on my sheet. It saves a problem if people forget their tickets. We can just check their names against the numbers. Members of the charity committee did the same thing with the tickets they sold."

That was something, at least. Bea's eyes slid to the bolted door of the ambulance. She looked a little fearful. "Who is it?"

"I don't know. I couldn't search through his pockets. I don't have any gloves."

"Where's Monty?" Bea looked suddenly stricken.

"He's in the barn," her husband said. "For heaven's sake, Bea, you saw him ten minutes ago! It's hardly going to be him in there."

"I know, I know." Bea turned to Ava. "Monty is our son."

"Right." Ava was relieved to see two uniformed police officers step into the building. She asked one of them to guard the crime scene, before returning to the barn with the other, along with Aubrey and Bea Stratford.

It was immediately obvious that word had spread. A small group of people, mainly middle-aged, had assembled in the area near the door.

"They're members of the charity committee," Bea whispered to Ava. A man broke through the group, and marched up to Aubrey and Bea.

"What's up? Everything alright, Aubrey? Is it true what these boys have been saying? Surely not!" Bea introduced the slightly dishevelled-looking man as Charles Unwin, Aubrey's friend from the village. Everyone in the group was wearing forties clothing, but Charles looked as though he lived in his attire every day. He seemed less in costume than in role.

Ava ignored the lot of them and asked the police constable her name.

"I'm PC Olivia Cotton. There's another patrol car from Langby on its way. ETA five minutes."

"Good." Ava looked at PC Cotton. "Stay here and make sure no one tries to leave without giving you their contact details." She turned to Bea. "I know you've got a list, but there could be some gatecrashers — or people who couldn't attend might have passed their tickets on." Nodding at the stage, she said, "I need to make an announcement. May I borrow the mike?"

Aubrey Stratford led Ava to the stage where a woman in a WAAF uniform was singing 'The White Cliffs of Dover', a song that normally brought a tear to Ava's eye because it reminded her of her grandparents. That evening, though, there was no time for sentiment. She marched up to the Vera Lynn impersonator and politely requested the mike.

Vera had obviously noticed the commotion over by the door and the presence of a police constable. She stepped aside immediately, clearing the stage for Ava. Ava scanned the dancers on the floor, noting that PJ was still coupled with her red-haired airman. People stared at Ava with expressions ranging from surprise to annoyance. Everyone wanted to know why the music had stopped so abruptly. Ava felt suddenly nervous as she cleared her throat.

"Good evening. I'm Detective Sergeant Ava Merry. I regret to inform you that, due to a serious incident, the dance will be ending now. I'd be grateful if you would all remain in the barn until the police have taken your contact details. We're expecting more officers to arrive shortly. I must stress that there is no need to be alarmed. The incident is under control." There was a screech of feedback, after which, she carried on. "We will try to ensure that you are all on your way as soon as possible. Thank you for your cooperation in this matter." Looking towards the door, she was relieved to see that more uniformed backup had just turned up.

That was a bit botched, she thought afterwards. She'd hadn't expected to be affected by stage fright. It wasn't as if she lacked confidence. Yet her fingers were numb from gripping the mike tightly, to stop them shaking.

Last time she'd been on stage was over a decade before in a school production of *Romeo and Juliet* — in which she had played Juliet. There had been no stage fright back then. She'd relished the attention.

PJ had pushed her way through the throng of people to the stage. She approached Ava as soon as she stepped down. "What's going on, Ava?" Her words were slurry. "Can I help?"

"Thanks for the offer, Peej. No offence, but you're not in a state to be of any use."

"I do feel a bit off. Must have been that burger I ate earlier."

"Yep, definitely the burger," Ava said, leading her friend to a table and sitting her down. In a hushed voice, she said, "It's going to be a long night. I'll call you a cab."

"Okaay. Arthur said—"

"I've got his number." She patted PJ's hand, glad that her friend had forgotten she'd asked a question about what was going on. But others were gathering to ask the same thing.

"What's going on?" a voice demanded behind Ava. People were curious, anxious. They wanted information. It was only natural.

"I'm not at liberty to say at the moment, sir."

"Bloody police!" another voice complained in a strong Stromfordshire accent. "You put the wind up people not letting them know what's going on."

"You'll find out soon enough. Excuse me." Ava pushed her way through the gathering of disgruntled bodies. She couldn't blame them for being annoyed. They'd come here for a night out and now they were likely to be hanging around at a loose end for a couple of hours. Ava wondered if she should ask the Stratfords to shut the bar. Probably too late for that already. Most of the guests looked flushed, and not just from dancing. People were flocking to join an already long queue.

Things started to pick up pace. Forensics arrived and, just behind them, Ava's colleague and fellow detective sergeant, Tom Knight, impeccably dressed, as ever.

"Have you been drinking?" he asked Ava. To her irritation he leaned towards her as if to catch a whiff of her breath.

"I had a couple. I'm perfectly sober." Still, Ava acknowledged that she could not take the lead here. With a sigh, she deferred to Tom. She led him to the outbuildings, with Aubrey and his friend Charles Unwin following on behind. Bea had disappeared.

Aubrey explained that the two nearest outbuildings housed his workshops, where he worked on his vintage cars and made scaled-down models of World War Two vehicles. "Tanks and the like," he said. "The odd battleship."

Ava watched from the sidelines as Tom and the CSIs suited up. Aubrey and Charles stood next to her, both looking tense.

One of the CSIs, Dan Cardew, slid back the bolt on the ambulance doors. He and Tom stepped inside.

Beside Ava, Aubrey Stratford muttered something under his breath. It sounded like, "Poor Ingrid."

She turned to him, raising her eyebrows. "Ingrid?"

He nodded at the vehicle.

"Oh, the ambulance?" For Ingrid Bergman, she supposed.

"Yes. Of course, the ambulance. She's my pride and joy. Restored her from scrap, you know. Took her along to the local stately home a few weeks ago, with Albert in the back."

"Albert?"

"He's an old mannequin. Rescued him from a skip outside Marks and Spencer's. I use him as a dummy patient to add authenticity. Looks very realistic wrapped up in bandages daubed with red paint. I even got complaints from parents that he was scaring their children . . ." His voice trailed off.

Had she made a terrible mistake? Was it only Albert lying in there painted in fake blood? Tom's voice, coming from deep inside Ingrid's bowels, was reassuring. "Victim is a white male, early to mid-twenties. Cause of death appears to be exsanguination." No doubt for clarification he added, "His throat's been cut."

Bea reappeared, accompanied by a man dressed in pleated trousers and a red moleskin waistcoat, two-tone shoes and a beige trilby, as if he'd been to a forties pick-and-mix store. Monty, Ava guessed.

She tried not to stare at the dreadlocks that spilled like a mane from under his trilby. A keen intelligence shone in his eyes but there was also a wariness about him that made Ava wonder if he had reason to be suspicious of the police.

Bea had apparently overheard her husband's reference to Albert. She rolled her eyes. "Not really appropriate in the circumstances, dear," she said.

Her son stood by, silent and intense, and Ava felt as if she was under scrutiny, even though Monty didn't look at her at all. His eyes were on the ambulance. He seemed watchful, inquisitive and slightly hostile, all at the same time. A complex character, if ever she saw one. How old was he? Late twenties, early thirties? It was hard to tell. He looked young, but with the wisdom of age. She could picture him as a character in a fantasy novel, which she read occasionally both for relaxation and so that she could talk to Ollie about them. Monty would be both the reluctant hero type and the wise old mentor rolled into one. But it turned out this wasn't Monty Stratford at all. Bea introduced him as Soren Hunter, an employee.

Hunter's eyes darted over the activity in and around the ambulance, taking everything in: Dan photographing the body; Tom bending low to look under the stretcher; the uniforms setting up a cordon around the scene. It was unnerving when his gaze finally landed on her.

"And you are?"

"Detective Sergeant Ava Merry." With reluctance, she added, "I'm off duty."

"Right. Not a lot of point in your being here, then, is there? Presumably you've been drinking?"

"Only a couple. I'm not drunk. I called this in." Why was she justifying herself to him? Ava felt herself bristle with annoyance. But he wasn't interested in her now; he was back to watching — no, *assessing* — everything that was going on around him.

He was right about her being superfluous, though. Tom was in charge here, for now. He'd mentioned that DI Kerry Short, as officer on call that night, was on her way to act as the senior officer in charge. The case was likely to pass to Neal on his return from Scotland the following day.

Still, Ava couldn't pull herself away. She'd be working this case, too, inevitably. How she regretted those two lime daiquiris that were keeping her from being in the thick of it. She'd only had them to keep PJ company.

Tom jumped down from the ambulance. Ava slipped under the cordon. She was eager to hear his thoughts.

"I found some ID in the victim's pocket." He lowered his voice. "His name is Nick Winter."

"Oh!" It was Bea Stratford. Turning around, Ava saw that Bea was covering her mouth. Hunter was frowning. Evidently, Tom hadn't lowered his voice enough to stop them catching a familiar name.

"You know the victim?" Tom asked.

"He was one of our guests," Bea said.

"Guests?"

"We run a glamping business on our land. Nick Winter was staying in one of our yurts."

"The *Game of Thrones* themed one," Aubrey said.

"His partner, Samantha Benrose, was staying with him." Bea looked panicky. "Oh dear! What if . . . ? We need to check if she's okay!"

"Is she in the barn with the others?"

"No, I haven't seen her — she should've been coming to the dance with Nick but they must have been running la—" Bea broke off, realising why they may not have arrived.

"I'll go," Hunter volunteered immediately.

"I'm coming with you," Ava said. To her relief, Tom didn't object.

Outside, away from the farmhouse and its outbuildings, the sudden darkness was a surprise. Ava had forgotten that they were deep in the countryside. No street lights here, only the moonlight. She could see constellations of stars bright with a cold, alien light. She shivered.

Soren was prepared. He passed Ava a torch, having already switched on another one for himself. Who carried two torches? she asked herself. He led the way across the crunchy, glittering field. With every inward breath, Ava felt the frosty night air scrape her throat and snake down into her lungs, making her chest feel tight. It didn't seem to be affecting Hunter, who was practically running. Fit as she was, Ava struggled to keep apace.

The darkness seemed to intensify the farther they left the farm behind. Presently, they came to an area of woodland. Here, the darkness was almost complete, inky black in the places where moon and stars couldn't reach. Ava shone her torch into black banks of tangled undergrowth, starting once when a pair of bright eyes shone back at her. An owl hooted, and all around them creatures seemed to stir in protest at their unwelcome human presence.

They reached a clearing. There was water gurgling nearby, Ava noted now that they'd stopped — a stream, most likely. In the daylight, it had to be an idyllic spot, but who would want to camp out here on a winter's night? Of course, it *was* Valentine's Day. Couples looking for a romantic get-away might be tempted by the woodland setting and the cosiness of a yurt with a wood-burning stove.

Hunter stopped abruptly.

"What is it?" Ava whispered. "Did you hear something? See something?" The latter was unlikely, given the darkness.

"It's more what I'm not hearing."

"What do you mean?"

"Nick and Samantha's yurt is behind those bushes. There's a wind chime in the trees outside. There's a slight breeze. We should be able to hear it."

Ava shuddered. Was Hunter trying to spook her? If so, he was doing a good job. "Maybe they took it down? Not everyone likes the constant jingling of those things. It might have kept them awake."

"It's not just that. It's a cold night . . ."

"And?"

"The yurts have wood-burning stoves. There's no smell of wood smoke — no sign of it, either."

"Right." Ava swallowed. Her heart had begun to beat faster. She sensed that something was very wrong. Why had Nick left the yurt without Samantha? And why hadn't Samantha come looking for him when he didn't return? She stepped forward, felt a restraining arm against her chest. "What the—"

"I'll go first." Hunter made it sound like an order.

"I'm the police officer here, remember? I have a duty to protect—"

"I'm aware of that. I'll go first," he repeated, to her intense irritation.

"Arrogant bastard," she hissed under her breath. She followed him to the other side of the hedge, where he pocketed his torch and instructed her to turn hers off, too. She appreciated the need for caution, but it didn't stop her resenting the easy way that Soren seemed to have assumed control — like some sort of macho alpha male. Like he was used to being the one in charge.

A bank of cloud passed overhead, plunging the whole area into darkness. After some moments it cleared, and the yurt loomed in front of them, its top section bleached white by the moonlight. Ava made out a picture of a grey wolf and remembered someone saying it was a *Game of Thrones* themed yurt. The wolf was the emblem of House Stark. She'd read the books and seen the TV series. Bad things happened to the Starks.

Hunter was moving towards the yurt, now, alert and stealthy, one arm outstretched to keep Ava at a distance. The other was raised in front of him. Ava thought she saw something glint in the moonlight, a flash of silver.

"What the—"

Hunter swung around, finger to his lips. His face had a feral look. Ava ignored him, ignored his determination to be first into the yurt. She sprinted forwards, pushing past him.

There was a sudden noise and the door of the yurt was flung aside. A shape — dark, human — hurled itself at her, knocking her to the ground. Ava was aware of the brief pain of impact, followed by a sick sensation in the pit of her stomach. Her head spun. Hunter swore, knelt beside her. She waved him away. "Just . . . winded. Don't . . . do anything . . . stupid—" But Hunter was already on his feet, ready for pursuit — precious time had been lost.

Panting for breath, Ava drew herself upright in the clearing, heart pounding, eyes darting between the gaping door of the yurt and the two dark shapes crashing into the woods.

Her decision made, she headed into the yurt. Immediately, her feet slid in something wet, sticky. There was that familiar coppery odour again, the same one she'd detected in the ambulance. With a sinking heart, Ava slowly shone her torch around the interior of the yurt, picking out wall hangings, an open bottle of champagne and two fluted glasses on a low oak table.

Whether from fear or the cold, she shuddered. Her hand trembled, sending the torchlight on a jerky dance around the room. As both steadied, the narrow beam of light came to rest on a scene of unspeakable horror.

CHAPTER THREE

The torch was starting to fail. Ava was glad. The strobing effect of its fading light spared her the full impact of the scene on the four-poster bed, at which it seemed she had stared forever, though in reality it had only been for a couple of seconds.

Then, her police training kicked in. She checked the woman's neck for a pulse, even though common sense dictated that no one could still be alive after losing that much blood. It looked as though every artery in her body had been punctured simultaneously, releasing the contents at high pressure to spurt in all directions at once. It was impossible to tell how many times she had been stabbed. Ava blinked her eyes against the flickering torchlight. She realised she had the shakes. It took several moments for her to get a grip.

Ava had seen her fair share of murders. She'd attended post-mortems where she'd seen bodies cut open, the organs removed and weighed with clinical precision. But she'd never seen anything like this. It was . . . She couldn't think of the right word. Then she had it: *inhuman*. Other descriptions tumbled into her mind then: *bestial*; *depraved*; *primal*. Bile rose in her throat. She stepped out of the yurt and threw up in some bushes, then knelt quietly for a few moments in an attempt to recompose herself.

"Are you okay?" Hunter's voice made her start. He was standing at the open door of the yurt. She'd heard no sound of his approach. The beam of his torch was pointed downwards, so as not to dazzle her.

"I'm fine. You . . . you've seen inside?"

"Yes. Are you sure you're okay?"

She ignored the question. "He got away?"

"Yes," Hunter growled. "I tripped over a tree root, turned my ankle." He handed something to her. Her torch. She must have dropped it in her haste to get out of the yurt. It wasn't much use now, anyway.

"You shouldn't have gone after him like that. He could be the killer." Then, "You had a knife."

"Yes." He made the word sound like a challenge. "I always have one with me. For work."

"I see."

Ava considered Soren's stealth in approaching the yurt, his almost detached sense of calm. And, before that, the way he'd read the situation as they entered the clearing, his observations about the wind chime and the lack of wood smoke. Grudgingly, she conceded that he seemed to know what he was about. She took out her phone. "Tom. We've got another body." She turned to Hunter. "Is that definitely . . ."

"Yes. It's Samantha Benrose."

Ava repeated the name into the phone. "There was someone in the yurt when we arrived. Male, I think. He fled the scene. Mr Hunter pursued him, but he had a head start. If he is the murderer, he's very dangerous. No one should approach him alone." She inhaled deeply. "It's a particularly brutal murder, Tom. Prepare yourself." She looked at Hunter. "Are any of the other yurts occupied?"

"No. Fortunately," Hunter said, his gaze on the door to the yurt. He didn't say any of the things that people typically said when they witnessed a murder. He didn't say anything at all. But he did seem affected by what he'd seen in there. Mostly, she guessed, he was angry about not catching his quarry.

22

"You act like you've seen this sort of thing before," she said, when the silence lengthened. No comment. *Surprise, surprise.* She was glad of his presence, though. Her nerves were on edge. She didn't want to think of the kind of person that was capable of killing two people so brutally.

"They're coming," Hunter said, his head cocked to one side, as if listening. Ava heard nothing. She was about to say so, but she had an idea that Hunter would tell her it was because she wasn't being attentive enough — which she hadn't been. Even though her body felt hyper-alert, her concentration was compromised — by the lingering sense of shock, she supposed.

Now that she was listening, she heard it too. The sound of a vehicle approaching. More than one car, in fact. Their headlights shone through the unadorned branches of the trees, the only bright thing in a place of terrible darkness.

Tom got out of the first car, accompanied by a woman in a parka. The fur-trimmed hood was pulled around her face, but Ava knew Kerry Short well enough to be able to identify her from her gait alone. Kerry was in her late forties, reputed to be a bit of a jobsworth, though Ava knew better. Kerry avoided putting in too many extra hours because she was bringing up three teenagers with no husband or partner to share the burden. She had nearly thirty years' service under her belt and made no secret of the fact that she intended to retire as soon as she'd put her youngest through university.

"This is an isolated spot, isn't it? A long way from the farmhouse." Kerry lowered her voice, melodramatically, "Nobody to hear you scream." Her attempt at dry humour fell flat. Ava and Hunter had seen Samantha's mutilated body and it was no laughing matter. Samantha had proba bly been surprised by her killer, her screams muffled in her throat. Kerry turned to Ava. "DS Merry. I understand you're off duty this evening."

"Yes, ma'am."

Ava half expected to be instructed to go home, but Kerry merely nodded. Then she said, "Lucky for us a trained person was on the scene." She looked at the yurt, before correcting herself. "Both scenes."

As Kerry and Tom donned protective clothing, Ava filled them in. "The victim is a white female, mid-twenties. Cause of death . . . er . . ." An image of the gruesome scene flashed in Ava's mind. She faltered.

"Ava?" Tom was looking at her with concern.

"There's a lot of blood. I think she might have been stabbed in the heart, among other places." It wasn't her intention to shock, but both Tom and Kerry recoiled slightly.

Tom turned his attention to Hunter. "Mr Hunter. I understand you pursued a potential suspect?"

"Yes." Tom waited, no doubt expecting Soren to elaborate. He'd be waiting a while, Ava thought. "Was there any contact between the two of you?"

"No." Hunter looked at Ava.

"He knocked me to the ground when he came charging out of the yurt," she explained. "Mr Hunter pursued him, but he checked to see if I was okay first."

"I stumbled and turned my ankle. That's why he was able to get away," Hunter explained.

"Don't feel bad about it, mate," Tom said. Ava doubted Soren Hunter was the type to waste time and energy in self-recrimination.

"That contact might yield some results, forensically speaking. You okay to stick around, Ava?"

She nodded.

"So . . . it's not a pretty sight, then?" Kerry said to Ava.

"No, ma'am. Worst I've witnessed."

"I like to think I've seen it all in my time," Kerry said. "Takes a lot to shock me these days, sadly. Not that I'm inured to violence or insensitive or anything. I've just learned professional detachment."

Ava sensed Kerry's jaded old cop act was a cover, something she used to prepare herself mentally for the worst the job could throw at her; if she really had seen it all, she would have no reason to fear stepping inside that yurt.

Ava looked at Tom and saw him grimace. He knew that Ava normally had a pretty strong stomach. If she said it was bad, he was likely to be nervous. Still, Kerry was right about the professional detachment. Ava hadn't had her guard up when she went in there.

Hunter stood aside, looking watchful. He turned away as Ava began peeling off her clothes and putting them in an evidence bag. In return, a CSI handed her some tracksuit bottoms and a sweatshirt.

Tom emerged from the yurt a shade paler than he'd gone in. "So," he said, joining Ava. "You weren't exaggerating, were you? Who would do a thing like that?" He shook his head. "It's like some animal's been in there ripping that poor woman apart."

"No, I wasn't exaggerating." Ava was glad someone was setting up some lights. In the tense, dark wood, she could almost have believed that Samantha Benrose had been attacked by a dire wolf.

"*No beast so fierce but knows some touch of pity. But I know none, and therefore am no beast.*" Hunter's voice. Again, he'd crept up on Ava without a sound. She and Tom looked at him, questioningly.

"Shakespeare. *Richard the Third.*"

Jim Neal would have recognised the quote. Hunter didn't seem the type to spout Shakespeare. He was full of surprises.

"Appropriate," she commented.

Kerry Short emerged from the yurt. "We need to find this animal." Professional detachment aside, Kerry was as shocked as the rest of them.

She whipped out her phone and began issuing instructions.

"Is this some kind of ritualistic killing, do you think?" Tom said. "What's the story with that yurt anyway? Is it meant to be medieval or something?"

"*Game of Thrones* themed," Ava said, surprised he hadn't caught on.

"That's sort of based on medieval times, isn't it?" Tom said.

"It's fantasy, really . . ."

"Now's hardly the time for a debate on genre distinctions." Kerry had finished her call. She was looking ragged.

"We should probably check the other yurts," Ava said.

"You should go home, Ava," Tom said. "You're off duty. No need to hang about here any longer. I can bring you up to speed in the morning."

"After we check the rest of the yurts." She turned to Hunter. "Can you show me where they are?"

Hunter led the way, limping slightly. The first yurt they checked out looked a bit like Bilbo Baggins's hobbit burrow in *The Lord of the Rings*.

Genghis Khan would have felt at home in the second, if he'd dropped through a time warp. It was lavishly decorated with plush cushions, exotic rugs and hanging tapestries.

The third yurt was clearly aimed at children. Disney characters abounded.

Ava had asked Soren to tell them if anything seemed amiss. He'd looked around the first three yurts without comment, but as they stepped into the fourth, an unthemed yurt, and shone their torch beams around, she sensed that he was wary. "What is it?" she asked.

"Someone's been here."

"How can you tell?"

Hunter flashed the beam of his torch around. "There's a scent." He shook his head. "Faint, but it's there. I don't know what it is. Some kind of cologne, maybe?"

Ava couldn't smell anything. She'd have to take his word for it. But she'd ask forensics to check it out.

As they walked back to join the others, she shuddered, imagining the killer was still in the vicinity, watching them, stalking them, lying in wait like some monstrous predator.

"Seen enough?" Hunter asked.

"For now. I hope the Stratfords don't have any bookings here for a while. This property is going to be crawling with police for quite some time."

Hunter shrugged. "Who's going to want to stay here now anyway?"

CHAPTER FOUR

On Saturday evening, Jim Neal and his son, Archie, were on the last leg of their journey back to Stromford. Thirty minutes and they'd be alighting on the platform of their adopted city. Much as Neal had enjoyed staying with Jock and Maggie, and much as he liked Edinburgh, the closest city to the West Lothian village where he'd been born and lived for the first eighteen years of his life, Neal was looking forward to getting home.

When the newly-weds returned from their honeymoon in Australia, they would be living in Stromford, in a rented house. An accident that resulted in nerve damage affecting his arm and shoulder meant that Jock, a surgeon, had decided to retrain in psychiatry. Neal was pleased that he would be seeing more of his lifelong friend, but now that Maggie would no longer be living with them, childcare would be more of an issue.

"Dad, Stan's just said he heard his mum say something about two savage murders in Stromfordshire this evening." Archie had been playing a game on his phone last time Neal checked. Looking down, he saw that his son's thumbs were now texting busily.

"Did Stan give you any more details?"

"It was a man and a woman. One of them was stabbed in a yurt. Stan stayed in a yurt last summer holidays. Sounded cool. Can we stay in one some time, Dad?" Stan, Neal knew, was short for Athelstan. His parents were the type Neal would have expected to go on a glamping holiday.

"How does his mum know about this?"

"Her niece is at some kind of dance at the farm where the murders happened. She sent Stan's mum a text."

"Right," Neal said. He should have guessed.

"Will you be investigating it, Dad?" Archie asked.

"I don't know. Maybe."

"Cool."

Was it disturbing that his son thought it was cool his father was going to be investigating two violent murders? Better that, Neal supposed, than Archie being anxious about the dangers of his father's occupation. There was still enough of the child in Archie for him to view the real world like one of the fantasy worlds in the age-appropriate games Neal allowed him to play. In these, good triumphed over evil and the dead came back to life. Archie had led a pretty protected life thus far, but Neal knew that when he started secondary school later that year, everything would change.

When Archie returned to playing his game, Neal searched for more information on the murders. He found only the barest details, as it was still breaking news. Tomorrow was Sunday, but he guessed that he would now be going to work. He wondered who the senior duty officer was that evening. Probably Kerry Short.

The murders remained at the back of his mind, preventing him from fully engaging with the book he was reading. He hoped he was managing to hide his distractedness from Archie.

Savage. The adjective bothered him. Reporters routinely resorted to hyperbole, though.

Later, at home, Neal checked the *Stromfordshire Courier*'s online news pages and found confirmation of the story, though the details were scant.

The bodies of two young people were discovered at a farm near the village of Langby in the Stromfordshire Wolds this evening. The police are treating their deaths as suspicious.

A senior officer at the scene commented that it was as harrowing a murder call-out as she had attended in her thirty-year police career.

Whatever happened to 'no comment,' Neal wondered. Had that been the detective's actual words or had the reporter sensationalised a throwaway line? Either way, the person responsible would likely be in for a reprimand from their boss, George Lowe. DI Kerry Short, most likely. She wasn't a woman who minced her words. And, it was no secret she was hoping to retire in around eighteen months. Discretion wouldn't be a big issue to her anymore, as long as she didn't blab enough to jeopardise her pension.

He could phone Ava for a briefing. Then, he remembered she wasn't working this weekend. She'd booked leave for the wedding.

Ava. Would his weekend have been any different had Ava managed to come to the wedding? Maggie would probably have seized upon every opportunity to throw the two of them together. Why did that make Neal feel uncomfortable? Or did it? As usual when he thought about Ava Merry, Neal felt slightly anxious and conflicted. And, as usual, he forced himself to think of something else.

The thought of two murders to investigate should have made him feel despondent about his return. Instead, he felt a thrill of anticipation. Should that worry him? He sighed. He wasn't used to having so much free time for introspection. The sooner he got back to work the better.

CHAPTER FIVE

Bea Stratford sat at the big oak table in her spacious farm-house kitchen. She took comfort from the sight of the shiny red range cooker, the uneven flagstone floor and the dark timber beams overhead that had supported the roof since the 1800s. Solid, familiar things.

The queasy feeling that she'd woken up with earlier was beginning to pass at last. It was probably all down to lack of sleep. A bad night often led to slight nausea and light-head-edness in the morning. Nothing a nice cup of tea wouldn't put right. There wasn't much a cup of tea couldn't help with, her mum had always claimed. The cup shook in her hand.

"You're up early this morning." Aubrey walked into the kitchen in his threadbare tartan dressing gown, the one she'd given him for Christmas twenty-odd years before, which Aubrey maintained was 'good for a few years yet.' The new one, a near-replica of the one he was wearing, was hanging, unworn, in his wardrobe upstairs. "Better keep it for best, in case I ever need to go to hospital," he'd say.

Bea was used to her husband's eccentricities by now. She'd long since stopped trying to change him. What right did one person in a marriage have to try to change the other anyway, or to mould them to fit their requirements? Odd shapes might not slot together perfectly but that didn't mean they couldn't exist harmoniously side by side.

"Couldn't sleep?" Aubrey asked, feeling the teapot to see if it was still warm. Bea had forgotten to put the cosy on it. She sighed. He said this to her most mornings. You'd think he'd have caught on by now that she was practically an insomniac. She never rose later than half past six. It was now almost seven thirty. If anything, she'd slept in.

"Oh, Aubrey. How can you ask me that? Besides, when do I ever sleep?"

He kissed the top of her head. "I know, love." She knew he knew. After forty years of married life, it wasn't what they said that mattered. It was what they understood to be true. Words were just words.

"Didn't sleep much myself, after — you know. All the upset."

Bea didn't bother to point out that he'd seemed dead to the world all night. She didn't think he'd been pretending.

"The murders, you mean."

"Well, yes, if you want to put it like that."

"Does *savage, brutal killings* sound any better?"

Aubrey was tipping lukewarm tea down the sink. He paused for an instant then got rid of the rest. Bea watched him pour boiling water into the pot and swirl it around, four times exactly. As always. Her husband was a fastidious man.

"I wish they hadn't reported the murders quite so graphically on the local radio this morning," she said.

"It won't be good for business, that's for sure."

"Aubrey!"

"It's true, though, isn't it?"

"Not necessarily. Some people like that sort of thing." It was Blue. She'd wandered into the kitchen and must have overheard. "Think how many people like to read about serial killers. There's a Jack the Ripper tour in London. They even named a pub after him, briefly. People complained. I wouldn't be surprised if we're overrun with bookings in the coming weeks."

"I hope you're not going to suggest we change the theme of that yurt to cash in on the horrible murder and mutilation of that poor young woman," Bea said.

"Mum!"

"Sorry, love. I'm still in shock. Have you seen Soren this morning? He was a hero last night."

Blue looked worried. "He shouldn't have gone chasing after the killer like that. He could have ended up a victim himself. What was he thinking of?" She placed a hand on her swollen belly. Instinctively, Bea reached out to comfort her. She pressed Blue's shoulder and pulled out a chair for her to sit down, but Blue remained standing, her cheeks blushing pink. Bea knew that her daughter was attracted to Soren. He was a good-looking man — despite the blond dreadlocks.

Bea wished Soren was the father of Blue's child. Unfortunately, it was impossible; eight months before, Blue and Soren hadn't even met. The identity of the baby's father was like a state secret. When Blue had informed her family that she was pregnant, she'd qualified her announcement with: "You don't need to know who the father is. So, don't ask. Ever." They all knew Blue well enough not to press her. Bea lived in hope that one day her daughter would relent, but she wasn't holding her breath.

It was impossible to gauge what Soren thought of Blue. Soren revealed little about the inner workings of his mind to those around him, let alone his heart. He didn't talk about what he'd done in the past much, either. Whenever anyone asked, he was vague, or evasive. He was a closed book, or rather a closed library; if he ever opened up, Bea was sure the story of his life would run to several volumes, not all of them with happy endings. She'd seen the scars, even though he went to some effort to hide them.

Bea wondered whether he had a secret in his past that he didn't want to talk about, some kind of trauma, perhaps, or some personal tragedy. One thing she did know for certain about Soren: he had saved the life of her son, Monty.

It had been seven months ago. Monty had gone to London to a brewing conference. Near his hotel in Bloomsbury, he had been set upon by a man in a mask brandishing a knife. When Monty tried to defend himself, the man had stabbed him in the arm. Monty was convinced he'd got off lightly, that the man had been aiming for his chest.

Soren, who had been sleeping rough in a shop doorway, spotted a man following Monty from the Tube station and had come to his rescue. He'd seen off Monty's assailant in a couple of swift moves and then used his phone to call an ambulance.

The following day, Monty sought out his Good Samaritan. He'd located his shop doorway to find only a rolled-up sleeping bag stuffed with old newspapers against the cold and a tattered paperback. He'd installed himself in a café across the street and waited patiently for Soren to return. When he did, Monty crossed the road with a coffee and a sandwich. Then, he sat on the pavement next to him. "One good turn deserves another," he said.

And that was how Soren had ended up at Northfields Farm. They had been talking about taking someone on for a while before his arrival. Apart from the fact that Blue's pregnancy meant she had to avoid the heavier work, the business had been doing so well that there was more work than the family alone could handle, particularly in the summer months when the yurts were always occupied.

Soren had slept in one of the yurts for his first week. A cancellation had come through and rather than take a last-minute booking, Bea had insisted on Soren occupying it. From there, he had moved into Bea and Aubrey's old caravan, which was parked in the field behind the farm. It was too old-fashioned to be used as a holiday let, but it was watertight, and was connected to water, electricity and gas.

Soren seemed more than content with his accommodation and, though Bea wished she could offer him a room in the farmhouse, she contented herself with the knowledge that at least he was no longer sleeping rough.

Over time, she had come to accept that Soren's past, like the identity of her coming grandchild's father, would have to remain a mystery for now. It wasn't as though the Stratfords were strangers to keeping secrets.

"Come on, love, have a cup of tea and some porridge, or at least a slice of toast. Or how about some scrambled eggs?" Bea's eyes flitted to Blue's bump, then swiftly away. The one time she'd suggested that her daughter wasn't eating enough for two, she'd got such a roasting from Blue that she'd never dared broach the topic again. Her urge to fuss this morning was probably a reaction to the events of the previous evening.

Blue sat down at last. To Bea's surprise, she said, "Maybe some porridge, then. You can tell me about last night properly."

Blue had missed all the drama. She'd spent the day helping with last-minute preparations for the dance and overdone it. She had left the barn at eight, complaining of backache and fatigue. She'd slept soundly through all the commotion, only learning about the tragedy when she encountered Bea on the landing outside the bathroom earlier that morning.

Aubrey put a mug of tea in front of his daughter. "I dread to think what state Ingrid will be in when the police are finished with her," he said.

"For goodness' sake, Aubrey. Two people are dead and all you can think about is that bloody ambulance." Bea knew how much the ambulance meant to her husband, but sometimes he needed to be reminded about priorities. Her hand shook as she stirred the porridge.

"Mum's right, Dad." It wasn't often that Blue took Bea's side over Aubrey's. His eccentricities were a source of humour for Blue and Monty. Normally Bea found her husband exasperating and endearing in equal measures, but not today. Today, she wanted him to be more like Soren. The sort of person you could depend on in an emergency.

"No fry-up?" Monty stood in the doorway. "I suppose this isn't a normal Sunday morning."

"Sorry, everyone," Aubrey said. "Don't feel much like cooking." Bea's heart went out to him. Perhaps she'd misjudged him. Even if he gave the appearance of being more concerned about that old ambulance than anything else, he, too, was shaken by the events of the previous night.

"It's okay, Dad. I don't think I've got the stomach for it this morning, anyway."

Bea ladled porridge into four bowls and put them on the table. Blue wobbled to her feet and fetched some spoons from the drawer.

"So, where were you when Soren was almost getting himself killed last night?" she asked her brother.

Monty glared at his sister. "I wasn't driving the pigs to market."

"I don't snore!"

"Do too."

Bea closed her eyes. She wasn't in the mood for sibling squabbles this morning.

"I was in the barn, helping the police keep people calm and helping to collect contact details from the guests. I didn't get to bed until four in the morning."

"None of us did," Aubrey pointed out. "Police have been here all night. That DI told us they'd be here for a while, maybe days or even weeks. You can expect a raft of cancellations in the next few days, Bea."

"Yes, well. As Blue said, some people are attracted by the macabre."

"They're not the sort of people you'd want staying on your land," Monty pointed out.

"I want to hear the whole story," Blue said. Bea sighed. It was left to her and Monty to put Blue in the picture. Aubrey seemed determined to focus on his porridge, contributing not so much as a grunt.

When Blue had been brought up to date, Bea said, "The police will be here soon. They'll want to question everyone. I don't think there's any need to mention what we all came

here to get away from, is there? Can we all agree on that?"
She looked around the table, noting with a mixture of anxiety
and satisfaction that Aubrey was engaged at last.

He looked up from his porridge and stared at her. Then,
he nodded. For a few moments, it was so quiet in the kitchen
you could have heard their collective hearts beating a little
faster.

CHAPTER SIX

DI Short ensured that Neal hit the ground running by bringing him up to speed on the killings at Northfields Farm in graphic detail. Neal's heart had skipped a beat when he heard the bit about Ava Merry approaching the yurt with the killer still inside. It was her job, and Ava knew how to handle herself, but it still made him shudder to think of her facing such a dangerous situation. Whoever this Soren Hunter was, Neal felt he owed him a debt of gratitude for being there with her.

Neal was aware that this was precisely the kind of thinking that he couldn't afford to pursue if he wished to maintain a working relationship with Ava. If his feelings for her — and Neal was now at a stage where he could acknowledge that he *did* have feelings for her — got in the way of either of them being able to do their jobs, something would have to give.

Ava wasn't the sort of woman who would allow a man's protective instinct to come between her and her ambitions. She was an excellent detective and would go far, but not if he held her back because he feared for her safety. It was a dilemma that he could see no way of resolving. And it was his problem to deal with, not hers.

It wasn't as if he was a rookie. He'd seen it happen to others, and he'd sworn to never be so idiotic as to become romantically involved with a colleague.

DI Short congratulated him on having two such dedicated officers as Ava and Tom on his team. "It's rare to encounter people who are ambitious and dedicated, and who also seem to work together without any apparent rivalry or discord," she said. Neal knew she was right, but for once it gave him no joy. It was one more reason for preserving the status quo. Tom would feel pushed out if he thought Ava and his boss were an item.

What Kerry had said about a lack of rivalry between Tom and Ava wasn't entirely true; ambitious people would always regard their close colleagues as rivals and Tom and Ava were no different. Still, they seemed to like and respect each other.

He went over Short's report before calling Ava and Tom into his office. Both looked ragged around the edges; clearly they'd had little sleep.

"Thanks for your good work last night," he said. "DI Short has briefed me, but I'd be interested in hearing your thoughts."

Tom spoke first. "The victims were killed separately, but Dr Hunt thinks the time of death for each of them was pretty close. We don't, as yet, know which of them was murdered first, although we observed someone fleeing the yurt, quite probably the killer, so Nick Winter was likely attacked before his girlfriend. Cause of death for each was the same. Massive trauma due to blood loss. The killings were brutal. The victims were stabbed over and over, including in the heart."

"As if the killer was in a rage," Ava added, somewhat unnecessarily. "Both scenes were gruesome. Complete overkill."

"So I understand," Neal said. "What do we know about the victims?"

"Nick Winter and Samantha Benrose. They hadn't been together for very long. A couple of months. They'd booked the yurt for a romantic Valentine's weekend when they read about the 1940s dance."

This piece of information seemed to lend an even sadder note to the murders. Neal, fresh from Maggie and Jock's wedding, nodded in sympathy. "Have their families been informed?"

"Yes, sir. They were visited by someone from their local force in the early hours of the morning."

"Nick and Samantha lived in Nottingham. They weren't killed in their own territory," Tom said. "For their killer to be someone they knew, he or she would have had to have been aware of their trip and planned the whole thing in advance. Either that, or we have a psycho on the loose."

Neal grimaced. His mind turned on logic and on making meaningful connections, looking at motive, means and opportunity. Anything else was chaos — and Neal detested chaos. He cleared his throat. "What do we know about the Stratford family. Are they local?"

Ava filled him in. "No. At least not Stromfordshire born and bred. They moved here from Brighton. Aubrey was an engineer. He worked abroad a lot in the past."

"And Bea Stratford?"

"She worked as an accountant for a firm based in Brighton. They'd always planned to retire early — escape the rat race, set up some rural business or other. You know the sort of thing."

He did. Stromfordshire, a largely rural county, attracted people like Aubrey and Bea. People who liked yurts and yoga, alpacas and rare breeds of sheep, making their own pottery and rescuing donkeys. Traditional farmers were having to embrace some of that stuff nowadays just to make ends meet.

"They run a glamping business?"

"Among other things," Ava said. "The kids, Monty and Blue, run a micro-brewery. There are also alpacas. Not sure if they're part of the business package or just kept as pets."

Neal nodded. He'd been right about the alpacas. "And this Soren Hunter?"

"There's a bit of a story there," Ava said. "Apparently he saved Monty's life when he was the victim of a random knife attack in London. The family was so grateful that they offered Soren work and accommodation at Northfields. Previously, he'd been living on the streets."

Neal raised an eyebrow. From what he'd heard of Soren Hunter's actions last night, it seemed unlikely that he was the type to end up on the street. He'd shown himself to be resourceful as well as brave. He sighed, acknowledging his own prejudices. Everyone who ended up homeless and living rough had once been someone else.

"We need to know more about him," he said.

"There were a lot of people on the Stratfords' land last night," Tom said, sounding a bit weary. Neal knew what he was saying. The list of potential suspects could be a long one.

"Do we have a list of names of the people who attended the dance?"

"Yes, sir. The tickets were numbered, in case anyone forgot them on the night."

Neal nodded his approval.

"We also took down people's contact details before we let them leave the barn."

"They'll all need to be interviewed. In particular, we need to know whether anyone saw anything suspicious prior to those kids mucking about with the ambulance. Maybe someone went outside for a smoke and saw someone hanging about — someone who obviously wasn't there just for the dance. You know the sort of thing. And I believe there was a charity committee, wasn't there? They'll need to be interviewed, too. I'll get PJ to start arranging for uniform to visit and take statements." Neal paused. "Where is PJ, by the way?"

Ava and Tom exchanged a look.

"She phoned in to say she'd be a bit late," Ava said.

"Right," Neal remembered that PJ had been at the dance with Ava, and guessed the reason for her tardiness. "Tom, I'd like you and DC Jenkins, when she arrives, to visit the families of the victims and anyone closely associated with them. Find out who knew where Nick and Samantha were going for their weekend break."

A flicker of something — resentment? — showed briefly on Tom's face. Did he believe he was being assigned the lesser task in not revisiting the farm with Neal? It made Neal question his choice. Did he want Ava with him for the right reason? Dammit. This was just the sort of dilemma he had always avoided in the past. He couldn't afford for things to get messy at work.

But this wasn't the time to stress about it. He turned to Ava. "We're going to speak with the Stratford family and Soren Hunter."

* * *

It was inevitable that Ava would ask about the wedding on the drive out to Northfields. Neal answered her questions curtly, with no unnecessary embellishments. He was aware that he must be coming across as distant, unfriendly, even. By the time they drew near to the Stratfords' property, Ava had fallen silent. Was she annoyed with him? He feared he might have driven a thicker wedge between them. Maybe it was for the best. One thing was certain: this wasn't the time to think about it. Neal nodded at the uniformed officer stationed near the front door.

A heavily pregnant young woman answered their knock. Blue Stratford? Ava had told him that she was eight months pregnant. Soren Hunter's arrival at the farm had been timely, as she'd planned to take some time off before and after the baby arrived. No one had mentioned a son-in-law or partner.

"Mum's in the study," the young woman said, showing them into the kitchen. Interesting that she'd automatically nominated her mother as the spokesperson for the family.

"Actually, we'll need to speak with you and Monty, and your dad, too," Ava said. Blue glanced at a clock above the range. "I have an antenatal appointment later this morning. Dad's driving me."

"It won't take long."

"Good morning, DS Merry." An older woman stood in the doorway. Ava introduced Neal to Bea Stratford.

"I understand why you need to question the family," Bea said. "We'll cooperate to the best of our ability. I can't bear to think of the monster who butchered that young couple being free to hurt anyone else. Imagine something like that happening here, in this rural haven."

It was a terrible thing to happen anywhere, but Neal understood what she meant. His eyes were drawn to the window with its view of the gently undulating contours of the nearby Wolds. People thought violence didn't belong in such idyllic settings. It was a fallacy, of course.

"Will you be alright, love?" Bea asked her daughter. At Blue's nod, she excused herself, tactfully.

"I remember seeing you at the dance," Ava said. "You were wearing a stunning forties evening gown. Cornflower blue. It draped beautifully over your bump."

"Blue's my favourite colour."

"Is Blue your real name?"

"No. I changed it by deed poll. My birth name was Scarlett. I don't like red."

Neal couldn't tell if she was joking. "When's your baby due?" Ava asked.

"Middle of March. The Ides."

"You left the dance early, didn't you?"

"That's right. I was tired, so I left at eight." Blue looked down at her bump. One hand rested on it protectively.

"You came straight back here?"

"Yes. I was tired. I went to bed."

"You walked back alone?"

"Yes."

"Apart from smokers or other party guests, did you see anyone on your way back? Or did you see anything unusual? Anything not quite right?"

"No. It's gross to think *he* was prowling our property . . ."

"I'm sorry if this is upsetting for you," Neal said.

Blue gave a shrug.

"Did you meet the victims? Nick and Samantha?"

"Yes. I booked them in. Mum was in the village when they arrived."

"How did they seem?"

"Normal. Nice. She was pretty."

"Did either of them seem nervous?"

"No. They were keen to get to their yurt. Couldn't keep their hands off each other."

"Did you take them there or just give them the key?"

"Monty took them across the field. Normally I'd do that, but I'm kind of slow these days and my back was killing me." Another glance at the bump. "Apparently they were at it almost immediately." She giggled. Neal raised a questioning eyebrow. "Monty showed them to their yurt and went off to check the shower block. When he passed by on his way back, he heard them."

"You slept through everything last night after you returned to the farmhouse?" Ava asked.

"That's right."

Neal recalled when his ex-partner, Myrna, had been pregnant with Archie. They had broken up by then, but he'd supported her throughout the pregnancy, ready to become his son's sole parent when he was born. He remembered that in her third trimester, Myrna had complained about not being able to find a comfortable sleeping position. She'd also needed to pee every couple of hours. It didn't make for a restful night. Maybe everyone was different.

"Had you ever met, or heard of Nick Winter or Samantha Benrose before they arrived at Northfields?" he asked.

"No. Why would I? I've never even been to Nottingham."

"They might have been to Stromford," Ava said.

"I'd never met them, period." Blue squirmed, shifted position. It could have been because she was physically uncomfortable on the hard oak chair, but Neal sensed her discomfort had a different source. She stared down at the limestone floor, avoiding eye contact.

"Is there something you want to tell us, Blue?" Neal asked, gently. Blue looked up suddenly, eyes shining.

"Don't take this the wrong way, right?"

A nod from Neal; a quiet 'okay' from Ava.

"I think Soren knew Nick."

Neal looked at Ava. This was certainly interesting. "What makes you say that?" he said.

"I saw them talking. On Friday afternoon, just after Nick and Samantha booked in. It was outside the window of the office. They spoke for a few minutes, then Soren grabbed Nick's arm and gave him one of those man hugs." She looked from one of them to the other. "Soren doesn't usually show his feelings much. I've known him six months and I've barely seen him smile. Why would he hug a complete stranger like he was his long-lost brother?"

CHAPTER SEVEN

"She's right," Ava said. They crossed the yard to one of the outbuildings, where Aubrey Stratford was allegedly tinkering with one of his vintage cars. "Soren Hunter doesn't give a lot away. I mean, he makes *you* look like you're emotionally incontinent." Neal glowered. Ava coloured. "Er, sorry, sir. But you know what I mean." Neal didn't. "He's got his emotions under control. Gives the impression of being self-sufficient and very capable."

"The strong, silent type?" Neal said, only half joking. He wasn't sure he liked the sound of this Soren Hunter. Sounded like your typical alpha male. "It's certainly of interest that he might have known Nick Winter. How did he react when he discovered it was him in the back of that ambulance?"

Ava pondered for a moment. "He didn't. I wasn't exactly looking at him at the time, to be honest, but he didn't seem upset. I'll be sure to scrutinise his face when we ask him whether he knew Nick. If he as much as twitches a muscle, I'll catch it."

They entered the outbuilding and Neal wondered what it might once have been used for. It probably housed cattle originally. Now, it had been converted into some sort of workshop, with whitewashed walls and an impressive array of tools and equipment, stored tidily on racks or suspended from wall hooks. More tools were attached to a pegboard, within easy reach of a large, cabinet-style workbench.

Aubrey Stratford was standing at the bench, working on a model tank. He was so engrossed in his work that when Neal cleared his throat to announce their presence, he didn't react to the sound of his voice. Suddenly, he threw his hands into the air and waved them around extravagantly. He thrust back his head, a look of sublime pleasure on his face.

"Earphones," Ava said, pointing at her ear. "He's listening to music. Conducting it by the looks of it." She walked up and tapped Aubrey on the shoulder. He gave a start then smiled.

"Sorry. I got carried away. Bruckner's Fourth." He nodded at the tank. "This is one of my projects. It's a scale model of a Second World War Sherman tank. Remote-controlled. I'll be able to put it through some manoeuvres on an assault course I'm building for it in one of the fields."

"It's a beauty," Ava said. Neal coughed. Ava made the introductions.

"Is here alright or would you prefer to go over to the farmhouse?" Aubrey asked. He didn't look at his watch or mention that he was taking his daughter to an appointment.

"Here's fine," Neal said. He couldn't help looking at the model tank with curiosity. Aubrey looked delighted that he was showing an interest.

"Splendid isn't she? Built her from scrap. Literally."

"Impressive," Neal said. "A hobby of yours?"

"My wife calls it tinkering. I suppose I've been tinkering all my life. Never happier than when I'm taking something apart and putting it back together again. Usually as something different. Been doing it since I was a toddler. Used to drive my mother bonkers when I was a teenager. She'd come home from work and find her food mixer or her vacuum cleaner in pieces on the kitchen floor."

Neal suspected that Aubrey would talk about his hobbies all day given the opportunity, so he explained that they were there to ask some questions following the murders.

Aubrey's face clouded over. He stood shaking his head, muttering repeatedly, "Bad, bad business."

They asked him the same questions that they'd asked his daughter. Like Blue, Aubrey had no connection to the victims that he could think of. He hadn't even met them. "Bea does all the bookings and looks after the guests. I'm no good at that sort of thing. *Socially compromised*, Bea calls me. They try to keep me away from the guests as much as possible in case I upset them or bore them to death."

He was presenting them with a certain image of himself. Too good at his job to take people at face value, Neal was wary of falling for the lovable eccentric act. People were seldom what they seemed, even to their nearest and dearest — *especially* to their nearest and dearest, in his experience. He'd lost count of the number of people who'd said of their partner, 'This isn't the man/woman I know,' after learning they'd committed some heinous crime.

"How well do you know Soren Hunter?"

"That young man saved my son's life," Aubrey said solemnly. It wasn't exactly an answer to his question, but Neal realised that Aubrey's opinion of Hunter would be forever coloured by that one act. To his surprise, Aubrey elaborated. "Soren and I are kindred spirits, in a way. Happiest in our own company or with close friends and family."

It seemed a peculiar thing to say about a man who seemed to have no friends or family to speak of other than the Stratfords. Where had Soren's friends and family been when he was living on the streets?

"He's a grafter too," Aubrey went on. "I respect that in a man." He waved an arm in the air. "I may spend my time on my hobbies now, but I worked damn hard for all of this. And it wasn't always a piece of cake, I can tell you. Living abroad for months at a time, moving from place to place, might sound exciting, but a man gets weary of all that after a while." Almost as an afterthought, he added, "Bea worked hard too, of course, holding down a job and bringing the kids up single-handedly a lot of the time."

"Well, you're sort of living the dream now, aren't you?" Ava said.

Slightly inappropriate, given recent events, Neal thought. "Do you spend a lot of time in here?" he asked.

"In here, or else in the other, bigger outbuilding. The one I call the garage, where . . . where the young man was found yesterday. That's where I work on my bigger projects, like Ingrid."

"The ambulance," Ava explained, before Neal could ask.

"Were you working on the ambulance yesterday?"

"Yes, for a few hours in the morning. I was quite busy in the afternoon. Charles, that's my friend, he came over and Bea had us helping out with the last-minute preparations for the dance. We were running around doing chores, like the proverbial blue-arsed flies."

Neal couldn't picture the bumbling Aubrey exerting himself much beyond tinkering with his machines. "What time did you leave the garage?"

"Charles came over around one to remind me to come for lunch. We walked back to the farmhouse together."

"Did you lock the garage after you left?"

Aubrey looked pensive. "I don't believe so. I'm usually in and out throughout the day, so I leave it unlocked. Monty always does a check last thing at night when he's finished in the brewery. If anything's been left open, he locks it up. I probably should have locked up, given I wasn't going back there that day. Oh dear, perhaps if I'd remembered to put the padlock on . . ."

If the ambulance was so dear to him that he'd given it a name, Neal wondered why he was so lax about the security of the building he kept it in, particularly on a day when Northfields was going to be swarming with visitors. Was he really that absent-minded?

"I doubt it would have made a difference," he reassured Aubrey. "Does your friend Charles . . . Unwin, is it? Does he spend a lot of time at Northfields?"

"Charles Unwin, yes. Lovely chap. A widower, you know. He's practically a member of the family. Bought two terraced cottages in the village and knocked them together to accommodate his collection of World War Two memorabilia. Absolutely fascinating collection. I highly recommend going to see it. I've told him he should open it up to the public by appointment. I could give you his number. I'm sure he'd show you around if you were interested . . ."

"Thank you, Mr Stratford." Neal doubted he'd take up the offer. Then again, maybe Archie would be interested if he did the Second World War in history.

"I appreciate that there were a lot of strangers on your property last night, but I'd like you to try and think whether you saw anyone acting oddly, or suspiciously."

Aubrey frowned. "I'm sorry, Inspector Neal, I can't think of anything to tell you. Everyone was just having a good time, until . . . the nightmare began."

"You said you were in your garage all morning and then helping with the preparations for the dance in the afternoon. Were you in the barn all the time from when the dance started, at — what was it, seven o'clock?"

"Yes, people started to drift in around seven."

"And Charles was with you?"

"Except for when he went outside to vape. He gave up smoking and took up vaping a couple of years ago. They say it's healthier, but I'm not so sure. Used to enjoy a puff myself, once upon a time. Gave it up, for Bea. She served me with an ultimatum. Her or the ciggies. Easiest decision of my life."

Neal looked at Ava to see if she had any questions for Aubrey. She hadn't.

Before interviewing Bea Stratford, they took a short break. They drove to the village, where they bought sandwiches and coffee from a machine in the local Co-op. Ava drove a little way out of the village and parked in a lay-by, knowing that their presence in the village would attract attention. When they returned to Northfields, Bea was waving goodbye to her husband and daughter, who were setting off for Blue's appointment at the antenatal clinic.

"I can't believe any of this is happening," she said to them. I keep hoping someone will tell me it's all a misunderstanding."

Unfortunately, Neal couldn't oblige. Bea invited them back into the farmhouse and once again, they found themselves sitting at the kitchen table. Neal had invited Ava to take the lead this time.

"Can you talk us through what you and the rest of the family were doing yesterday before the dance started, Mrs Stratford? Don't worry, it's just so that we can establish a timeline of people and events."

"I hope it's not because you think one of the family is capable of hurting those young people," Bea said, fiercely. Ava neither agreed nor disagreed. She simply encouraged Bea to answer the question.

"We were all busy for most of the day. I was in here all morning baking cakes for the dance and for the raffle. Aubrey was in the garage tinkering with the ambulance. I'd asked him to come over for lunch around one. I wanted to get him to do some chores afterwards. Preparations for the dance, mostly. His friend Charles arrived on time, but of course Aubrey had forgotten all about lunch. He's oblivious to everything when he's busy with his machines. I sent Charles over to remind him.

"After lunch, Aubrey and Charles iced the cakes and buns I'd made in the morning. The members of the charity committee arrived around two and went straight over to the barn. I left Aubrey and Charles clearing up, while I went over to the barn to see if I could help with the decorations. They joined me later, as did Blue. She'd joined us for lunch then had a short nap. Monty was in the brewery most of the day. He came over to the barn around four."

"What about Mr Hunter?"

"Soren? Soren was away most of the day. It was his day off. He went to Nottingham and didn't get back until ten in the evening." Bea turned to Neal. "Soren works very hard. He's become invaluable to us. My son and daughter run a micro-brewery — very successfully, I might add. They've won an award for one of their beers. Soren's been helping out with the brewery and the yurts since he arrived. Actually, Blue and Monty have asked him to become a partner. They want to grow the business and there's already too much work for two. Blue's having to take it a bit easier now she's in her third trimester. Only two or three weeks to go until the baby's due. Very exciting. I do hope all this . . . business won't upset her."

"What other duties does Soren have?"

Bea seemed to think for a moment. "Do you know, Soren helps out with so many things that I don't know how we managed to cope before he came here. He's good at fixing things, too. That much he has in common with Aubrey." A deep sigh. "But unlike Aubrey, Soren actually gets around to doing the repairs I ask him to do." She rolled her eyes. "What else does he do? There are the yurts. He helps clean them and makes sure they're stocked with wood for the burners. He also shops for groceries and delivers them to the guests, helps with cooking breakfast. There's a communal kitchen for the guests to use, but some people like a cooked breakfast, so one of us will go over and do that. He cleans the shower block and the kitchen area. I help with all of that as well as doing the admin. Blue and Monty pitch in, too, if we have a lot of guests staying. It's a real family affair." It didn't sound as though Aubrey was very hands on with any of the chores. Maybe he fed the alpacas.

"Was the baby's father here last night?" Ava asked, none too subtly. "If so, we'll need to question him." It was a question that they should have asked Blue when they spoke with her earlier. It seemed to unsettle Bea.

"The father? No . . . He . . . he wasn't here."

"Perhaps you could give us his name and contact details?" Ava said.

Bea was silent for a moment. "I'm afraid you'll have to ask Blue," she said at last.

It was an awkward moment. Neal cleared his throat. Not for the first time in his police career, he asked what he considered to be an intrusive question. "You aren't on good terms with the father?"

Bea sighed. "I'm not on any terms with the father, Inspector Neal. I wish I were. Good or bad it would at least be something. I don't even know who he is. None of us do. Blue won't tell us."

"Ah," said Neal. "We'll speak with your daughter again, then."

"Good luck with that."

"How well do you know the committee members, Mrs Stratford?" Ava asked.

"Quite well. They all live in the village. I met some of them through the local branch of the Women's Institute. I can give you their names and contact details if you like. Oh, you have them already, of course. One of the policemen wrote them down last night."

"It would still be helpful if you could write them down for us and we'll collect them before we leave. It might save us some time. A lot of contact details were taken down last night." Neal then asked Bea where they might find Monty.

"At this time of day, he'll be in the brewery. It's the outbuilding with the red roof tiles on the other side of the barn."

Waiting outside while Ava used the bathroom, Neal watched some chickens pecking their way across the yard. Northfields had been a working farm once. There would have been animals in the sheds, not vintage vehicles and toy tanks; crops in the fields instead of glamping yurts and accessories; proper farm animals instead of alpacas. He wondered what the real farmers thought of outsiders like the Stratfords, buying up land and properties like this, and turning them into holiday camps. Did they resent them?

When Ava re-joined Neal, they walked to the brewery. She shared her thoughts with him as they went. "What on earth was Nick doing in that garage?"

"He could have been lured in, or gone in there voluntarily with his killer." Neal veered to avoid a wayward chicken.

"Aubrey told us he left his garage unlocked. I don't know what to make of that man," Ava continued. "Everyone seems to regard him as a sort of affable buffoon — socially inept, eccentric. Does he play up to the image a bit, do you think? I mean we're talking about a man who's had a successful career in engineering and worked on projects all over the world. He's no fool."

"I agree," Neal said. "But if it's an act, he either has his own family convinced, or they're all part of the smokescreen. On balance, I think he's genuinely eccentric. I hate to stereotype, but engineering is one of those jobs that attracts . . . well, for want of a better word, *geeks*."

Ava nodded. "I just can't picture him tinkering with his ambulance, icing some buns with his friend Charles, then going out and committing two brutal murders. Be interesting to hear what Soren Hunter has to say about him."

Neal felt a pinch of resentment at Ava's apparent confidence in Hunter's judgement. He suppressed it immediately, saying, "As an outsider, you mean? Someone at a remove from the immediate family?"

"Yes. And he struck me as someone who has the measure of people."

"He's a suspect, Ava." Immediately, Neal wished he could retract his words. In the first case he and Ava had worked on, Ava had slept with a suspect — one with a cast-iron alibi, it was true, but she'd brought a lot of trouble on herself for doing so and had been lucky to escape with a warning from their boss. She'd redeemed herself in her subsequent cases and shown that she was an excellent detective, capable of self-restraint. His subtle reference to the episode now made him feel slightly shabby. Thankfully, Ava didn't respond.

As they entered the brewery, Neal sniffed the air and detected a distinctive, malty aroma. A fair-haired young man was standing over a large stainless-steel vat containing what looked like porridge, but which Neal knew from his attempts at home-brewing with Jock was known as the *mash*, a mix of hot liquor and malt.

"Hi," the young man said, recognising Ava. "Is it okay if I keep an eye on this while we talk? I need to get the temperature just right. It's kind of crucial to the process."

"Sure," Ava replied. She introduced Neal.

"It doesn't seem right for me to be in here carrying on as normal after what's happened," Monty said. "I love brewing. I feel guilty for doing something I enjoy when two people have been so brutally slain on our land."

"People often feel that way in the wake of a murder," Ava assured him. "But life has to go on for the living."

"I suppose it does help to be busy." His expression lightened. Monty struck Neal as the sort of person who felt things deeply, without taking them too much to heart. He looked a bit like his sister and therefore like their mother. But he came across as more personable than Blue, less touchy. Blue had a guardedness about her, a sullenness. He wondered what was at the bottom of that.

"How is business?" Ava asked.

"Good, good." Monty beamed. "Very good, actually. One of our brews won an award last month." There was pride in his voice.

"Yes, your mother told us. Congratulations." Ava looked around. "There's a lot of equipment, isn't there?"

Neal looked around, too. The brewery was housed in two adjoining outbuildings. They were standing in the one where the actual beer-making took place. Neal could see the edge of a table and some shelving through a half-open ledged and braced door into the other room. Monty immediately seized on Ava's interest to start explaining how the magic took place.

"This is the hot liquor tank," he said, indicating the first of a row of four large stainless-steel casks. "It's basically a giant kettle that heats the water — or liquor as it's called — once it's been mixed with gypsum to achieve the right pH balance." He moved on to the second cask, saying, "This is the mash tun. We transfer the hot liquor into here and mix in the malt grains to produce the mash, which is what you can see at the moment."

"The porridgy stuff?" Ava said.

"Yes. It's important to keep the mash as close as possible to seventy degrees Celsius, which is why I can't leave it at the moment."

"The sparging comes next, doesn't it?" Neal said, showing off his remembered knowledge. It earned him a look of respect from Monty.

"Yes, that's right," Monty said, enthusiastically. "Do you brew?"

"Not anymore."

"What's sparging?" Ava asked.

"It's basically the process of running hot water through the grain to rinse out the sugars and produce the wort from which the beer is made. The wort is run off into the copper." He pointed to the fourth cask. "Then it's fermented in this last cask. If you stand on that little step you can see the beer inside." Ava mounted the step. The rim of the cask was sticky with the residue of a foamy substance, like the head on a glass of beer. Inside, the beer was dark and enticing.

"Cool," she said.

"I can let you have a taste of some that's ready to drink, if you like," Monty offered.

"I wish," Ava said. "But we're on duty."

"How long have you and your sister been brewing?" Neal asked.

"Here? About two years. I started while I was still a student. I did a degree in microbiology, so I understood the science of beer-making, but it's not really necessary. Anyone can do it." He looked at Neal. "Blue did a marketing degree, so she mostly looks after that side of the business, although she does like to help with the actual brewing." He grinned. "She's really catching the bug. I began as a hobbyist, blew all my savings on a home-brewing kit and experimented with it." He paused. "I had a friend at uni who was going to go into business with me, but . . . er . . . it fell through. When Mum and Dad bought Northfields, they suggested Blue and I set up our business here."

"I understand you've invited Soren Hunter to be a partner?" Neal said.

"Yes. Soren saved my life. Did you know?"

Neal and Ava nodded.

"It's not just that, though. Soren's sound, you know? It's not his fault he ended up homeless."

"Oh?" Ava said. "How did that happen?"

Some of Blue's guardedness crept over Monty's face. "You should probably ask Soren about that."

"Mr Stratford . . ."

"Please, call me Monty."

"Monty, can you give us an account of your whereabouts yesterday?"

"Sure. In the morning I was here, cleaning some of the equipment. Blue was here, too, until around one, when she went over to the farmhouse for lunch. I often bring a sandwich over and eat it here. That's what I did yesterday. I was here until around four, then I went across to the barn to see if there was anything I could do to help."

"Please think carefully, Monty," Ava said. "Did anything seem amiss on the farm yesterday?"

"Amiss? No, but it wasn't anything like our normal Saturday evening. There were lots of people about because of the dance, all in 1940s fancy dress. Lots of strangers, hard to tell who people were because of the costumes."

Unfortunately, Monty was right: how could anyone spot something out of place when nothing was as it usually was? It was the perfect cover for a murderer.

"I wish I had seen someone, or something," he said, unhappily. "Nick and Samantha might still be alive if only I'd gone into the garage."

"Don't distress yourself," Ava said. "There was probably nothing you could have done. Nick and Samantha's injuries were . . . catastrophic."

"Thanks," Monty said, quietly.

"That time Soren Hunter saved your life . . . can you tell us what happened exactly?" Ava asked.

"Sure. I was in London at a sort of brewer's convention. It happened when I was making my way back to my hotel."

Neal frowned. "How late was it?"

"Around midnight. It was dark. I was drunk. I went down an alleyway." Monty looked embarrassed. "To . . . er . . . to relieve myself. My attacker must have followed me from the Tube station, seen the state I was in and waited for the right opportunity. I certainly made it easy for him."

"And Mr Hunter?"

"He was in a shop doorway, in his sleeping bag. I was singing as I walked along and caught his attention. Just as well, as it turned out. Soren noticed that I was being followed and shadowed us. When he saw the man follow me into the alley, he sensed I was in danger, and instead of turning away, he launched himself at my attacker."

"Your attacker had a knife," Ava prompted.

"Yes, that's right." Monty took a breath. "I didn't even know he was there until he was nearly on me. I'll never forget the moment I saw he had a knife. The fear I felt. I thought, *This is it, I'm going to die here,* you know." Monty trembled slightly. He was starting to sweat. The memory was obviously traumatic. "I was certain he was going to cut my throat. Because of Soren's intervention, he only managed to nick me in the arm."

Neal gave him a moment to recover before gently asking, "Did he speak to you? Ask for your wallet, or your phone?"

"No," Monty said. "But I assumed that's what he was after, so I sort of croaked out that my wallet was in my inside jacket pocket and told him to help himself. Then, suddenly Soren was there, pitching in like some hero in an action movie. My attacker took off pretty fast."

"And Soren called an ambulance for you?"

"Yeah. He stayed with me until the ambulance arrived, then he just sort of . . . vanished, before I could even thank him properly. But I recognised him. I'd seen him in a doorway earlier in the day and asked him if I could get him anything — like a coffee or a sandwich. He didn't want anything, but maybe he remembered me and thought he'd do me a good turn. What he did for me was way out of proportion to my offer of a sandwich."

"You felt indebted to him?" Ava asked.

Monty's expression said *do you really need to ask?* "Sure, wouldn't anyone? I mean that guy wasn't messing about. I could have died in that alley."

"It was a heroic thing to do," Ava agreed. "I take it the police interviewed Mr Hunter? Got a description of your attacker from him as well as from you?"

There was a pause. "I guess so," Monty said at last.

"Don't worry if you can't remember everything. We can check the details with our colleagues in the Met."

"Why?" Monty said, suddenly defensive. "That incident has nothing to do with what happened here."

"Just covering all the bases, Monty." Another pause.

Monty looked from Ava to Neal. "Okay . . . look . . . I didn't mention Soren to the police, alright? I mean . . . I told them a passer-by intervened and scared my attacker off. Soren asked me not to give a description of him. I just told the police he was a Good Samaritan who didn't want to get involved any further."

"Right," Ava said. "It didn't occur to you to wonder why Mr Hunter didn't want to be identified to the police?"

"Why would it?" Monty said, hotly. "It made no difference to me what his reasons were. He'd just saved my life. Actions speak louder than words, don't they? I didn't need to know his business. I already knew he was a good man. No wonder the police get a bad rep if they go around being suspicious of people who just want to keep themselves to themselves. I hope you're not going to stereotype Soren just because he was homeless. He's not into drugs, and he doesn't have a mental health problem."

"We're not in the business of stereotyping people, Monty," Neal said. "But, unfortunately, in a murder investigation, we do have to look into the backgrounds of people who have a potential connection with the victims."

"Soren didn't know the victims. None of us did. They were just murdered on our land." A note of petulance had crept into his voice.

"When we spoke to your sister, she told us that Soren had greeted Nick like a long-lost brother when he arrived. Are you sure they didn't know each other?"

Monty looked surprised. "Blue said that? She must be mistaken."

"Was Mr Hunter here in the brewery with you yesterday morning?"

Monty shook his head. "It was his day off."

"Thank you, Monty. If you can think of anything else that might be relevant to our investigation, please get in touch."

Monty nodded and turned back to his mash tun.

"He got quite tetchy over Hunter, didn't he?" Ava said when they were back in the farmyard once more.

"Well, he did have a very frightening experience. He believes Hunter saved his life."

"Believes?"

"It was probably a mugging. Muggers don't usually kill. Hunter probably got involved before Monty's assailant had an opportunity to make his demands known."

"True," Ava said. "We need to check with the local Met. See if there were any similar attacks in the area. Not many people would do what Hunter did. I mean, the fact that he followed Monty, knowing the man at his back was suspicious. He was the same when we were approaching the crime scene out at the yurts — noticing things that most people wouldn't notice. The silence . . . the absence of wood smoke. Like he'd been trained to be alert to things."

Neal listened. Earlier, Ava had expressed a theory about Hunter perhaps being ex-army. It made sense. And ex-forces personnel did figure amongst the numbers of those living rough on the streets, for a variety of reasons.

"Why do you think he was shy of the police?" Ava asked.

This intrigued Neal, too. "I'm hoping Hunter will be able to provide us with the answer to that when we question him."

Of course, it didn't really matter if he failed to cooperate. Checking whether he had a record would be a routine part of the investigation. If Hunter — or any member of the Stratford family — was harbouring secrets, these would come to light. Their lives were no longer private. But Neal also knew that people often harboured secrets that could not be accessed readily. Forensic science could help uncover the truth, but when you were dealing with people, the truth was often found in places beyond the scope of scientific tests, places where the human qualities of perseverance, intuition and intellect came into their own.

"Do you think Monty lied about not knowing that Soren and Nick knew each other?" Ava said.

"Hard to say. I doubt he'd volunteer the information even if he did know."

"You're right. They're all so protective of Hunter, aren't they? He seems to inspire loyalty."

"Yes," Neal said, without enthusiasm. He'd heard enough about Hunter's overabundant virtues for one day.

CHAPTER EIGHT

PJ clocked immediately that Tom was a bit sullen this morning. She'd apologised for her lateness, but he was still probably peeved about having to hang around waiting. Also, she sensed that he would rather have been at Northfields Farm than driving to Nottingham with her. Perhaps because he'd been on duty at the farm the night before, he had taken it for granted that he would be the one to accompany the DI.

It was probably just as well he wasn't in a talkative mood; she was feeling a bit delicate after her excesses. With luck, he wouldn't notice if she just dozed off for a bit.

It turned out to be more than a bit. Next thing she knew, the satnav was telling them they had arrived at their destination.

"Wake up," Tom said, curtly.

"I am awake." Well, she was now, wasn't she?

Tom knocked a little too loudly on Mr and Mrs Winter's front door. It reminded PJ of the pounding in her head when she'd woken up that morning.

The door opened and Nick's father appeared in front of them. He was a balding man in his late sixties, who until recently must have been looking forward to a future that included his son. It seemed to put PJ's own disappointment over her recent break-up in perspective.

Mr Winter showed them into a small sitting room, where his bird-like wife sat straight-backed on an unyielding chair. PJ's eyes flicked to an array of photographs along the mantelpiece, some of which included babies and young children. She was glad to see that Nick had not been an only child. The Winters could perhaps take some comfort in their extended family. Now, though, it was probably small consolation to them.

Tom began by offering his condolences for their loss. PJ followed suit. Then it was down to grim business.

"Tell us a little about your son." Tom offered them an opportunity to be as intimate or as general as they cared to be. PJ expected the usual outpourings of grief along with gushing accounts of their son's personality and accomplishments, so she was somewhat surprised by what followed.

"Nick was our youngest." Mr Winter's voice was flat and emotionless. "We had four children in all." He pointed to the mantelpiece. "That's them in the photos there, with the grandchildren. All three of them." His wife's gaze lingered lovingly on the photographs. As Bernie Winter reeled off the names of their children and grandchildren, PJ had a sense of something amiss. It took a few moments for her to realise what it was. Amidst the portraits of smiling siblings arrayed across the mantelpiece and around the rest of the room, there was only one of Nick, as a baby. There had to be a reason for that. She didn't have to wait long to find out what it was.

Bernie sighed. "Nick was always . . . difficult."

"That's an understatement." Alice spoke for the first time. "Might as well be up front about it, Bernie. Nick was no good."

Bernie looked apologetic. "I hope you won't think us hard, officers — speaking this way about our own flesh and blood. But, like my wife says, Nick was the odd one out in this family. Difficult behaviour at school, truanting and getting into fights. He was what used to be called a juvenile delinquent

— always in trouble with you lot. Drink, drugs, shoplifting — Nick was into it all. Alice and I . . . we couldn't do a thing with him. We had three other kids who were like bloody angels — and then Nick. How do you explain a thing like that?"

Tom and PJ nodded. PJ had a nephew who was going through a rebellious phase. Her sister and brother-in-law had sought her advice on how to keep him from crossing a line. PJ didn't have any answers. The reasons for young people's behaviour were many and complex. She'd volunteered to act as a sort of mentor to young Jack, and they were all hoping it was just a phase. It sounded as if, for Nick, the phase had become permanent.

Despite her natural empathy, PJ didn't feel immediate sympathy for the Winters over their wayward son. She sensed that, although neither was likely to come right out and say that they were better off without him around, that was how they truly felt. Moreover, she had the sense that there was more to this than was immediately apparent.

"We're not here to judge, Mr and Mrs Winter," she said. "It's a total mystery why some kids go off the rails. You shouldn't blame yourselves."

"We don't," Alice said. "Like Bernie says, we had three perfect kids. We didn't deserve a son like Nick. We should have stopped after we had our Jenny." Her gaze, full of resentment, settled on her husband, as though she considered Nick's provenance solely his responsibility.

Something about that adjective *perfect* bothered PJ. It seemed clear that the Winters hadn't planned or wanted a fourth child. Had Nick been treated differently from his siblings? Had he understood that he wasn't loved in the same way? *Many and complex*, PJ reminded herself, wary of the trap of indulging in amateur psychology. Tom had noticed something was amiss, too. She'd seen his eye twitch, a sure sign that he was irritated by something.

"Did Nick have enemies?" he asked. "By which I mean anyone who might have wished to harm him?"

The Winters didn't seem to need time to ponder. Alice deferred to her husband. "I wouldn't be surprised, sort of company he kept. Bad enough when he was here. Who knows what sort of people he was involved with in London?"

"London?" PJ said.

"Nick had only been back here for about a year. Before that he was living in London. Must have been about . . ." Bernie Winter looked to his wife.

"Best part of two years," Alice Winter said. "We lost touch with him after the first ten months. His sisters and his brother, Adam, all went down to see him from time to time — to try and persuade him to come back to Nottingham. He was living in squalor in a flat in . . . where was it, Bern?"

Bernie shrugged. "Cricklewood?"

"Then, our Jenny went down one time and found he'd moved on from there. The people who lived in the flat said the last they'd heard, he was on the streets. Jenny was persistent. Asked around . . . visited hostels and the like. She tracked him down eventually and persuaded him to come back to Nottingham."

PJ looked at Alice. She was sitting ramrod straight in the chair, her posture as unforgiving as her attitude to her son. PJ wanted to believe that the woman had trained herself not to care as a defence mechanism. She never liked to believe the worst of people. But it seemed telling that Alice had said *back to Nottingham* and not *back home*. It made her wonder if this had ever been a loving home for Nick.

"Did Nick move back in with you?" she asked.

"No," Bernie answered. "Jenny contacted a homeless charity and got him a place in a hostel. She knows people, our Jen. She's a solicitor. Knows how to pull some strings."

"She's a legal secretary," Alice corrected her husband.

"Same thing, isn't it?" Bernie insisted.

"And how did Nick get on?" Tom asked.

Alice and Bernie exchanged a look. Alice said, "What you have to understand is that we'd been there before. We didn't believe Nick would be able to turn himself around, not with his track record, so we didn't have a lot to do with him. Our Jen stuck by him — all credit to her. She told us recently that Nick was like a different person. Off the drugs. He'd enrolled at college to retake his exams — wanted to be an electrician. He'd even got himself a girlfriend. Samantha. There was talk of us going around to Jen's for a family dinner to meet her." Alice gave a bitter little smile that PJ found hard to interpret. "Last week Jen called us and said that Nick was going away with this Samantha for Valentine's weekend." Her voice trembled, accompanied by a slight slouching of her shoulders — corrected quickly. "We'll never know now whether Nick had really changed. I like to think so, I really do." PJ sensed a *but* coming. *Don't say it*, she urged Alice, silently. *Look for the good in your son, for once.* She was relieved when Alice said nothing more.

Tom cleared his throat. "Do you know who Nick was staying with in London? It would be useful if you could find out the address for us. Perhaps one of his siblings would know?"

"They might," Bernie said. "Will you be speaking to them?" He sounded concerned.

"Yes. Is that a problem?"

"It's just that they've had a lot to deal with over the years, having Nick as a brother. They've got their own lives. They shouldn't have to be dragged into all this unpleasantness."

PJ winced internally at Bernie's use of euphemism for the murder of his own son. From what she'd heard of Nick's siblings, they hadn't given up on him as readily as his parents, especially Jenny. "Just to be clear . . . are you saying that neither of you ever met Nick's girlfriend, Samantha Benrose?"

"No," Alice said. "Jenny said she was a nice girl. Hard to picture Nick with a nice girl." Perhaps Alice hadn't meant it the way it sounded. "Is it true what they said about her on the news? That she was stabbed right through the heart?"

PJ swallowed. "Yes, it's true."

"Poor girl . . . though Nick would probably have ended up breaking it for her anyway."

There was a prolonged silence. Then Tom cleared his throat. "I think we're done here." He looked at PJ. She had nothing more to add.

***

"Don't get me wrong," Tom said. "I don't know what their life with Nick was like. Maybe it was hell. But . . . you know . . . they seemed a hard-hearted pair to me. And that remark she made at the end . . ."

They were progressing slowly in heavy traffic along the A6005 towards Beeston, where Jenny Winter worked for a small firm of solicitors. She'd agreed to meet them on her lunch break. As they passed Nottingham University campus, PJ thought of a party she'd been to a few years back with one of her cousins, Daisy, who'd been a student there. Daisy was helping out with mentoring young Jack, too. PJ couldn't envisage ever giving up on a member of her family completely. Then again, Jack's misdemeanours had been fairly mild thus far. She might think differently if, when he was sixteen, he robbed her to pay for a drugs habit. "Yeah, well, like you say . . . we don't know the background."

They left the car in a nearby Tesco car park and walked to Jenny Winter's workplace. A young man on the reception desk called Jenny down. She led PJ and Tom upstairs to a small room furnished with a table and some chairs. "We use this room to interview clients," Jenny said. "Never thought I'd be in here myself being interviewed by the police."

Tom and PJ gave their condolences. Jenny's reaction differed completely from her parents. She wept into a handkerchief and displayed body language more typical of the recently bereaved: restlessness; tearfulness; eye contact expressing an unspoken need for reassurance.

"Perhaps we could begin with you telling us a bit about your brother. The kind of person he was . . ." PJ coaxed, gently.

"I know you've been to see my parents this morning," Jenny said.

"That's right."

"I can guess what they said about Nick. Difficult. A bad seed. Not like the rest of their kids. Too much trouble." She met PJ's gaze. "Am I right?"

"More or less," PJ said. There was no point in denying it.

Jenny sighed. "Nick was . . . what do people say when they don't want to say a *mistake*? A late baby. I know that late babies are often seen as a blessing, but that wasn't how my parents looked on Nick. Mum and Dad were in their mid-forties when he was born. They'd almost got their lives back and suddenly they had to start all over again. Poor little Nick was dumped on the rest of us as much as they could get away with." She sniffed and blew her nose.

It always helped to see things from another viewpoint. PJ found her sympathies tipping even further towards Nick. She'd begun to suspect a case of emotional neglect arising from Nick's arrival at a time when the Winters had run out of enthusiasm and love for another child.

"Not that Rach, Adam and I minded," Jenny continued. "We all loved little Nick. He was the cutest baby . . ." Another sniff. "But Rachael was eighteen when he was born, Adam was sixteen, and I was fourteen. We did our best to love Nick and give him the attention he didn't get from our parents, but we were normal teenagers, doing normal teenage things. We were at school or out with friends, or . . . you know. Rach left home and went to uni — then Adam did too. I was at home until Nick started school. Then I met my partner, Joe, and I moved in with him. I offered to have Nick come and live with us. Nick was seven or eight by then and starting to cause Mum and Dad a lot of grief with his behaviour."

"That was kind of you," PJ said.

"It caused a big row." Jenny fiddled with her engagement ring; it was loose and she slipped it off and put it on her middle finger. "Mum and Dad didn't like the implication, you see. That they weren't paying enough attention to Nick.

They aren't the sort of people who can admit to being bad parents."

At this, Jenny looked around the room, as if afraid Alice or Bernie might be listening. "To give them their due, they were good parents to me and my brother and sister. But then, we weren't like Nick. He was the sort of kid who just seemed to need that little bit . . . more, you know?"

PJ nodded, thinking of Jack. Jack wasn't a bad lad; he just needed the right kind of guidance and encouragement to keep him from being overwhelmed by life. *Parenting plus*, her sister called it. That was the way she saw it, too. A little love might have gone a very long way with Nick.

"I took him off their hands as much as I could. And Rachael and Adam did what they could, too. Had him round to stay. Took him on outings. It just didn't seem to be enough. Nick knew, you see. He knew our parents didn't love him." Jenny made a sort of choking sound. Tom, who had been listening intently, crossed the room to a water cooler. He filled a paper cup and offered it to Jenny. "Thank you. I was about to tell you what Nick said to me once. It was when he was about eight years old. He said, 'I wish you could be my mummy. My real mummy and daddy don't love me.' It broke my heart." She took a sip of water. "Oh, God! I hope you're not thinking Nick was abused or anything like that. Mum and Dad never laid a finger on him. It's hard to explain. They just weren't . . . engaged the way they'd been with the rest of us."

PJ thought she understood. Somewhere, in the two differing accounts of Nick's childhood, there was probably some overlap. Alice and Bernie, in their mid-forties, looking forward to a spending more time together and enjoying a new relationship with their grown-up children, suddenly finding themselves embarking on parenthood again. They must have hoped for an easy child, but that wasn't what they got. PJ didn't doubt that Nick had been difficult. Some kids just were. If Nick had been easy and likeable, perhaps his parents would have loved him more. He might have stood some chance.

Somewhere along the line, intervention, perhaps from school or some kind of family support service, might have bridged the gap. But PJ knew that in a time of austerity, kids with problems didn't get much of a share of the budget. Time and again in her work, she'd seen the truth of that.

She was reminded suddenly of Ava, who had a troubled relationship with her parents. Her father had remarried and moved to the States; her mother was enjoying being single again. Ava's brother, Ollie, had felt unhappy and unsettled with the changes in the family set-up and was now living with Ava. There was no such thing as the perfect family. PJ's own extended clan came pretty close, but she was aware that there had to be a few skeletons lurking in their cupboards, too.

"Tell us about when you went looking for your brother in London, Ms Winter," Tom said. "Your parents said that you went to visit him and eventually persuaded him to come back home."

"Not home," Jenny corrected him. "My parents would never have let him across their doorstep after all the *trouble* he'd caused them." For the first time her tone towards her parents had an edge of bitterness. "Poor Nick! He moved to London with a boy he met in prison when he was only nineteen. He sent me a postcard of Buckingham Palace. He drew a little arrow pointing to one of the windows and wrote, 'My new gaff.' Really, he was sleeping on the floor of someone his ex-cell mate knew. They were all addicts. I suppose my parents told you about Nick's drug habit and the life of crime that supported it? The money he stole from them?"

Tom nodded. PJ wondered if Nick had stolen any money from Jenny, or his other siblings.

Jenny answered her question. "Nick never took a penny from me, even when I offered."

"How did Nick fund his habit? Did he get a job in London?"

Jenny stared at her hands. "He did odd jobs. Mostly cash in hand. He told me he wasn't dealing."

"He ended up sleeping rough, is that right?"

"Yes. I went down to see him at that awful place he was staying in and he'd gone. They told me he was probably on the streets. That was a terrible time."

"But you did find him."

"Yes. I took a week's leave and spent the whole time looking for him, asking questions of strangers until I got some leads. It wasn't as hard as it sounds. One of the people at his old flat told me where Nick was most likely to be. I concentrated my search in those areas."

"It's still amazing that you tracked him down in a city the size of London. A lot of people who go missing, stay missing. You must have been very determined."

"All for nothing, wasn't it, though?" Jenny wiped a tear from her cheek. "You know what I find so hard to stomach about all of this?" She gave a fleeting smile. "I rescue my brother from the streets of London, bring him back here, and he goes and gets himself murdered in a bloody field in the middle of nowhere. In an *idyllic rural retreat*, as it said on the blurb on the website."

PJ looked at Tom, thinking of his description of how Nick had died with his throat sawn raggedly but deeply, as though his murderer had inexpertly hacked away at it with a serrated blade. His torso had been punctured all over with knife wounds. *Savage* — that's how the media had described it.

Samantha had also been stabbed over and over before her killer had plunged his knife into her heart. Two unspeakably violent killings. And, thanks to the more prurient reporters going to town on all the lurid details, the families of the victims could read all about how much their loved ones had suffered.

"I'm so sorry," PJ said.

"I understand now how some of the clients we deal with here feel," Jenny said. "The ones who go on about bringing back capital punishment for people who commit crimes like this. You want something more than a prison sentence for them. You want them to suffer like their victims did. Make the punishment fit the crime." She shook her head. "Sorry, I'm angry. I hope I won't always feel this way. It's not really who I am."

She was a good person. No one could blame her for feeling the way she did, but PJ was relieved to hear that her essential humanity was intact.

"Do you know if your brother made any enemies in London?" Tom asked. "Or here in Nottingham?"

Jenny frowned. "You probably think the kind of company he kept in London brought him into contact with the lowest forms of life. It's not like that really, though. Everyone has a story to tell, you know? I've heard so many sad stories — at work and from Nick's acquaintances. So when you ask me if he had any enemies, the answer is none that I can think of. Nick had nothing. Most of the people he knew had nothing. Why would anyone want to kill a person who had nothing?"

PJ could think of plenty of reasons. She suspected Jenny Winter was being disingenuous. Working for a company of solicitors, she had to be aware of the multitudinous reasons for people resorting to murder. A person with nothing could still experience rage or jealousy or any of the extreme emotions that could lead to murder.

"Nick was living in a hostel when you found him, wasn't he?" Tom asked.

"Yes. He'd met a kind of Good Samaritan on the streets. A man who helped him when he was at his lowest. He took Nick to the hostel, befriended him."

"Who was this man?" Tom asked. "Do you know his name?"

"Sorry. Nick didn't tell me."

"Was he staying at the same hostel?"

"I don't know. I can give you the name of the hostel. Maybe he's still there, or someone might remember him."

Jenny looked at her watch. "Is there anything else? Only my lunch break's almost up, and I'd like to grab a sandwich and a bit of fresh air before I go back to work. My boss did say to take some extra time if I needed to, but I don't like to take advantage."

They took leave of Jenny. She cut a sad figure as they walked away, standing there, looking like she didn't have the strength to return to her office.

"She's such a lovely person," PJ said when they were out of earshot. "Did you hear what she said about everyone having a story to tell? So true."

Tom's voice was grim. "There's only one story I'm interested in hearing and that's the one Nick and Samantha's killer has to tell."

CHAPTER NINE

Neal and Ava sought out Soren Hunter. Bea Stratford had informed them earlier that she'd asked him to collect some groceries from Langby, a market town about six miles from Northfield. When he returned, he was off duty for the rest of the afternoon. With the yurts still cordoned off by the CSI team, there was less for Hunter to do than usual.

Hunter was unloading bags of shopping from a 4x4 parked near the entrance to the farmhouse when they returned from interviewing Monty. He greeted Ava with a curt nod and carried on unloading. "Like a hand with these?" she asked, picking up some bags.

"Thanks. I'm guessing you want to talk to me."

"That's right."

"I'm Detective Inspector Jim Neal." Neal stepped forward and also hoisted up a couple of bags.

"You know who I am," Hunter said.

"Is there somewhere private where we can talk?" Neal asked.

"I live in a caravan on the other side of the barn. We can go there."

Bea met them at the door of the farmhouse. As soon as they'd piled the bags up on the kitchen table they left her to empty them and followed Hunter around the side of the barn.

"Monty tells us you like to keep yourself to yourself," Neal said.

"That's right. The classic loner. That's me." Hunter grinned darkly as if referring to the stereotypical recluse who suddenly goes off on a psychotic killing spree. "Not a crime, is it, Inspector?" There was no antagonism in his tone. Neal noticed Ava smile. Hunter had those twinkly eyes that women seemed to love and men distrusted. It made it very hard to tell what he was thinking.

"Welcome to my humble abode."

The caravan wasn't modern, but it had been well looked after and was comfortable — homely even. There were colourful throws over the seats, and some scatter cushions. These must have been provided by Bea. Hunter would have had few possessions when he came in off the streets. There was a jar of wild flowers on the windowsill behind the sink and a stack of books on the coffee table. Hunter's additions?

"It's generous of the Stratfords to let me live here," Hunter said. "Not as draughty as my previous digs."

"That's how you came to be here, isn't it. You met Monty Stratford when sleeping rough in London. We heard the story about you saving his life."

Hunter didn't answer. He offered them tea, and when both agreed, set about preparing it. Loose leaves, Neal noted — the way he preferred it. Ava was more of a coffee person. Soren apologised, saying he didn't have coffee. The tin said green tea. Neal wondered, absently, whether Soren was a vegan. Surely not with that much muscle mass. The man was *ripped*, a word Neal had heard his sister use and which he disliked, but in Soren's case it was appropriate.

Now that Hunter had removed his coat, it was also apparent that he was no stranger to the tattoo parlour. Both of his arms were intricately adorned. Neal recalled *The Illustrated Man*, a story he'd read as a teenager about a man whose tattoos came to life at night and predicted the future.

But it was Soren's recent past that he would have preferred to see brought to life.

"I just happened to be in the right place at the right time," Soren said, finally answering Neal's question. "Monty's assailant soon got the message."

"How does a man like you end up on the streets?" Neal asked.

"A man like me?" Hunter said, with a wry smile.

"I think you know what I mean. I've heard how you reacted last night. If you hadn't turned your ankle, I doubt our yurt man would have got away." It was a compliment of sorts, but Neal's intention wasn't to flatter.

Hunter shrugged. "I'm not invincible." He stared down at the table. "I suppose you'll be checking my background?"

"Is that a problem?"

"Do what you have to do. I have nothing to hide." The glint in his eye suggested otherwise.

"Did you get a look at his face?" Neal asked. Ava had told him how things had happened quickly, and that she'd been unable to see anything in the dark.

"Too dark, and he had a dark hoodie pulled around his face."

"What are your thoughts on what happened here?" Neal didn't often seek opinions from suspects. He sensed Ava's surprise.

"Obviously it was extreme, in Samantha Benrose's case especially. No doubt people will read something into the fact that she was stabbed in the heart on St Valentine's Day, but I'd be wary of making assumptions. The killer was certainly enraged. Or wanted to give the impression of being so."

Neal found himself warming to Soren Hunter, despite his reservations. A reasoned, logical mind was something he could relate to.

"How well did you know Nick Winter before his arrival at Northfields?" Ava asked.

"I didn't." There was no hesitation in Hunter's response, but he must have known they'd question him about that and prepared not to react. Neal watched him closely as Ava continued.

"Blue Stratford seems to think you did. From the way you both behaved when you greeted each other . . . like old friends."

"Blue's mistaken."

"And Samantha?"

"I'd never met her either, until the day she arrived here."

"Can you give us a description of your whereabouts yesterday?"

"It was my day off. I borrowed Bea's car and drove to Nottingham. And no, I have no way of proving that's what I did."

"So you didn't see Nick Winter or Samantha Benrose during the course of the day?"

"Actually, I did. I cooked breakfast for them before I left, to help Bea out. There's a kitchen out at the yurts where guests can prepare their own food. We provide a cooked breakfast on request."

"How did they seem that morning? Did they appear worried about anything? Any raised voices, arguments or other behaviour that might suggest something was up?"

"Nothing like that. They behaved like a pair of young people in love." Hunter's expression stayed neutral as his eyes flicked from Ava to Neal. "Poor kids. They had no idea what the day had in store for them." His words were surprising, the first he'd uttered unprompted.

"What time did you get back from Nottingham?" Neal asked.

"Around ten. I knew that there were plenty of people to help with the preparations for the dance, so I didn't worry about hurrying back. In retrospect, obviously, I wish I'd been here."

"Did you go into Aubrey's garage workshop on your return?" Ava asked.

"Not until I went there with Bea. You saw me then." His face tightened. Neal thought he understood what Hunter was thinking. If he had been there earlier and had noticed that the garage was unlocked, he might have gone in and had a look around. He might have intercepted the killer or found Nick's body sooner. He could have raised the alarm. Nick or Samantha or both might still be alive — if he'd noticed. A man who seemed to notice everything had missed something important. Hunter didn't strike Neal as the type of man who would let himself down lightly for a perceived failure.

"I suppose I'm a suspect now?" Soren asked. "I'm not so naïve as to believe that the man who ran out of that tent was necessarily the same one who killed Nick and Samantha."

No, but it was an assumption that most people would make, and Neal wasn't in any hurry to correct it.

"What's your opinion of the Stratford family?" Ava asked.

"Any one of them in particular, or collectively?" Hunter asked.

"Let's start with Aubrey, then. Is he all that he appears?"

"You mean a lovable oaf? Or clever dissembler?"

Ava nodded.

"I think he's one of life's eccentrics. A bit unworldly, despite his apparent ability to hold down a job as an engineer. My guess is that he found his niche. But he's happier now, tinkering, as Bea puts it. Away from the pressures of work. Perhaps he sometimes plays up to people's perceptions a bit, behaves in the way that people expect him to. But we're all of us acting to a certain extent. Keeping up a façade." His gaze rested a moment on Neal, the shadow of a smile on his lips. He hadn't touched his tea. Now he picked up his mug and drank it down in a single gulp. "Want me to psychoanalyse Bea next? Wonderful woman. Long-suffering where Aubrey is concerned." Hunter stroked his dreadlocks and smiled. "That's it. No further comment."

"What about Blue? Do you know who the father of her child is?"

"No. That's Blue's business."

"I'm afraid it's also our business now," Ava commented.

"Blue is—" Hunter stopped abruptly, looked uncharacteristically flustered. "I don't know her that well. She seems . . . nice." Neal thought he'd just glimpsed through a chink in Hunter's armour. Was it possible that he had feelings for Blue?

"And Monty?" Ava asked. "He and Blue have asked you to become a partner in their brewing business, haven't they?"

"With Monty, what you see is what you get. He's a genuinely good person. Not too many of those about. But he's slightly naïve. He has a very trusting nature."

"Will you take them up on their offer? Do you see yourself developing a passion for brewing too?"

"I'm considering my options."

"The murders haven't put you off?" Ava asked. "I'm guessing you have any number of transferable skills. You must have plenty of other options. Not tempted to move on?"

"I like it here. And I have no intention of going anywhere while there's a killer on the loose."

"Yes, well, we're working on that," Ava said. "Be sure to let us know if you remember anything that might be relevant to our investigation. Sometimes details come back at random. Often they're triggered by seemingly unrelated things."

Hunter looked bored, as though she were teaching him to suck eggs. They left him to his own thoughts.

"Convenient for the killer that Hunter wasn't around all day yesterday," Ava said. "He's probably the only one who might have been able to stop him. Unless he was the killer, of course. As he pointed out, Yurt Man isn't necessarily the murderer — although if he *was* the killer he'd hardly point that out. Or would he?" She sighed. "What do you want to take a look at first, sir, the garage or the yurts?"

"The garage."

On the way, they passed the barn where the dance had been held. Neal stopped to look inside. The shabby red, white and blue bunting above the tables fluttered in the draught from the open doors. Tables had been abandoned as they were, cluttered with glasses and platters of food. The bar was still set up. It felt like a place that had been abandoned suddenly after some disaster, which of course it was.

When they reached the garage, they donned protective clothing before being permitted inside. Nick Winter's body had been removed from the ambulance, but his blood remained, most obviously on the thin mattress of the stretcher.

Ava waited while Neal took a look in the ambulance. When he jumped back down, he caught her eye.

"If you think that's grim, wait 'til you see the yurt."

Neal had, of course, heard all about it. He'd also seen photographs of both scenes first thing that morning. They'd made the porridge he'd had for breakfast heave slightly in his stomach.

Dan Cardew approached, shyly. He was one of the least assertive people Neal had met, always hanging on the edges of a conversation, waiting to be invited to speak. This morning he was looking a little ragged. Like the rest of the forensics team, he had been at the scene all night.

"Do you have anything for us, Dan?" Ava asked.

"The usual. Fingerprints. Lots of them. And fibres, of course. The ambulance was shown at an open day at a nearby stately home three weeks ago, and the inside hasn't been cleaned since. Aubrey Stratford reckoned he swept out the interior with a broom to get rid of a small amount of litter and dirt from people's shoes, but that's all."

This wasn't particularly good news. But Dan had more. "We did find something a bit interesting, though." He walked across to a trestle table loaded up with equipment and neatly labelled evidence bags. "In here." He held up a bag with a small blue plastic peg inside.

"Okay, I give up. What is it?" Ava asked, after peering into the bag.

"It's called a tut," Dan answered.

"And? What's that, exactly?"

Neal thought he knew. "Used on beer casks, isn't it?"

Dan nodded. "Yes. Basically, a tut is found in the middle of a thing called a shive, which is placed over a bung hole on the side of the cask. I retrieved this one from the folds of Nick Winter's jacket. If it was in the killer's pocket, it could have dropped out as he lifted Nick onto the stretcher."

Ava whistled. "Okay, so that makes your little bit of blue plastic a lot more interesting. Then again, plenty of people must have climbed in the back of the ambulance at the recent open day. Some of them might have been brewers. So, it doesn't necessarily originate from here, I suppose. Or from the killer."

Neal agreed. "Is it possible to find out more about it? Where it originated from? Is it the type used in the brewery here?" It seemed like a tiny and inconsequential object in which to place so much hope, but Neal had known convictions arise from less.

Dan studied the small plastic peg. "If there's something to find, we'll find it," he concluded. He was not being boastful, merely putting his faith in the efficacy of his profession.

Neal noticed Dan stifle a yawn. "Keep up the good work!" Neal said.

Ava led the way to the yurts, where another team of white-suited officers was at work. As they approached, one of the team turned off the radio, which had been blasting out an eighties rock anthem. It wasn't lack of respect for the victim. God knew, they needed some distraction from the grim business they were about. If Guns n' Roses sufficed, so be it.

"Morning, sir, ma'am." A stocky woman with purple hair greeted them. It was Janine Watts, one of the senior CSIs. She was forty-five years old, hailed from the West Country and was a fervent gamer.

"Hi, Janine. Got anything for us? Dan had a tiny plastic peg. Can you beat that?" Ava asked. Neal looked at her. He'd heard she'd thrown up outside the yurt the night before. Not something she did routinely, but she seemed unruffled about returning to the scene. Unless the flippancy was a front.

Janine screwed up her face. "You know better than to ask at this point, Ava. We've got the usual stuff. It'll be up to the boys and girls in the lab to do their thing." She grinned. "Actually, we did find a charm. In the grass, a short distance from the yurt. From one of those Pandora bracelets. Samantha was wearing one, but the charm isn't necessarily hers. Maybe we can check with the Stratford family, see if any of them recognise it."

Janine was non-committal. Neal had no issue with that. He preferred caution to unbridled enthusiasm.

As they stepped inside the yurt, Neal did a double take at the sight of the four-poster bed and lavish furnishings. It was not what he'd been expecting, although he had been informed of the yurt's theme. He hadn't seen *Game of Thrones* but he was acquainted with some of the characters and certain elements of the plot from conversations he'd heard around the station. Something called 'the Red Wedding' had been dissected by Tom and Ava in all its gory detail. He'd have thought they saw enough blood and death in their work without seeking it out in their leisure time.

"The dragons are cool." Janine drew their attention to three fearsome winged creatures suspended on coloured strings from the ceiling, one of them breathing a trail of paper fire. "Shame they can't speak. Almost makes you wish the owners had installed secret cameras."

"Hmm. I'd be worried about one of those dragons dropping on my head in the middle of the night," Ava commented. Her eyes flicked to the bed and she fell silent.

"She was stabbed fourteen times, I hear. Poor lass. You've got to hope he got her in the heart first and that she died quickly. Who knows what his motive was?" Janine shrugged. "I'll leave it to you lot to figure out all that psychological stuff."

Neal considered what strong passions drove an individual to break a basic societal taboo and commit this most heinous of crimes. Love . . . hate . . . the desire for revenge . . . any of these could provide motives for murder.

He thought back to something Archie had asked him recently. "If there was one mystery you'd like to be solved before you die, what would it be?"

"Dark matter," he'd answered, without giving the question too much thought. It was one of those seemingly unsolvable mysteries of the universe, after all. Right now, though, he'd probably change his answer. After what he'd seen and heard this morning of Nick and Samantha's terrible deaths, the only mystery he wanted solving quickly was who had killed them and why.

CHAPTER TEN

Soren Hunter poured himself another cup of green tea and sipped it slowly as he thought over his interview with Inspector Neal and Sergeant Merry. It was a long time since he'd been in an interview scenario and, all in all, he felt he'd acquitted himself less well than he would have done a few years back. He was out of practice. He'd been interrogated in far more hostile situations and by more terrifying interrogators, yet managed to give nothing away. Or, more precisely, he had been in control of the information he was feeding his interrogators. When and how much he revealed had been his choice.

In reflecting on the questions that Neal and Merry had asked and the answers he'd given, he was trying to evaluate not how much information he'd ceded, but how much of himself he'd revealed. This was not something he'd worried about in previous interrogations, where no one cared what sort of person he was, only what he knew. The only psychology involved on his interrogators' part back then had been to work out how quickly they could find his breaking point.

It was different in a murder investigation. The police had an interest in finding out what made you tick. He'd managed to deflect Neal when he'd asked how a man like him ended up on the streets. Let Neal and his attractive DS uncover the truth of that for themselves.

He worried that he'd betrayed himself over Blue, the way he'd faltered when asked his opinion of her. He might as well have proclaimed his love for her right in front of them. Still, that was irrelevant. It mattered only in as much as he hated other people finding a way in. Emotion was dangerous in that respect. Allowing people to see that you cared could be the most dangerous thing of all. It made you vulnerable.

The tea was cold and the pot almost empty, but Soren strained the last of it into his mug. He'd been in survival situations where the dregs in that pot could have saved him from dying of thirst. Waste wasn't in his vocabulary anymore.

He got up and walked into his bedroom. He picked up a small backpack and took out a tin that had once contained assorted toffees. He smiled at the picture of the jolly Santa on the lid. He'd received it in a Christmas stocking at one of the foster homes he'd lived in after the death of his parents when he was nine years old. For some reason, he'd held on to it, despite not considering himself a sentimental man.

Soren removed the lid and looked at the patch of material inside. While he'd been answering the detectives' questions, he'd had to employ all his inner resources to resist the magnetic pull of that tin and its contents. He hadn't dared glance over at the door to his bedroom for fear of giving away that something significant was in there. Maybe that's why he'd let his guard down over the other things.

He was acutely aware that he should give the scrap of material to the police. There was a brown mark on it that could be blood. They could test it for DNA. It was the sensible thing to do. And yet, he felt compelled to hold it back just a bit longer.

Soren stared at the cloth, a frayed, faded patch of green and blue check. He touched it, as if hoping to trigger a psychic connection. The only thing that made it interesting was that it had been torn from the sleeve of a man who might be a killer.

He replaced the lid and stuffed the tin back in his pack. As he tidied up the tea things, he considered what he would do to this man if he ever found out who he was.

* * *

Bea watched the two detectives drive off in their car. Overall, the questions they had asked had been reassuring, all about the night of the murders and where people had been throughout the day leading up to the dance and what they had been doing. Nothing about that other business, which they'd all feared would be dredged up.

She sighed. It was only a matter of time. The longer this went on, the more likely it was that the police would be back asking more questions relating to the more distant, though still, in Bea's reckoning, too recent past. She had been right to mention it at breakfast that morning and insist that none of them talk about it.

Her thoughts turned to Soren, the man who had saved her son's life, for which she, and the rest of the family, were eternally in his debt. But who was he really, this man who guarded himself so closely that she hardly knew him at all? He was so expert at deflecting her questions that she had all but given up asking anything about his past. But that didn't mean she'd ceased to be curious.

It seemed that no one else in the family cared about Soren's background. All Aubrey said when she raised the subject was, "He's a hero. He saved Monty. He's a good grafter. What else do you need to know?" Likewise, Monty. And Blue, bless her, was head over heels in love with him despite being eight months pregnant with another man's child.

So, she alone of the family had been left to wonder whether Soren's past was as irrelevant as they all seemed to think. One thing Bea was certain of now was that the murders put a different slant on things. Nothing was likely to remain private for long once those detectives started digging around.

Bea had to ask herself if she believed that Soren Hunter was capable of killing. The answer was a resounding *yes*. The fact that he had done one good thing in rescuing Monty didn't mean he was one-dimensional, that he had no flip side. Everyone was multi-faceted. Not everyone presented such an inscrutable demeanour to others as Soren, though. She couldn't help but wonder what he had to hide.

But although Bea believed she was a good reader of people and sensed clearly that Soren was capable of killing, she couldn't conceive of him being capable of these murders.

She knew that Aubrey, Monty and Blue would claim they didn't care if Soren had something to hide. When it came to this man, they were like Buddhists, believing that only the present mattered.

Soren had no alibi for the time of the murders. He claimed to have been away, but he could easily have returned undetected. It wouldn't have been a challenge for someone with his skills.

Come to think of it, any of the family could have slipped out of the barn and killed Nick and Samantha. They had all told the police that they were in the barn all evening — with the exception of Blue, who had left early to go to bed — but Bea had gone out herself at one point to fetch an extra cake tin from the kitchen. Nobody had mentioned missing her. Similarly, any other member of the family could have slipped out unnoticed. The question was why would they? Nick and Samantha were complete strangers to the family, and, as far as she knew, to Soren. What possible motive could any of them have to murder them?

The thought of Monty being a murderer almost made her laugh. From childhood, her son had seemed to exude goodness. She remembered one of his teachers at primary school complaining, "That boy doesn't have a bad bone in his body," as though it were a defect in his personality. She'd been hinting that he needed to toughen up. Monty had been the kid who cried when other kids got hurt, or at the slightest cruelty to any animal. His first thought on moving to

Northfields was that they had plenty of space to run a donkey sanctuary! They'd got the alpacas instead — family pets, as it was turning out. So, even though it contradicted her theory about everyone having a flip side, and even looking at it objectively as though she were not his mother, Bea couldn't see her son as the perpetrator of those evil murders.

What about Aubrey? There were some who already believed that he was a murderer. Bea closed her eyes. She opened them abruptly at the sound of a car drawing up in the farmyard, Aubrey and Blue returning from Blue's antenatal appointment. Aubrey got out first and opened the passenger door for their daughter. He offered his hand and she took it, which surprised Bea. Blue rarely accepted help even when she needed it. Had she received worrying news at the clinic?

"How did it go? Are you both alright?" she asked as soon as Blue waddled into the kitchen. Her eyes came to rest on Blue's bump.

"My blood pressure's up a bit." Bea felt her stomach lurch. "Relax, Mum. It's not a cause for concern at the moment. I don't need to go into hospital or anything. When I explained what happened here last night they said it was understandable and advised me to try to take it easy." Blue rolled her eyes. "That seems to be all I've been doing for weeks now. Anyway, how can I be relaxed when people have been murdered here?"

Bea suppressed a mild feeling of panic. She wanted to tell her daughter to go and lie down for a bit, but she was aware that such a suggestion would be met with resistance. Instead, she suggested they could all do with a cup of tea, and was relieved when Blue lowered herself into a chair and asked for a slice of cake as well.

"Did they question Soren?" she asked.

Bea unwrapped the fruitcake that a shy young CSI had allowed her to rescue from the buffet table in the barn. She'd baked it the previous afternoon and it was still untouched in the tin. He'd seemed pleased when she'd invited him to share the other cakes with his colleagues.

"Of course," she said in response. "And Monty." It irritated Bea slightly that Blue's first concern had been for Soren.

"They're bound to be prejudiced against Soren, given that he's an outsider and that he was homeless before he came here."

Bea glanced at Aubrey. Soren wasn't the only one the police were likely to be prejudiced about once they started doing background checks.

"They're just doing their job." She set a lump of cake in front of her daughter. Surprisingly, Blue didn't moan about the size.

"I wish I could have a big glass of wine," she sighed. "I'm sure that would bring my blood pressure down faster than anything." She took a bite of fruitcake then brushed away the crumbs that scattered over her bump.

"Not long now, love," Bea said.

"Did they ask you or Monty about . . . you know . . . ?" Aubrey ventured.

Bea shook her head. "They mostly wanted to know about our movements yesterday."

"Did they talk to your WI friends and the others on the charity committee?" Aubrey asked.

"They took names and addresses. I expect they'll follow up. They have a list of the people who were here during the afternoon setting up. It was just the committee members — Linda Holmes, Tracy Burrows, Rita Coleridge . . . Terry Boswell . . ." Bea struggled with the two remaining names. There was no point looking to Aubrey. He was no good with names — or faces, for that matter. People in general were a bit of a mystery to him. He was looking blank-faced now.

"Meredith Whatsit and Pete Coates?" Blue said.

"Yes. Meredith Price. That's the one. Can't see any of that lot being able to kill anyone. They must have a combined age of five hundred."

"And the rest," Blue agreed.

"Someone must have invaded our land," Aubrey said.

"Trespassed, not invaded." Bea sometimes got weary of her husband's tendency to use war-related metaphors. But she didn't usually bother to snap at him over it.

"Soren would have seen them if he'd been here," Blue said. "He doesn't miss a trick."

It was true. Soren was hyper-alert. Not much got past him. Only a few weeks after he'd started working for them he'd solved the mystery of the stolen eggs, which had been puzzling everyone for weeks. It had been a couple of lads from the village, sneaking in early in the morning. They'd all assumed it must have been a fox.

"Well, he's not infallible," Bea pointed out — although Blue probably thought he was. "And he *wasn't* here, was he. Anyway, someone killed those poor kids, and whether it was a deranged madman or a cool psychopath who planned the whole thing with military precision . . ." Damn it, who was using war-related metaphors now? "I hope the police catch him before . . . before . . ." She choked. "Sorry, piece of cake went down the wrong way." She crossed to the sink to get a glass of water for her pretend cough. When she turned back to Aubrey and Blue, she saw concern on both their faces. Blue's especially looked strained and pale.

She'd stopped herself from finishing her sentence just in time; the last thing she wanted to do was raise her daughter's blood pressure another few notches by suggesting that more murders might follow. Everyone was used to her being the strong one in the family. She couldn't let them down. So instead of giving into her own sense of fear, she said, "I hope the police find him before I do or he'll wish he'd never been born."

CHAPTER ELEVEN

Ava scrutinised the board depicting the information they currently had on the Northfields Farm murders. Like the other members of the team, she awaited the arrival of Jim Neal, who was running uncharacteristically late. Now that his sister, Maggie, was no longer living with him and providing backup childcare, he'd no doubt had to do some juggling concerning his son, Archie. Rumour had it that the childminder had let him down that morning. She hoped that didn't mean he'd arrive harassed and in a dark mood.

Ava quickly turned her attention back to the board. Sometimes she felt like she was back at school when she saw the pictures and arrows and other visual information. It reminded her of montages on the art room wall or story boards in English. In fact, it was a bit of both. A visual representation of the story they were attempting, step by cautious step, to piece together: how Nick Winter and Samantha Benrose had ended up brutally murdered. If they were lucky, the story would end with an arrest and a successful conviction, an outcome that still seemed a long way off.

Also pinned on the board was an enlarged satellite view of Northfields Farm. Photographs of Nick and Samantha had been placed at their separate murder sites.

The farmhouse and its various outbuildings were labelled with dotted lines depicting the interconnections between the locations. A red line denoted Nick's final journey from the yurt to the garage.

There were also photographs of the four members of the Stratford family, of Soren Hunter and of Aubrey's friend, Charles Unwin. The members of the charity committee, all of whom had been at Northfields on the day of the murders, were also represented, as were two other groups: hired staff and attendees of the dance. None of them seemed to be likely suspects, and Ava was acutely aware that the killer's image was probably not even on the board.

The buzz of conversation in the operations room stopped abruptly as Neal walked across the floor and took up his place by the side of the board. He didn't look harassed — a good sign — but he was plainly embarrassed. He began by apologising for his tardiness, which Ava knew he would regard as a personal failure to live up to the standards he liked to set for his team. She felt for him. She knew he couldn't let his guard down in the presence of his colleagues in the way she'd seen him do with his family and close friends, but she wished he would be a bit easier on himself, maybe show the more personable side to his colleagues. No one in the room was going to be upset if the boss was a bit late occasionally — or if he smiled a bit more.

The room was full. Besides Ava, PJ and Tom Knight, there were some constables who had helped with taking statements from people at the dance. Neal spent a few minutes summarising the events of Saturday evening. Ava felt eyes dart in her direction when he recounted her gruesome discovery of the bodies.

He reminded them all that the case had already captured the attention of the media, and was exciting the imagination of the public. His face became taut when he was obliged to mention that the killer had been dubbed 'the Beast of Northfields' and that one journalist had already referred to the murders as 'the Valentine's Weekend Massacre.'

"I take it I don't need to remind people not to discuss any of the elements of this case with anyone not involved in the investigation?" he concluded. Heads nodded in agreement.

Then it was down to the business of assigning tasks. Follow-up interviews were still required to ascertain whether any of the guests at the dance or any of the catering or bar staff or the entertainers could provide any useful information. This would be the job of the uniformed constables.

"Listen to everything, discount nothing," Neal reminded them. It was to be hoped that he didn't have to remind them of how an investigation could turn on a single comment or a seemingly throwaway remark. He ended by exhorting everyone to flag up anything that sounded suspicious, inconsistent or just plain odd.

As the room began to empty, Neal signalled for Ava, PJ and Tom to remain.

"Tom, how did it go with Nick's parents yesterday?" he asked.

Tom and PJ exchanged glances. "Bit of an eye-opener, actually, sir," he said. "We expected the whole grieving-parent thing, but that wasn't what we got. Turns out Nick wasn't the apple of his mum and dad's eye. Not a lot of tears were shed over him. Well, none while we were there, anyway."

"He was a late baby," PJ chipped in. "Unwanted. Unloved."

"Yeah. Way they described him he was a deviant from birth. Lucky for him, his siblings looked out for him a bit. One sister in particular, Jenny. She's the one who went to London to look for him and persuaded him to come back to Nottingham."

Tom summarised the interviews with Bernie and Alice Winter and with Jenny. PJ chipped in with snippets of information as well as personal judgements on their characters. Ava couldn't help smiling at PJ's attempts to depict Nick's parents in a sympathetic way. Tom had no such concerns. "With such shit parents, it's no wonder the poor kid made a balls-up of his life."

"Jenny did an ace job of tracking him down," PJ said. "Went around the hostels until she found him."

"Did you ask about enemies?" Ava said.

"She didn't really know. He had a friend on the streets, though. A Good Samaritan, as she called him. He was the one who got Nick into a hostel."

"Name?" Neal asked, sharply.

"She didn't know, sir. Sorry."

Ava caught Neal's eye and intuited that he was thinking exactly what she was thinking: could Soren Hunter have been Nick's Good Samaritan, as he'd been Monty's?

"Sir?" she said.

"It's possible," Neal said. PJ and Tom exchanged puzzled looks.

"Soren Hunter, the man who accompanied me to the yurt where we found Samantha's body, lived rough in London for a time. He came to Monty Stratford's aid when he was mugged at knifepoint. Perhaps he did Nick a favour too. It's not a wild guess. When we questioned Blue Stratford, she mentioned that Hunter greeted Nick warmly when he arrived at Northfields, although Hunter denied it. Claimed he'd never met Nick before. But it's a possibility that he did meet him, and that they'd kept in touch. Soren could have told Nick where he was staying and Nick could have looked it up online, seen the idyllic rural setting and decided it was the perfect place to spend Valentine's weekend with his girlfriend — and surprise his Good Samaritan friend." She glanced at Neal to see if he approved of her theory. He was nodding his head. "We know the name of the London hostel Nick stayed in. One of the staff might remember who brought him there well enough to give us a description. Or even a name."

"Okay," Neal said. "We need to get in touch with that hostel ASAP. Show them Hunter's picture. If Hunter's lied to us about not knowing Nick, he might have lied about other things, too. Or been selective with the truth."

"Yes, sir."

"Did you have time to speak with Samantha Benrose's parents?"

Tom shook his head. "No, sir. We're scheduled to speak with them later this morning."

Neal nodded. "Find out what they thought of Nick and ask if there are any ex-boyfriends we should be aware of." He turned back briskly to the board and tapped the satellite photograph of the farm. "And we need to find out how Nick ended up in Aubrey's garage workshop."

"There were no messages on Nick's phone," Tom reminded everyone. "Or Samantha's."

"Nick and Samantha had tickets for the dance," Ava said. "Which means that if they intended to arrive right at the beginning, they would probably have set off from their yurt around 6:45. Nick was already in costume when he got to the garage. Samantha wasn't in costume when she was found. Could there have been a problem with her outfit? That might explain why Nick went on ahead."

"Could have been her hair," PJ suggested. "These 1940s hairdos aren't straightforward. Maybe she needed to borrow some clips or some curling tongs. What was her hair like when you found her, Ava?"

"I wasn't really looking at her hair," Ava replied. "But now that I think about it, I don't remember it being styled in forties fashion."

Neal was beginning to look impatient. "Perhaps Mr Hunter can enlighten us on the state of Samantha Benrose's hair. He seems to be the eyes and ears at Northfields."

"From what you've told us, Ava, he does seem pretty clued up," Tom said, missing the sarcasm. "How did he end up on the streets?"

"Good luck finding out," Ava said. "He's pretty adept at deflecting questions he doesn't care to answer. Still, it won't be a mystery for long. We're running background checks on him and the Stratfords."

She had to admit she was intrigued by Soren Hunter. He'd assumed the role of leader and protector instinctively, suggesting some sort of professional training. He'd also demonstrated observational and field skills that went far beyond those of the average boy scout. Neal hadn't commented much about her theory that he might be ex-army.

"Ava, we're going to London this morning on the 10:35," Neal announced, taking her by surprise. She'd need to let her mum know that there was a chance she wouldn't be back in time to go to the theatre with her that evening. It was some seventies tribute band playing at the Stromford Theatre Royal. Guiltily, Ava hoped their train back would be delayed. Now that Ollie was on the mend, there wasn't really any reason for their mother still to be there, but she'd insisted on staying until the end of the week. The weekend couldn't come soon enough.

"Er . . . okay. I'll just grab a few things, sir."

The last time Ava travelled to London with Jim Neal was on their first proper case together. Neal had read his book most of the way and she'd listened to music. Though they were better acquainted now, she didn't think they'd be having a cosy chat all the way to King's Cross, so she double-checked that she had some earbuds. She could catch up on an episode of that Netflix drama she'd been watching with Ollie before his accident. He'd got ahead of her during his convalescence.

They left ten minutes after the meeting ended. Even so there was little time to spare. Ava's hopes of grabbing a coffee before boarding the train were dashed when she saw the length of the queue in the café, only to be raised again when it was announced that the train was running ten minutes late. "I'll just go and grab—"

"I'll have a tea and one of those breakfast baps," Neal said, handing her a tenner. "No time for breakfast this morning with all the hassle over childcare. I'm bloody starving now." He took out his phone.

The train drew up to the platform just as Ava was waiting for her change. It was busy and they couldn't find a seat together, so there was no question of having a chat, cosy or otherwise. Ava settled down with her drama and the next thing she knew they were pulling into King's Cross.

Monty Stratford had been staying at a budget hotel in Bloomsbury. The nearest Tube station was Russell Square, thankfully, only one uncomfortably congested stop on the Piccadilly Line from King's Cross. Ava was pressed close against Neal in the carriage and felt her breathing quicken. Neal cleared his throat and ran a finger around the inside collar of his shirt to loosen it. Maybe he was feeling the heat, too. Or was she imagining it? Squashed together like sardines, everyone was probably half suffocating. Still, she made sure that when they reached the station she got into the lift a few seconds behind him, so that she was pressed up against a total stranger this time.

It was a relief to step into the open air. "Hunter slept rough in the area around the Brunswick Centre, the Tube station and Woburn Place, according to Monty," Ava said. "He followed Monty and his attacker from the station. It's about a five-minute walk from here to the hotel where Monty was staying."

She looked around as she spoke. Hunter wouldn't have lacked neighbours. The homeless were in evidence up and down the street, either begging on the pavement or suggested by lumpy sleeping bags and heaps of belongings. Yet to the passers-by they were either invisible or a nuisance. She wondered which doorways Hunter had preferred.

"Hard to imagine him like that," Neal said, his gaze on a man across the street outside a busy café. He was sitting cross-legged against a tree, chin resting on his chest. A sorrowful-eyed dog was curled up in the bow of his legs. Ava thought of Hunter's competence, his air of being in control. Neal was right. It was unimaginable.

"I can picture him living rough in a jungle or surviving up a mountain, though. You know, like Bear Grylls. Hunting and killing his own food."

Neal didn't comment.

They crossed the street. Ava showed the startled beggar Hunter's picture on her phone. He shook his head. But he also pointed to a woman further down the street who'd been in the area longer than him.

"Do you recognise this man?" Ava asked, showing her the picture. The woman was barely able to focus.

"Leave it," Neal said, quietly. "She's on something." But as they began walking away, the woman called them back. Her hand curled around Ava's arm, pulling her closer until her rank breath was in her face. "He helped me, he did," she said. Ava waited. "Used to sleep around here sometimes. Not seen him around for a while, mind."

"Tell me how he helped you," Ava said.

"One night last summer, it was. Couple of lads set on me. They do that for a laugh, you know. Sometimes they just piss on you, but those two were nasty. Anyway, your man soon saw them off. He was no stranger to fighting, I'll tell you that."

"Show her a picture of Monty Stratford. And Nick Winter," Neal said. But they'd lost her. Her eyes had taken on a glazed look and when Ava showed her the pictures the woman turned her face away. Neal slipped some money into the pocket of her coat. Ava hoped the eyes on the street hadn't noticed.

Their route to the hostel where Jenny Winter had found her brother took them past the location of the modest hotel where Monty Stratford had stayed on his trip to London. He'd been attacked a short distance from the entrance, in an alley that ran alongside the hotel. A pity he hadn't just waited until he got inside to relieve himself. The alley was poorly lit. The security lighting looked like it had been vandalised. There were no cameras.

They went inside and asked to speak to the manager. He remembered Monty and confirmed what they already suspected: no one had seen or heard anything.

"You might want to get those lights fixed," Neal said. "It's an obvious place for a potential mugger to lie in wait."

"Yeah," the manager said, without taking his eyes off his phone. "The Met already suggested that. Suggested a camera, too."

Not in a hurry then, Neal mused wryly. It was seven months since Monty had been mugged.

They let it go. They weren't there to investigate Monty's mugging. The purpose of their visit was primarily to find out whether the hostel manager recognised Hunter as the man who had brought Nick to the hostel. And to see if the local Met could give them any additional information on him.

It didn't look like a hostel from the outside. Not that hostels looked like anybody's idea of them, these days. From the pavement it could have been a private apartment block, revealing no clue that its residents had sadder backstories than most. Still, they were the lucky ones. At least they had a roof over their heads. Ava wondered if the hostel's name, Hope House, was inspirational to the people living there or whether it reminded them that, in their case, hope was often elusive.

Neal showed his ID at the reception. The duty manager was summoned to speak with them. She was a large woman, dressed in ripped black leggings and a loose black T-shirt bearing a picture of some comic book character. Her eyebrows were pierced with silver rings and there was an inflamed red patch on her nose. The missing stud must have caused an infection. Ava was reminded of Janine Watts. The woman led them into an office and introduced herself as Pixie. No surname. She was anything but Pixie-like. Maybe it was an ironic nickname.

Pixie seemed a bit irritated, but it turned out not to be due to the presence of two detectives in her domain. "Bloody hot-desking," she complained, in a broad Scots accent. She swept aside books, papers and other objects on the desk. "I can't stand clutter. Night manager's a right hoarder." She smiled at them. "How can I help?"

They'd already explained on the phone. Ava showed her Soren Hunter's photo. Pixie's face showed a flicker of recognition. "Yep. That's Soren Hunter. But I hope you're not expecting me to give you his life story, because that man is a complete enigma." She looked at Neal. "To tell you the truth, I wouldn't be surprised if his name wasn't even Soren.

Or Hunter." She paused, then added, "Actually, Soren's a bit of an urban legend around these parts."

"How so?" Ava asked.

Pixie's expression darkened slightly. "He's no' in any trouble, is he?"

"He's a person of interest in a double murder we're investigating."

Pixie was sharp. "OMG! Stromfordshire! This is about that Valentine's massacre, isn't it?"

Ava heard Neal's sigh of exasperation. "I tell you what though . . . if you're pegging Soren for that Beast of Northfields, you're barking up the wrong tree. Soren's more superhero than supervillain, though I'll no' deny he has a dark side."

They seemed to be entering the realms of fantasy. Ava gazed at the image on Pixie's T-shirt. She thought the lizard-like creature depicted was called Venom. Ollie was a big fan of Marvel and DC comic books and movies. He talked about the characters as though they were real people, and so Ava was acquainted with the more memorable heroes and villains. She sensed Pixie and Ollie would get on well.

"Soren's sort of a witness," Ava said, not untruthfully. It sounded better than *suspect* and seemed to quell Pixie's wariness.

Pixie nodded. "He'd be good at that. I honestly believe Soren's got superpowers when it comes to seeing stuff that other people miss."

Ava cleared her throat. "What else can you tell us about him?"

"Well, he knows how to handle himself, if you know what I mean."

Ava nodded. "What was that you were saying about him being an urban legend in these parts?"

Pixie picked up a cube from the desk. It was comprised of lots of little magnetic silver balls, which she ran her thumb over thoughtfully.

"He looked out for people," Pixie said. "You know. Street people. He protected them." She seemed suddenly hesitant. It wasn't too much of a stretch to imagine that protecting people might sometimes have involved the use of violence. Ava thought of Soren beating up the men who'd set about the woman at Russell Square, of him seeing off Monty's mugger. Even she was starting to believe in him as a kind of Dark Knight figure.

"You mean, like a sort of vigilante?" She remembered PJ saying that Jenny Winter had referred to the man who'd taken Nick to Hope House as a Good Samaritan. The two weren't the same.

Pixie looked pleased at Ava's description. "Yeah. You nailed it."

Ava recalled something Pixie had said. "You said Soren had a dark side. What did you mean by that? Did you ever witness that side of him?"

Pixie's 'no' was a beat too quick. Perhaps she'd just caught on that being depicted as a vigilante wasn't to Hunter's advantage. After a thoughtful pause, she said, "He never did anything to anybody that they didn't deserve."

Ava looked at Neal. "Go on," she said.

But Pixie was no longer in a cooperative mode. "That's all I'm saying. You can think what you like, but Soren is a good man."

At least they'd got some information. It was enough. For now. Ava showed Pixie the picture of Nick and asked her to confirm that Soren had brought him to Hope House. Pixie's eyes widened and she gasped. She'd heard about the murders at Northfields Farm but clearly hadn't made the connection. "I saw about the murders on the news, but I didn't take in the names. I didn't realise . . . it was the same Nick who'd stayed here last year. I never asked his surname."

"It's alright," Ava said.

"Soren wouldn't have . . . He helped Nick. He doesn't *hurt* people."

Unless they deserve it. Pixie had said it herself.

* * *

Before they left Hope House, Ava had asked Pixie what she could tell them about Nick Winter. He was no stranger to drugs, she'd told them, but he wasn't an addict. He'd been in bad shape when he'd arrived with Hunter. By then, Pixie was being more circumspect about mentioning Hunter. She did hint that Nick had injuries consistent with a beating and that it might have been a lot worse if Hunter hadn't come to his rescue. She didn't mention how Hunter had dealt with Nick's assailants. Presumably they had not come out of it unscathed.

"You've been really helpful," Ava told her just before they left. Pixie asked them to remember her to Hunter.

"So, what did you think of my vigilante theory?" Ava asked Neal. They were on their way to the Met station where Monty Stratford had reported his mugging.

Neal made a grunting sound. "I think you've been watching too many superhero films." But his tone was flippant, rather than critical. Archie liked comic book heroes and Ava suspected Neal did, too — though getting him to admit it might prove challenging.

"I'm more concerned with his dark side," Neal said. "Perhaps he's more devil than avenging angel. Let's not forget that we have two brutal murders to account for."

As if she could. Her mind flashed back to the macabre sight of Nick and Samantha's mutilated corpses — reality, not fantasy.

"The killer could be someone Nick crossed while he was here in London. They wouldn't have taken kindly to Hunter's efforts at playing the hero, running around fighting crime on his own. If Nick was into drugs, who knows what sort of villains he might have pissed off? Pixie said he wasn't an addict, but he could have been dealing, despite what his sister said. Or cheating dealers who'd have no qualms about pursuing him to Stromfordshire for revenge."

"Great," Neal said. "That's all we want. Getting mixed up with London drug dealers again." It was a reference to a case they'd investigated the previous year.

At the station, they were shown the report on Monty Stratford's mugging. He'd mentioned that a stranger had come to his rescue and that the stranger had asked to remain anonymous. This prompted the desk sergeant to comment. "That happened a few times last year, funny enough. People being mugged around that area or being beaten up, reporting that a member of the public had come to their aid, but declined to be named. It's not that unusual, though. People have their reasons for not wanting to get involved with the police." He rubbed his chin. "Still, almost seemed like a pattern was developing. Most of them didn't want to give a description of their rescuer, but a few did, and we suspected it was the same person." He looked from Neal to Ava. "Which was a little bit troubling." He paused. "On one occasion we think he might actually have put a perp in hospital."

"How so?"

"The perp attacked a homeless woman. He turned up in A&E with a knife wound. The man the victim described matched the description of our mystery hero. Funny thing was, Mystery Man administered first aid at the scene, and got the mugger's victim to call an ambulance. It was said that he knew exactly where to inflict a wound without causing serious damage." He shook his head. "Then, all of a sudden, we never heard about him again."

"When did it stop?" Neal asked.

"Let me think. Probably around the end of July last year. I went to the Canaries with my missus the last fortnight in July and when I got back the lads at the station joked that the local Caped Crusader had gone strangely quiet while I was away." He gave a short laugh. "As if he might be me."

"So, Monty Stratford was the last person he helped, then?" Ava asked.

The sergeant looked thoughtful. "Yes. Yes, I suppose he was. That we know of, anyway."

She slid her phone in front of him and showed him the picture of Soren Hunter. "Could that be your mystery hero?" The sergeant stared at the picture for several moments before confirming that it matched the description, although he couldn't say it was definitely the same person.

On their way back to King's Cross, Ava said, "Are you going to get Tom to bring Hunter in? He was lying when he said that he didn't know Nick. And if he is the Met's mystery man, he's already used a knife to cause injury."

Neal seemed to consider, then said, "Tomorrow will do." He quickened his pace. "Come on. If we catch the 3:30, I'll be home in time to eat with Archie."

CHAPTER TWELVE

"The boss and Ava should be in London by now," Tom remarked. He wasn't convinced PJ was awake. They'd driven in complete silence for about fifteen minutes now. With any other person that wouldn't be unusual, but PJ was naturally chatty. Except when she had a hangover. A glance to his left confirmed his suspicions, although he highly doubted it was down to alcohol this time, given her condition the previous day.

He turned the radio on. It was tuned into a local station. The news reader's accent sounded like PJ's. Maybe that's why she woke up at that precise moment. Probably thought it was one of her legions of relatives speaking to her.

"Welcome back, Sleeping Beauty," he said.

"Ha ha. I hardly slept a wink last night. My neighbours were partying until all hours."

"They didn't invite you?"

"They don't know me. I've just moved in, remember?"

"No excuse. Still could've asked you. Good way to get to know you."

"Not sure I want to know them."

"I'm sorry about your break-up." Tom had heard the news but had never got around to saying anything. Who knew what the etiquette was in those situations? The only other person he knew who'd been jilted was a lad he'd gone to school with, and he'd seemed more relieved than heartbroken.

"Thanks. It was probably for the best. I heard from a friend in Bali at the moment. Bali! This is the bloke who complained when I booked a holiday in Spain." She mimicked a whining Steve. "*What do you want to be going abroad for? There's plenty of places we haven't been to in this country.*"

"Yeah, well, he did have a life-changing experience," Tom said, not altogether tactfully.

PJ grunted.

Tom focused on the road ahead and fifteen minutes later they drew up outside the Benroses' house. It was in a village six miles north-west of Newark, in Nottinghamshire.

"Here we go again," he said, as they waited for someone to answer their knock. More grieving parents to deal with.

Samantha's father, Neil Benrose, showed them into a bright living room where they found his wife, Pearl, just finishing a phone call to the vicar. Samantha's body wasn't likely to be released for some time to come, but arrangements still had to be made. Tom gave his condolences, followed by PJ, and both accepted the offer of a cup of tea, mainly because the Benroses seemed eager to provide refreshments. It was a delaying tactic. Putting off the interview that would remind them not only that their daughter was dead but that she had died in such a brutal way. Just before Tom was about to start, a young woman entered the room and sat down next to Pearl.

"This is Natasha. Samantha's sister," Pearl said, slipping an arm around her surviving daughter's waist.

Tom nodded. "I'm sorry for your loss." PJ did the same.

It was obvious from the start that Neil and Pearl hadn't approved of Nick. "He used to be a junkie," Neil said. "And he'd slept rough on the street." He shook his head. "How did our daughter get involved with a person like that?"

Through her work as a social worker, Tom knew. Which Neil Benrose must have known. He wasn't really asking how, but why. Why did a nice middle-class girl like Samantha bother with a low-life like Nick? It was in his tone, his choice of words. Tom felt a stirring of empathy with Nick; as a mixed-race man, he'd been judged and dismissed in similar fashion by the prejudiced parents of an ex-girlfriend.

"Samantha was engaged for two years to a wonderful man, Toby Swallow," Pearl Benrose said. "A doctor."

"Did the engagement end because of Nick?" PJ asked.

The Benroses exchanged glances. Pearl cleared her throat. "No. Toby had a brief affair with another woman. Samantha found out and broke off the engagement. Toby was distraught. He would have done anything to get Samantha back."

Anything? Tom wasn't sure he liked the sound of this Dr Toby. Strange, also, that Pearl's focus was on Swallow's distress and not her daughter's. "And this was how long before Samantha met Nick?"

"About three months," Pearl said.

"And Toby was still trying to persuade Samantha to forgive him? Even after she started seeing Nick?"

Pearl looked to her husband. "I don't know where you think you're going with this, Sergeant," he said. "Toby loved our Samantha. He would never have hurt her. Never."

"Never," Pearl echoed. Tom wondered why they needed to keep repeating the word.

Natasha, who had been sitting quietly, now spoke up. "You know that's not true, Mum." Both parents glared at her.

"Did Dr Swallow hurt Samantha?" Tom's question was directed at Natasha.

"No," Pearl said.

"Yes, Mum. He did." Natasha removed her mother's arm from around her waist. Her face flushed with anger. "You should stop defending him. It's despicable. Especially now that Sam's . . ." She gulped. "Gone."

"It was only the once," Pearl said. "Toby had had a bit too much to drink. He apologised immediately. Bought Samantha the most beautiful gold bracelet the very next day."

Tom was fast losing respect for Samantha's parents. He had to remind himself that they were grieving.

"Maybe it was only the once that we know of," Natasha said. She turned to Tom. "Sam turned up here one night with a fractured wrist from where Toby twisted her arm. But she told me Toby was always telling her what to do, what to wear, which of her friends she could go out with. He was a controlling bastard."

"Did your sister tell you this after her wrist was fractured?" PJ asked.

"Yes. She told my mum and dad, too. But they kept telling her it was just because he cared about her. That he hadn't meant to hurt her. 'Didn't realise his own strength,' Mum said. But Sam was thinking of leaving him before he had that affair. She told me she was afraid of him."

PJ addressed Neil and Pearl. "Is this true? Did your daughter say that Dr Swallow was excessively controlling?"

"He wasn't excessively controlling. He just liked her to look nice. Samantha was a beautiful girl, but didn't always make the most of her appearance. Always dressed down in tatty jeans and baggy shirts . . ." Pearl looked at her daughter, less sure now. "She said she was afraid of him?"

Natasha nodded. There was a brief silence. Then, she said, "Nick was like a breath of fresh air for Sam. He loved her the way she was."

"Apart from Dr Swallow, can you think of anyone else who might have wanted to harm Samantha?"

No one answered. Tom suspected Neil and Pearl would have brought up Nick if he hadn't been dead already. He took out his phone and showed them a picture of the Pandora charm that had been found near the yurt where Nick and Samantha had been staying. "Do any of you know whether Samantha had a charm like this one?"

"Yes," Natasha said. "Toby gave her a Pandora bracelet for her birthday the year before last. That was one of the charms he gave her at the same time. Is . . . is it Sam's? What happened to the rest of the bracelet?"

"It's safe. It will be returned to you in due course," Tom said.

"Sam wondered if she should give it back to Toby. I persuaded her not to. She felt a bit guilty about wearing it, but she liked it a lot. She got rid of everything else that reminded her of him, but kept the bracelet and the charms."

Tom and PJ thanked them all for their time. It was Natasha who accompanied them to the door.

"Do . . . do you think Toby might have killed Sam, and Nick?"

"We don't know yet, Natasha. But we will find the person responsible, and he will be punished."

She watched them from the doorstep until they reached their car. She had her arms wrapped around her body, holding the sides of her cardigan together, but it was herself she was trying to hold together, Tom thought.

He had not mentioned that there had been minute traces of blood on the charm, giving rise to speculation that it might have been removed from the bracelet after Samantha had been killed. That was a detail the family didn't need to know about. Not yet, at any rate. It would all come out at the trial, no doubt — when, not if, they caught the killer.

He was unsurprised to discover that PJ's opinion of Neil and Pearl Benrose matched his own. "Pathetic. They obviously knew what was going on but chose to overlook it for the sake of their daughter marrying a bloody doctor. I can't understand that sort of attitude. It's the twenty-first century, for heaven's sake! So, what do you think? Could Swallow have been at Northfields that night? Did he take the charm as a sort of trophy, then lose it when he was fleeing the scene?"

"It would have enraged him to see her wearing it," Tom said. "It was a reminder that Samantha had once been his, and now, to his way of thinking, she belonged to another, lesser man. Natasha described him as controlling and possessive. It's not much of a stretch to picture him being sent into a jealous rage." He sighed. "It's hard to ignore the symbolism of a jealous ex-lover stabbing his girlfriend in the heart on

Valentine's Day, isn't it? Jealousy would also give Swallow a motive for killing Nick, his rival in love."

"If his prints are on that charm, he'll have some explaining to do," PJ said, then added, "I'm starving. Do you think we could stop for a bite to eat?"

"Great idea. There's bound to be a pub in the village."

"There is. I checked while we were talking. Straight ahead, first left, second right. The White Horse." Tom put the car in gear.

"He's a plastic surgeon," Tom said ten minutes later inside the White Horse. "Private." As soon as they'd left the car, he'd looked up Toby Swallow on his phone. "Specialises in cosmetic surgery."

"Why am I not surprised?" PJ sighed. "Maybe he'll create his perfect woman under the knife to replace Samantha."

"I think we should pay him a call. Check if he has an alibi for the weekend. His practice is in Nottingham." He reached for his phone again.

Swallow's receptionist was less than accommodating. Tom needed to use his heft as a police officer to get her to arrange a slot for them to speak to him. "The great doctor can fit us in at three," he said to PJ. "We've got a couple of hours."

He could think of worse places to pass the time than sitting in this pleasant country inn. A pint would have been nice, but he was on duty. His eyes travelled along the row of craft beers on offer behind the bar. One of them was familiar. Blue Monty. He nudged PJ, who agreed.

Tom asked to speak with the publican. He showed his police ID to the barmaid.

The manager confirmed that the beer came from Northfields, adding, "Prize-winning brew, that. It's one of our top sellers."

"I'd love to try it, but alas, I'm on duty," Tom said. "Do you know the brewers, Monty and Blue Stratford?"

"Sure. They approached us about a year ago about sampling their beer." His face clouded suddenly. "Is this about the murders?" He looked at the cask, perhaps wondering if his supply of Blue Monty would dry up if one or both of its brewers were to serve time for double murder. "A tragedy for the Benroses. They're regulars here."

"Yes?" Of course, someone who owned a pub in the village where one of the victims lived would be clued up on the case.

"The family have booked our lounge for the wake."

"I'm one of the investigating officers," Tom said. "What can you tell me about the Stratfords?"

"Good brewers," the publican said. "Strong on sales and marketing, too. Seem like good people."

"Right." What had he been hoping for? Blue Monty was stocked by a number of independent public houses. There was nothing meaningful about it being sold in a pub where one of the victims lived. This was one of those connections that wasn't causal, just coincidence. He was about to go back and join PJ when the publican spoke.

"I suppose you're asking because Monty knew Samantha Benrose and her boyfriend, Nick." He picked up a beer mat, rubbed it on his sleeve then set it down again. "Hey, young Monty's not a suspect is he? I wouldn't believe that of him. His mate with the dreadlocks maybe, but never Monty."

"Monty Stratford knew Nick and Samantha?" Tom looked over at PJ. The barmaid had just brought their order to the table but PJ wasn't paying attention to the food. She'd heard Tom's question and was looking over with acute interest.

"I think it was his mate who knew Nick. He came along with Monty on a delivery — the usual delivery driver had let them down that week. That was . . . let me think. Back at the beginning of January. Nick was here with Samantha. He got up and shook hands with Monty's friend and they all sat down and had a drink together."

The manager had mentioned dreadlocks. Definitely Soren Hunter, then. Tom returned to their table and eyed his lunch appreciatively. He was hungry and the plate was loaded. PJ's plate was piled high, too. Tom approved of women who enjoyed their grub. Despite PJ more often than not being on some faddy diet to lose weight, to him she looked just fine as she was.

"Well, well, well," she said. "The boss is going to be interested in this development."

"Yeah. Confirmation that Hunter knew Nick. And Monty met him too, even if it was only on that one occasion." He blew on his forkful of chips. "He didn't mention that little nugget when the DI and Ava interviewed him. He and Hunter have got some explaining to do."

"I'll be interested to learn whether Ava and the DI have been able to establish a London connection between Nick and Hunter," PJ said.

They ate and chatted for a while. When their plates were almost clear, the barmaid came over and asked if they'd like to order dessert. Tom declined but PJ asked to see the menu. "I'll have the warm chocolate fudge cake, with an extra dollop of cream."

The waitress nodded, and hovered. Then she looked at Tom and said, "Has anyone ever told you you're a dead ringer for Bradley Cooper. Except you're . . . er . . ."

"Black?" Tom said. It wasn't the first time he'd heard this. For someone with his skin tone it was rather bemusing. The waitress looked a bit embarrassed and hurried off to get PJ's order.

"She's right, you know," PJ teased.

Tom grinned. "Always knew I had star quality. Poor Bradley . . . he probably gets mistaken for me all the time."

That raised a smile. Tom was pleased. The old PJ was still in there. The fudge cake also cheered her up. "Perfect," she said when she'd demolished the lot after initially offering Tom half because she was sure she couldn't eat that amount of cake by herself. "Do you mind if I finish off with a quick coffee?" It, too, arrived piled high with whipped cream.

Lunch over, they drove to Nottingham. Swallow's practice was located south of the city centre in a small retail park. The building itself looked like just another outlet store. Inside was a different matter. A lot of effort had been made to suppress any hint that medical procedures took place there. The décor was minimalist and modern, all shiny floors and clean lines.

A goddess in a spotless white uniform greeted them at the reception. The uniform, more of a dress really, was pulled in at the waist and cut low to emphasise perfectly sculpted breasts that couldn't possibly be real. "She looks like a nurse in a *Carry-On* film," PJ whispered when, after showing them to a waiting area, the woman tottered off, high heels tip-tapping on the polished marble floor.

Swallow kept them waiting for twenty minutes. "I'll bloody nick him for wasting police time," Tom grumbled after the first fifteen.

At last, the receptionist called over. "Dr Swallow will see you now."

Swallow's consulting room was smart and lavishly furnished, nothing like an NHS consulting room; no plastic chairs or vinyl floor in evidence here. Everything was plush and leather. Swallow was suave and expensively attired. Not the kind of man who'd want to be seen with a woman who favoured old jeans and T-shirts.

"I'm not sure how I can help with your inquiry," Swallow said, once the introductions were over. "Samantha and I split up some months before she started seeing Winter." There was no emotion, Tom noted. No expressions of upset over the fate of his ex-fiancée, the one for whom, so her parents alleged, he would have done anything to win a second chance.

"How would you describe your relationship with Samantha Benrose, Dr Swallow?" Tom began.

"We were engaged to be married. I loved Sam. I was devastated when she called off the engagement."

"Ms Benrose broke off the engagement after discovering that you'd been having an affair, isn't that right?"

Swallow sniffed, in a manner that suggested disdain. "Hardly an affair. More like a couple of one-night stands. I told Sam how sorry I was. But she just couldn't forgive me."

A couple of one-night stands. So, Swallow had cheated on Samantha more than once. Had she seized on the second affair as an opportunity to get out of a toxic relationship?

Tom decided to come straight to the point. "Did you ever hit Samantha?"

"I see you've been speaking with her sister."

"Natasha Benrose claims that you twisted Samantha's arm so badly you fractured her wrist." Sam's parents had also confirmed it in not so many words, albeit they'd written it off. But Tom didn't think it'd be helpful to bring that up just yet.

"Natasha was jealous of Sam's relationship with me. She came on to me on a number of occasions while Sam and I were together. Her claim is vastly exaggerated. I caught Sam by the arm when she stumbled one day and she turned awkwardly. It was an accident. I took her to A&E myself."

"Natasha also claims that your behaviour towards Samantha was excessively controlling."

Swallow laughed. "Look around you, Sergeant. I'm a successful and respected medical professional. Natasha's what? A teenager who was jealous of her sister and had a chip on her shoulder against a man who resisted her persistent sexual advances. Are you going to take her word against mine?"

Yes. Tom had been around enough sexual predators to sense that he was in the presence of one now. He wouldn't be surprised if it was Swallow who'd made inappropriate advances towards Natasha. She hadn't mentioned it, but perhaps that was one truth too far to raise in the presence of her already disbelieving parents. Could she be persuaded to bring a case of sexual harassment against Swallow? It was unlikely. As Swallow had hinted, who would a judge be more likely to believe?

"Did you ever meet Samantha's new boyfriend, Nick Winter?" PJ asked. She'd been quiet until now. Swallow looked at her. A little too long, as if he were appraising her. Tom wondered how women could stand that sort of thing.

"No, thank God. He sounds like a complete waste of space." He didn't need to say it. His disbelief was written on his face. How could Samantha have preferred a man like that to him?

Swallow glanced at his watch. "Is there anything else I can help you with?"

"Yes, actually," Tom answered. He showed Swallow the picture of the Pandora charm on his phone. Swallow was a beat late in hiding his surprise.

"You gave Samantha Benrose a charm like this for her birthday, didn't you?"

"I gave her one *like it*, yes."

"This was found near the yurt where Samantha and Nick were staying the weekend they were murdered."

"I don't understand why you're showing it to me, Sergeant."

Tom put his phone away without offering Swallow an explanation.

"Can you tell us where you were and what you were doing on Saturday?"

"I was in surgery in the morning." He looked directly at PJ. "Liposuction. We offer a very good rate for that here."

"And the afternoon?" Tom asked, his anger stirring at the implied insult to PJ.

"I had a migraine. Took some pills and slept well into the evening."

"Right. No alibi for the time of the murders, then." He had the satisfaction of witnessing Swallow's sly confidence waver slightly.

"I'd love him to be guilty," PJ said, as soon as they were back outside. "Dr Toby is a total prick."

"Thought you liked to look for the good in people," Tom teased.

"Hmm. Proves there's always an exception to the rule."

"Never really got what that meant," Tom commented.

"It means Dr Toby's a total prick."

CHAPTER THIRTEEN

Blue Stratford woke with a start. It was amazing that she'd actually managed to sleep at all, given that it was practically impossible at this late stage in her pregnancy to find a comfortable position. Her mother had bought her one of those V-shaped cushions, but the bump was too massive for even that to be of much use now. She glanced at the display on her clock radio: 2:35. She must have been exhausted to drop off so quickly and sleep like the dead for four and a half hours.

She lay still, waiting for the baby to move. It was uncomfortable when it kicked, but she preferred the discomfort over the panic that consumed her when it went for long periods without moving. Then there were the Braxton Hicks contractions, which made her stomach tighten painfully, mimicking labour. Much as she dreaded the real labour and birth, she couldn't wait for this third trimester to be over.

Anxiety gnawed at her. Ever since they told her at the clinic that her blood pressure was a bit high, she'd been worrying about it, though she'd tried not to make a thing of it in front of her mother. She knew her mother must have been bursting to tell her to go and have a lie down when she broke the news. That's why she'd accepted the tea and cake when she didn't really feel like eating. Anything to distract her from

115

fussing over her. Then again, wasn't a bit of fuss preferable to taking a risk with the baby?

It was a girl. They'd asked Blue if she wanted to know when she had her scan at sixteen weeks and she'd said yes. Relief had flooded through her at the news. A girl would be less likely to look like the father, she reasoned, though she didn't know enough about genetics to know that for sure. She hoped that once her family set eyes on the baby they would stop asking about the father, and just accept her as a Stratford.

Does the father even know you're pregnant? Blue never reacted to her mother's questions about the baby's father. Unfortunately, her mother had taken her lack of response on that occasion to mean that Blue hadn't told him. Her mother was nothing if not persistent. *Don't you think he has a right to know?* Blue had maintained the stony silence and impassive expression that she reserved for any and all questions about the baby's provenance.

She doubted the rest of the night was going to be restful. She felt wide awake and uncomfortable, and now she needed to pee. Sighing mightily, she rolled onto her side and pulled herself up. The hush on the upstairs landing enfolded her as she tiptoed to the bathroom.

Afterwards, before getting back into bed, she crossed to her bedroom window. She liked to look out and imagine Soren asleep in the caravan. Even more than that, she liked to imagine herself curled up against him. Did he even notice her, she wondered?

It had been cloudy when she'd turned in for the night, no hint of a moon, the farm and its outbuildings shrouded in darkness. When they'd first moved here there had been talk of installing security lighting on the outbuildings, but it always seemed to move down the list of priorities. They'd all felt safe here, deep in the countryside. Before the murders.

Blue pulled the curtain aside and looked out. She gasped. The night sky wasn't dark. It was alive with fire.

* * *

Blue learned later that her scream had struck panic into the hearts of the various members of the household. Her mother told her she had awoken with a start and assumed that her daughter had gone into labour. Her father had sat bolt upright in bed, convinced they were under enemy attack. Monty came running out of his bedroom to find her half-collapsed on the landing, yelling hysterically, "Fire!" He'd looked around him, as if expecting to see flames licking around the oak banisters of the staircase or curling around the gap under Blue's bedroom door.

"Where?" he said.

"Outside . . . I think . . . it's . . . the caravan. Oh God! What if Soren's—"

"Have you called 999?"

"No . . . I . . . I didn't think . . . I—"

"For goodness' sake, Blue!" Monty dashed off to his bedroom. He emerged seconds later, phone clamped to his ear as he struggled to pull on a pair of jeans one-handed. Her mum and dad joined her on the landing and, on hearing that there was a fire, her dad bolted off downstairs after Monty, still in his pyjamas and dressing gown.

"It's alright," her mum said, arm around her. "Soren will be fine. You know he has a sixth sense about danger. He would have got out as soon as he caught a whiff of smoke."

"What if there was . . . an explosion?"

"We would have heard it. Try to calm down, Blue. It's not good for the baby you getting into a panic. Your blood pressure . . ."

But Blue was already making her way cumbersomely down the stairs. Realising, perhaps, that there was nothing that she could say or do to stop Blue going out to the caravan, her mother followed behind her. She grabbed a couple of jackets from the rack near the kitchen door and she and Blue pulled on wellies in the porch before going outside.

Blue had seen clouds of thick black smoke and leaping flames from her bedroom window. Now, as they neared the barn, the sky above it appeared to glow orange, as though a fiery blood moon brooded on the other side.

Her worst fear was realised when she emerged from the side of the barn and caught sight of the blazing caravan. It looked like some molten creature had dropped from the sky and been reduced to a carcass by the inferno. Fiery tongues erupted from its mouth and leapt into the air, like living torchlight. The creature spat out sparks that landed in the grass and sizzled with menace. The air around it was electric. Choking.

Blue stared at the creature and the creature stared back. Without realising it, she'd moved too close and its scorching breath seared her face. Her mother pulled her away. "Come back, Blue! It's not safe!" Blue felt hysteria rising within her. How could she tell her mother that she would willingly walk through fire to save Soren? From somewhere far off came the sound of sirens. Blue uttered a heartfelt plea. "Oh, please, don't let them be too late!"

She turned to her father and Monty. "Where is he?" she demanded.

Monty shook his head. "We don't know, sis. The caravan was engulfed in smoke when we got here, and when the smoke cleared a bit we could see that the inside of the van was a furnace. We couldn't get anywhere near it."

"Oh no!" Blue pictured Soren waking to the sound of fire crackling all around him, choking on toxic fumes, dying alone. It was unbearable.

Monty squeezed her arm. "If anyone could survive that, it would be Soren."

"Then where is he? If he got out, he could be lying somewhere horribly injured . . ."

"We've checked the immediate area. There's no sign of him, Blue."

"The fire engine's here," her dad said. There was no siren. It must have been turned off when the vehicle left the main road. Now, Blue could hear the sound of its engine and, within moments, its headlights dazzled. A member of the crew jumped down and strode towards them as his team mates began unwinding the hoses.

"Was anyone inside?" he asked.

"We're not sure. One of our workers lived in the caravan, but we don't know if he got out before the fire started." Monty paused, looked at Blue. "He doesn't seem to be in the immediate area."

"Right." The fireman looked grim-faced. He might as well have just come right out and said that anyone still in there would be burnt to a crisp.

Blue stood in a miserable huddle with the rest of her family. There was nothing to do but watch and wait as jets of water rained down on the fire from powerful hoses, slowly but steadily winning the battle of the elements. At last, the flames were extinguished. The caravan's charred, skeletal remains dripped and smouldered, reeking of burnt rubber and acrid chemicals. Otherwise, the scene was strangely still and peaceful after the recent conflagration. Wisps of ash fluttered dreamily in the faint night breeze.

When one of the fire crew ventured inside the carcass of the burnt-out caravan, Blue feared the worst.

"Clear!" he called to the captain.

Blue's heart leapt. Did that mean Soren was alive? He'd escaped the furnace?

"No victims," the captain confirmed. He turned to the family. "Your worker clearly wasn't at home when the blaze started."

"What now?" Blue's mother asked, gazing at the bones of the caravan.

"Now we sift through the remains to establish the cause of the fire."

"Do you think it might have been deliberate?" her mother asked. Blue stared at her. Such an idea would never have occurred to Blue. The captain seemed to consider. He must have dealt with a lot of fires. He'd probably developed a sixth sense about probable causes. In the end he didn't comment, unwilling to commit himself, no doubt.

The fire engine had not arrived alone. A police patrol car was parked a short distance away and now two uniformed officers approached, one with a notebook in hand. "Did I hear someone say that you thought there was someone inside the caravan?" she asked.

Monty gave her Soren's details. Blue stood by, shaking slightly. "I'm the one who saw the f-fire f-first," she said. "F-from my bedroom window."

"What time was that?"

"About 2:45. But it must have started before then."

"This is the farm where the murders occurred last weekend, isn't it?" the PC said. "There can't be two Northfields in this area."

"Yes," Monty said. "Same farm."

Blue had begun to shake more violently. Her teeth chattered.

"Come on, love," her mother said. "There's nothing more we can do out here. Let's go indoors. You're shaking."

The PC looked at Blue's bump. "You should do what she says. Maybe have a cup of hot sweet tea? You don't want to be going into shock in your condition."

"Fuck my condition!" Blue said under her breath. It didn't seem right to go back to the farmhouse while the police and firemen were still on the property and Soren was missing. Now that her relief that he hadn't been burnt to death was subsiding, Blue's main concerns were with his whereabouts, and his safety.

As if reading her mind, Monty whispered, "Go on, Blue. If anyone can take care of himself, it's Soren. Dad and I will wait here. We'll let you know if there's any news."

Suddenly, she felt exhausted. It was an enormous effort to walk back to the farmhouse. Once back and seated at the kitchen table, she even allowed her mother to fuss a little. There was no question of going back to bed before Dad and Monty returned, so they drank tea and waited. Finally, at around half past six, they returned. She searched their faces. Her dad shook his head.

"Soren's still missing." Grim-faced, Monty pulled off the boots he'd forgotten to leave at the door. For once, their mother didn't comment on the mud he'd trailed across the kitchen floor.

"Well, no news is good news, isn't it?" she said.

Blue winced at her mother's feeble attempt to raise their spirits. But before she could respond, she was gripped by a pain in her lower abdomen that made her gasp aloud. It was quickly followed by another, sharper pain. She felt a sudden warm gush between her legs and, when she looked down, she was shocked to see blood soaking through her pyjamas. Her first thought, before she managed to tell her family that she was losing the baby, was *Bad luck comes in threes.*

CHAPTER FOURTEEN

"Daaad, have you found them yet?" Archie called from the upstairs landing. Jim Neal sighed. He considered his detective skills to be above the average but he'd been hunting for his son's lost PE shorts for the best part of ten minutes and he'd run out of places to look. With five minutes before they were due to leave for the childminder's, he did what he swore he wouldn't do. He called Maggie in Australia. She sounded worried.

"Hey, Jimmy. Is everything alright? What do you want?" A pause. "Is it Archie? Is he okay?"

"Archie's fine. Where the hell are his damn PE shorts?"

"In the basket in the bottom of his wardrobe where they always are."

"Right." Why the hell hadn't Archie known that? Why hadn't *he*, come to think of it? Neal apologised for waking his sister and took the stairs two at a time to retrieve the shorts. He was now angry on two counts: firstly, for not having known that Archie had PE today so that he could have reminded him to get his kit together the night before — it was unforgiveable to be so disorganised; secondly, for having allowed Maggie to slip into the role of domestic servant during her time with them. He'd never intended for that to happen when she'd moved in two and a half years previously after breaking up with her then boyfriend.

Neal had told his sister from the outset that he didn't want or expect her to be a live-in childminder and house-keeper. With a stab of guilt, he acknowledged that Maggie had taken on more and more of the chores. The last time they'd had a conversation about it, she'd dismissed his concerns, saying that helping out was her way of paying for living there for free.

Neal made sure he did his share when he was around, but when he was on a case there was no such thing as regular hours. "Bloody shorts," he muttered under his breath, kicking a discarded towel on the upstairs landing out of his way. "Archie! Is that where the towel's supposed to go?"

"Sorry, Dad," his son said, meekly. Then, cheerfully, "Great you found my shorts!"

Neal's temper didn't improve when he caught the child-minder glancing at her watch when they turned up at her door ten minutes late. "Sorry, traffic was bad on Stromford Road."

"Not a problem," said the childminder, whose name was Trish and who was actually very nice. She had grown-up children of her own. "I'm expecting a new charge this morning. Another boy around your age, Archie. He goes to your school. His name's Joe Rice. Do you know him?"

"He's in the year below me," Archie said, dismissively.

Neal wished Archie was Trish's sole charge. "I never have more than three, including Bertie, and he's only really here occasionally when his parents need a break," she'd assured him. Bertie was her two-year-old grandson. "And Archie's the only one I'll be looking after at odd hours of the day and night."

He was lucky to have her, really. She'd even agreed to look after Archie in the evening and cook him a meal if Neal was going to be too late home to cook. She was also available for babysitting in the evenings if he was stuck. In fact, Neal already had someone for that, but she hadn't been called upon all that often. He and Maggie had managed between them. Neal didn't really have a social life.

"See you later, Archie," he said, managing to plant a kiss on the top of his son's head as he ducked to avoid it. He was at that age. Neal gave a heavy sigh.

* * *

At least he was on time this morning. Early in fact. He made a quick cup of tea and settled in front of his emails. As soon as Tom and Ava arrived, he'd get them to bring Soren Hunter in for questioning.

His phone rang. George Lowe. The boss. What the bloody hell did he want? As if he didn't know. The Northfields murders was becoming a high-profile case. That meant more interference from above. But Lowe hadn't called to lecture him about the need for fast results on the investigation. He'd been at his desk even earlier than Neal and he'd been briefed on an incident that had occurred at Northfields Farm in the early hours of the morning. Could Neal get out there ASAP and find out what the hell else was going on at that damn farm?

Neal called Ava, Tom and PJ into his office as soon as they arrived, one after the other, as though they'd all caught the same bus.

"I just want to share a piece of information with you all before we brief each other on yesterday's interviews," he began. "Emergency services were called out to a fire at Northfields Farm in the early hours of the morning. The caravan that Soren Hunter was staying in was completely destroyed."

Tom gave a low whistle.

"Hunter wasn't in the caravan, and his whereabouts are currently unknown. Ava, you and I will be driving out there this morning. Tom, I'd like you to coordinate a search for Hunter. We need to find him as soon as possible."

"Yes, sir," Tom said.

"PJ, I'd like you to continue to read through the statements we've got from the dance guests and the charity committee. Flag up anything that looks interesting."

"Sir." PJ sounded a bit dejected to be assigned a desk job.

"Ava, would you like to fill the others in on our findings yesterday?"

Ava described their visit to the hostel and their conversation with Pixie.

"So, Soren Hunter definitely knew Nick Winter prior to Nick's arrival at Northfields. And, we now know that, not only was Hunter in the habit of carrying a knife before he arrived at Northfields, but he's also capable of using it. And not just for odd jobs around the farm. Add the fact that he possibly sees himself as some sort of vigilante . . ."

"Sir," Tom said. "Hunter had met Samantha, too. In a pub in the village where Samantha Benrose's parents live."

"A free house," PJ chipped in. "It stocks Monty and Blue's prize-winning beer, Blue Monty. Soren accompanied Monty on a delivery there. The publican remembers the four of them having a cosy chat."

Neal raised an eyebrow at that. "Good work," he said. "We'll have a nice chat with Monty Stratford this morning."

"We also paid Samantha's ex-fiancé a visit," Tom said. "He's a Dr Toby Swallow. A cosmetic surgeon. Samantha's sister told us that he was controlling of her, and that he was violent towards her on at least one occasion. He fractured her wrist. He has no alibi for Saturday afternoon and evening. We have to consider him a suspect."

"I agree," Neal said. "PJ, see what else you can find out about this Dr Swallow. And arrange for his picture to be shown to everyone who was at that dance. Someone might remember seeing him there."

They were interrupted by a knock at the door. It was PC Serena Cole with an update on the background check into Soren Hunter. She seemed apologetic when she informed them, "There's no record of a Soren Hunter in any of the usual databases. There's no current British passport or driving licence holder with that name matching the description and age of our suspect. No National Insurance number." Serena offered a tentative, obvious explanation. "He must have changed his name."

"Thank you, PC Cole," Neal said. The young PC gave a funny sort of bow and hurried from the room.

"Not really a surprise, is it?" Ava remarked. "Every vigilante hero needs a secret identity." Neal was not amused.

* * *

Ava waited for Neal outside. She sidled into the driver's seat of the car and glanced at herself in the rear-view mirror. Did she look too severe with her hair pulled back in an unforgiving ponytail? She'd been accustomed all her life to people remarking on her looks. If anything, she tended to play down her attractiveness, dressing in jeans and muted colours and wearing little or no make-up. Of course, there had been times when she'd used her looks to her advantage, even at work. It was a sad fact that even now, a woman with blonde hair and a pretty face was often underestimated. Still, it often meant that she could command an element of surprise in dealing with people who harboured such prejudices.

Ava had the additional advantage of being a pretty blonde trained in karate and kick-boxing. Anyone who underestimated her was in for a shock.

Leaning forward to peer more closely at the mirror, she felt an unaccustomed stab of anxiety about her appearance. PJ was forever complaining about this or that aspect of her looks. Her nose was too big, her lips not full enough, she wasn't curvy but morbidly obese . . .

Ava always took care to be supportive when PJ was feeling insecure about her looks, but she'd never truly understood her friend's need for constant reassurance. Friends in the past had accused Ava of taking her looks for granted, but she had disagreed. She preferred to believe that what people looked like wasn't important. Most of them came back with, "Easy for you to say."

She flipped the mirror back, but not before pulling a few strands of hair loose to soften her appearance. She hoped this wasn't going to be a 'thing.' She glanced out the window and saw the source of her unaccustomed self-consciousness striding across the car park.

Neal slid into the seat beside her and slammed his door shut. He probably wouldn't notice what she looked like this morning, anyway, given the grumpy vibe he was giving off. She considered asking him how he was adjusting to Maggie's absence, then changed her mind. Not a good idea to touch on the probable explanation for his ill humour. Safer to stick to work.

"Do you think Soren torched his caravan deliberately?" she said. "If he wanted to disappear, he could have done it in a way that would attract less attention. And if we assume for a moment that the fire wasn't an accident, the obvious assumption is that someone wanted him dead. Or at least out of the way."

"But why?" Neal said. "Something he knows? We know he's not trustworthy, whoever he really is. People don't reinvent themselves to such an extent unless they've got something to hide. Let's hope the family can shed some light on the matter."

It was Monty who answered the door when they arrived at the farmhouse. He looked as if he'd been up all night and more. He ran his fingers through his hair as he stepped back to let them in. Worry showed in his face, but it wasn't about Soren, or the fire. "Everyone's at the hospital. Blue collapsed in the early hours of the morning."

"What's happened?" Neal asked.

"She's got something called pre-eclampsia. They were prepping her for an emergency caesarean last time Mum gave me an update. I'm waiting for news."

Neal nodded. "Try not to worry. It's a serious condition, but I'm guessing your sister was near her due date?"

"Two, three weeks away."

"Hopefully, everything will be fine." Ava was about to agree with Neal, when Monty's mobile rang. He looked at them, panicked.

"It's Dad."

"Answer it, son," Neal said, gently.

There was no need to wait for Monty to tell them it was good news. As he listened, a grin spread across his face and his eyes welled up with tears of relief. *Dammit.* It was going to be hard to take a stern approach with him after this.

"It's a girl!" Monty announced. "Seven pounds, five ounces. They're both okay. Her name's Esmerelda. Esmé, for short. Pretty, isn't it?"

"Congratulations!" Neal and Ava spoke simultaneously.

"Thanks. It's kind of cool being an uncle," Monty said. He beamed, but then his expression altered suddenly. "I guess you're here about the fire?"

"Amongst other things," Neal said. Monty sat down, gesturing for them to join him.

"Soren's still missing," he said, without prompting. "I know you're going to think he's done a runner because he killed Nick and Samantha, but you're wrong."

"Monty, we know you and Hunter had met Nick and Samantha previously. You and Soren lied to us."

"I only met them the once. At a pub that buys our beer. It's in the village where Samantha's parents live."

"Right. And Hunter? Did he tell you how he knew Nick?"

"Soren met him in London. They were both living on the streets, but Nick wasn't like Soren. Do you know what I mean?"

Ava knew. She could tell from Neal's nod that he did too. Hunter might have been homeless, but he was never vulnerable. A man with Soren Hunter's skills adapted and thrived, whatever his environment.

"Nick was in a bad way. Like he was really messed up. He'd been kicked out of the flat he was staying in. Wasn't looking after himself. Soren rescued him when he was attacked by some lowlifes. I'm not the only one Soren saved. He's a hero, not a murderer."

Saved. There it was again. Soren the Good Samaritan. Or perhaps, more appropriately, the vigilante hero.

Monty's eyes flashed with sudden anger. "He was right to ask me not to mention that he knew Nick. He said it would only make you suspect him, and he was right."

Ava rolled her eyes. She wondered at Neal's patience. As a rule, when someone asked you to keep a secret around a murder, it wasn't for a good reason. Also, she was irritated by Monty's petulant manner.

"Do you know where Soren Hunter is, Monty?" she asked.

"No." Monty crossed his arms and met her eye. *And I wouldn't tell you even if I did,* was what she guessed he was thinking.

"How did you persuade Hunter to come and work here?" she asked. "Did he tell you what he'd been doing before he ended up rough sleeping? I'm asking this because, as I'm sure you'll agree, Soren Hunter doesn't seem like the sort to end up homeless and jobless."

"I offered him a job and he accepted. That's it."

"You weren't at all curious about his background? Didn't want him to provide you with a CV?"

Monty shook his head. "Actions speak louder than words. Soren put himself at risk to help me. A person who does that is okay in my book." Still the same intransigence over Hunter.

"Did he ever show you some ID?"

"I didn't ask." For the first time a flicker of doubt showed in Monty's eye. "Why?"

"He was about to become an employee of the family. I'm assuming the business is run legitimately. At the very least, Soren would have been required to provide you with a National Insurance number."

"I . . . You'd have to ask my mum about that. She deals with all the admin stuff."

Ava sighed. "I think you're being evasive, Monty. Hunter didn't provide you with a scrap of evidence to prove his identity. Am I right?"

Monty didn't answer.

"You might be interested to learn that nobody knows who Soren Hunter is. Because officially, on paper, he doesn't exist."

That got a reaction. Monty unfolded his arms and stared at her. "What do you mean?"

"It means we've run some checks on Hunter, and drawn a blank."

"You mean he's like, living off the grid?" Not quite the reaction Ava had been expecting. There was something like excitement, admiration even, in Monty's voice.

"This isn't a game, Monty. Two people have been murdered. The man we know as Soren Hunter is living under an assumed identity. There has to be a reason for that. And not necessarily a good one."

"Well, maybe it's for his own protection or something. He could be in witness protection."

Give me strength. Ava looked at Neal, who shook his head.

"Changing your name doesn't mean you've done something wrong, though, does it? Blue used to be called Scarlett."

"No, but surely you must be able to see why this is a bit different, and why we're interested in speaking with him," Ava said.

Neal took over. "At the very least, it suggests to us that he has something to hide. Or that he's in some sort of trouble. So, once more, do you have any idea where Hunter might have gone? Or do you have any information that might help us locate him?"

Monty shrugged. His only suggestion was unhelpful. "Back to London?"

Neal thanked Monty politely for his time, then said, "If you hear from Hunter, contact us immediately. You trust him because he saved your life, and he may well turn out to be the man you believe him to be. But if you're wrong, you could be putting the lives of your entire family at risk." He let that sink in. "If I find out you've failed to provide us with information — *again* — I'll charge you with obstructing the course of justice."

Monty looked worried, but he said nothing more.

They needed to see the site of the fire before leaving Northfields. Fire investigators had been there since the early morning.

"Anything?" Neal asked a white-suited investigator.

"I can confirm that this fire was no accident," he said. "Most likely cause is something like an old towel soaked in accelerant, set alight and chucked through a window. There's something else. Wait here."

"Useful to learn that the fire was definitely arson," Neal commented. "As we suspected, but who was responsible? The killer? Or did Hunter start the fire to cover something up?"

Ava favoured the former theory. But it begged the question: why had Hunter disappeared?

"If Hunter believed the arsonist was after him," Neal said, "he might have gone to ground to evade a further attempt on his life."

"Or because he wanted to track down the arsonist — who may also be Nick and Samantha's killer — alone. We know he doesn't trust the police. He might have gone into vigilante mode."

"All the more reason why we need to find him — and fast," Neal said. "Problem is, police resources for a full-scale manhunt are practically non-existent. The last thing we need is a man like Hunter running around thinking he can take the law into his own hands."

The investigator returned holding a clear, sealed bag, which he held up so that they could see the contents. "We retrieved this from the grass outside the bedroom window."

"Dog tags." Neal took the bag and inspected them closely. "Belonging to Lance-Corporal Glen Bolton." He looked at Ava. "I think we've just unmasked our superhero."

CHAPTER FIFTEEN

It was like his first few nights on the streets. Keeping himself to himself, trying not to attract attention, Soren was confident that he could evade being located by the police. But it was different here; in rural Stromfordshire it was less easy to be anonymous than in a busy city like London.

He thought back to the events of the night. At two in the morning, he had been lying awake in the Stratfords' caravan contemplating how the murders had rocked his sense of complacency. Prior to the atrocity, he'd considered a farm near a sleepy village on the edge of the Stromfordshire Wolds to be about the safest place in the world. He couldn't have predicted becoming involved in a double murder investigation when he agreed to Monty's offer of a job at Northfields.

Soren was tired of running. Tired of hiding. Until the murders, he'd begun to entertain fantasies of staying on at Northfields, becoming Monty's business partner, maybe even telling Blue about his feelings for her. He sensed he wouldn't be rejected. He was a good judge of people, and he could tell that Blue was attracted to him. But he sensed that Blue, too, had her secrets — one of them glaringly obvious. Soren didn't give a damn about the identity of the baby's father. Given half a chance he'd love and protect the child as fiercely as if it were his own. But chance was a fine thing.

Of course, he'd known all along that his fantasies could never be realised. Monty hadn't asked any questions about his background when he invited him to work at Northfields. The Stratfords had been paying him cash in hand, but only the previous week, Bea had given him a gentle reminder that this situation couldn't continue. He could only fob her off for so long with excuses for not providing her with his National Insurance number. If he became Monty's business partner, everything would have to be legal. He would need to prove his identity. And how would Blue react if he told her he could never marry her because the minute his real name entered a government database, it would set off alarm bells that would bring the police right to his door? The murders had been a timely reminder that an ordinary life was forever out of his reach.

In the aftermath of the murders, he'd asked himself how long he could remain at Northfields. As soon as the police discovered that Soren Hunter didn't exist, they'd be back to arrest him for obstructing the course of their investigation. He'd be elevated to the rank of prime suspect, if he wasn't there already. Worse than any of that, they would quickly establish his true identity. Logic told him that he should have been on his way already. So, what was stopping him?

It was complicated. The murders had happened on his watch. Okay, he had been elsewhere on the day they took place, but that didn't excuse him. He should have known that something was in the offing. There had to have been signs, and he'd missed them. Remaining at Northfields when his instinct told him to take flight was therefore also a matter of self-respect. How could he live with himself if he fled without attempting to make amends for his laxity?

He was surprised to have fallen asleep that night. For the first few weeks after arriving at Northfields he'd refused to surrender to sleep fully. In London, as in his previous life, his safety had relied on remaining alert, so he'd slept with one ear and one eye open. Then, as the months passed, he had begun to relax and permit himself the luxury of a sound night's sleep. So, when the fire had started, he'd been off his guard.

The smell of smoke had alerted him, so perhaps he hadn't switched off all his senses entirely, but the fire had already taken hold by the time he was aware of it. It was beyond what could be tamed by the extinguisher in the caravan and had worsened by the second. His instinct had been self-preservation. He'd grabbed whatever of his belongings were to hand, broken the safety restrictor on the window of his tiny bedroom and hurled himself out. He'd landed on soft grass in time to see smoke and flames engulf his home. And then, fearing an explosion, he'd begun to run.

At a safe distance, he'd watched the blaze for a few moments. From somewhere not far distant, he heard the sound of an engine revving up. It was too far off to be any of the vehicles on the farm. The road was quarter of a mile distant, but at night sound travelled — and he was trained to listen. It was in that moment that he knew for certain what he already suspected. The fire had been no accident.

He had walked around the outside of the barn and looked towards the farmhouse. A single light was showing in one of the bedroom windows. Blue's. He thought he caught a glimpse of her standing there like a ghost in her white pyjamas. She had to be able to see the glow of the fire in the night sky above the barn. For the first time in years, he'd experienced a stab of doubt. Blue would raise the alarm. The police would come. He would be back on their radar, the focus of their attention. It was time to leave. But what about Blue and her family? He couldn't just abandon them with a killer still at large.

And that was why he was still here. He had a mission now, just as he'd had one on the streets of London. To protect the innocent and the vulnerable.

The police had been swarming around Northfields and the surrounding fields and villages all day. At least they weren't using dogs. He hoped that meant they were after him because he was missing and not because they thought he was Nick and Samantha's killer. Still, he had to be on their list of suspects. He wasn't about to walk into their arms and answer all their prying questions.

He waited until dark before doubling back to Northfields. The light was on in the kitchen, but he didn't intend on going up to the house. Monty would be going out to the brewery sometime in the next hour to sterilise the equipment and measure out the malt. He did it most evenings. Soren took a monocular spyglass from his bag and observed the kitchen more closely. Monty, Aubrey and Bea were assembled for a family meal but there was no sign of Blue. Perhaps she was having an early night.

Soren felt a stab of guilt. What if Blue was absent because she was still upset about the fire? He was certain she cared for him, and his disappearance must be worrying for her. Surely the family had been reassured that he hadn't died in that inferno? He tried to read the emotion in the faces of Bea, Aubrey and Monty, to observe their body language and guess at their mood, but the monocular wasn't powerful enough to pick up the nuances.

He glanced up at Blue's bedroom window. The curtains were open, the room in darkness. He hoped she wasn't lying up there, awake and alone, worrying about him. Then again, the thought that she might be thinking of him at all gave him a warm glow.

The barn was still cordoned off with police tape but there was no longer a guard. He was about to slip under the cordon when he noticed a large padlock on the door. He slipped around the back of the barn, wincing when he caught sight of the burnt-out caravan. It was also surrounded by tape. Some would say he'd had a lucky escape, but he didn't trust to luck. His training had saved him, even while asleep.

He made his way to the brewery. The door was unlocked. He was disappointed but unsurprised. His efforts to encourage the Stratford family to be more security conscious had fallen on deaf ears, even after two murders on their property.

He breathed in the familiar aromas of the brewing room, feeling a sudden sense of nostalgia. He stepped up to see over the side of the fermenting tank. Although it was dark, he could sense that the tank was full. He cupped his hands, scooped up the cool, delicious beer, and slaked his thirst.

Afterwards, he opened the rough wooden door to the adjoining room used for storing casks and as an office space. He sat down and waited.

Monty arrived at eight. He flicked the light switch and walked straight across to the office, flicking on the light in there, too. Soren looked at him and smiled. Monty's reaction on catching sight of him raised Soren's spirits for the first time since he'd escaped from the burning caravan.

"Soren! Mate! You're okay!" He peered at him. "You are okay, aren't you?" Monty placed his hands on his shoulders and searched his face with concern.

"I'm good," Soren answered. "I'm sorry if anyone thought I'd come to harm."

"They told us you weren't in the caravan," Monty said. "But we didn't know if you were hurt — or why you'd disappeared."

"Yeah. Sorry about that."

Monty lowered his voice. "You were right, though. The police were here asking questions about you."

Soren hoped Monty didn't feel the sudden tension in his shoulders. "What did they want to know?"

"They wanted to know if you'd ever shown me any ID." Monty looked embarrassed. "They said you're not who you claim to be. They said Soren Hunter doesn't exist. What's going on, mate?" He released Soren's shoulders. "Look, I told the police I don't care what your name is. You put yourself in danger to help me. That tells me everything I need to know about what sort of person you are. Nothing's changed."

"Thanks, Monty." To his relief, Monty just nodded and didn't press the issue. "So, have the police confirmed that the fire was started deliberately?"

"Yes. An old bath towel soaked in paraffin — set alight and lobbed through one of the windows. Dad or I should have upgraded the locks on those windows. A child could have opened the ones that were on there."

"Don't blame yourself. The arsonist would have smashed the window if it was the only way."

"Do you think it was the same person who killed Nick and Samantha?"

"Probably."

"Why would they want to kill you?"

"I'm working on that. Can I trust you not to tell the police where I am?"

Monty didn't hesitate. "Course you can, mate. Can I tell Mum, Dad and Blue that you're okay?" His face lit up. "Hey, Blue's had a baby girl. Esmé. They're still at the hospital but they're both fine."

"That's great news! Congratulations, Uncle Monty!"

"Thanks. Look, where are you going to stay? I doubt the police will be back here looking for you. There's a kind of general assumption that you've gone back to London. You could stay here. Blue's going to be busy with the baby when she comes home, and nobody really comes to the brewery except me."

Soren considered his options. Nothing like hiding in plain sight. "Okay," he said, at last. "I'd appreciate it if you could keep quiet about it, though, even to the rest of the family — for now."

"Sure. No problem. They'll be worried about you, though. I'll bring you some food. You must be starving."

Soren helped Monty complete the evening tasks then Monty left the brewery. He'd promised to bring some food and a sleeping bag for Soren as soon as Aubrey and Bea had gone to bed.

Soren sat in the dark. He didn't want to draw attention to the shed by putting the light on. His stomach rumbled. He hoped Monty would return soon. To distract himself from his hunger, he went over his first encounter with Nick Winter in London.

* * *

It had been close by the Brunswick Centre, near Russell Square Underground station. Nick had been huddled in a doorway looking like he was new to the streets.

It was around two in the morning. The only people still around were stragglers returning late from the West End or those for whom the street was their habitual accommodation for the night. As soon as he saw the three drunk lads turn into the street, Soren knew they were trouble.

At first, they only abused Nick verbally, but then one of them took it a step further by landing a kick. Nick was passive. He covered his head and seemed resigned to a beating. Perhaps it wasn't his first. His strategy seemed simply to endure. Maybe he believed antagonising his attackers would only make the thrashing worse. Soren tensed as a second man kicked Nick in the groin. The third gave a laugh and began to unzip his fly, no doubt to piss on Nick.

"Hey! Shitface!" Soren's voice startled the trio — ruined their fun. He took a step towards them, making sure the knife in his hand was visible. One of the men held up his hands in a gesture of surrender.

"No worries, mate. We were just having a bit of fun. No harm done."

Another piped up. "Yeah, we were just on our way." The third, Fly Man, pulled up his zip hastily and took a step backwards. They weren't looking for a fight, Soren knew. They were cowards, bullies picking on the vulnerable. He saw them off with little more than his initial address and a step towards them. It was almost funny watching them turn tail and run off down the street like three frightened children.

"You alright?" Soren turned his attention to their victim.

"Yeah. Thanks, mate."

"Haven't seen you around these parts before." He hunkered down beside Nick to check if he was injured.

"I tend to move around a bit," Nick said.

"Well, shove up. I'll share your doorway tonight, make sure you don't get yourself into any more trouble."

The following day, he'd introduced Nick to Pixie at the hostel. Unlike a lot of rough sleepers Soren had encountered, Nick was amenable to being offered help. There were some who preferred the streets for one reason or another — usually, in Soren's experience, because of an underlying issue with their mental health. As usual, Pixie had offered Soren a bed for the night, too. And, as usual, he'd turned her down.

"Who are you really, Soren Hunter?" she'd asked him. "You don't belong on the streets." But she knew better than to press him. That was the good thing about Pixie. She knew that people weren't always ready to tell their stories, and she didn't pry.

Soren and Nick met up a number of times over the next few weeks until Nick's sister, Jenny, turned up and persuaded him to go back to Nottingham. Before leaving, Nick gave Soren his contact details and asked him to get in touch if he was ever in his area. Soren had thought that unlikely. Then he'd met Monty and been offered work and a place to stay at Northfields. When he was settled there, he'd sent Nick a letter — Soren didn't do mobile phones — to let him know he was no longer in London. After some consideration, he'd let Nick know where he was, never guessing that he would actually turn up.

Should he regret rescuing Nick from his assailants that night in Russell Square? Would Nick still be alive if he had never met him? Usually, Soren would dismiss such thoughts as unproductive, but he couldn't help wondering if the killer had some connection to him — to his time in London — or to Nick or Monty.

He dug in his backpack and pulled out the tin containing the scrap of material he'd torn from the sleeve of Monty's assailant in London. He rummaged around in the bag again with a growing sense of dismay and then anxiety.

He tipped the contents out across the desk and picked out a torch. He shone the beam over his small pile of possessions and saw at once that what he was searching for wasn't there. It took a few moments for him to recognise the sensation of tightness in his chest as fear.

CHAPTER SIXTEEN

Ava woke to the sound of her mother singing in the shower. She had a good voice, but why did she have to use the shower just when Ava was ready to use it? Still . . . just another couple of days and her mother would be gone. Ava and Ollie could settle back into their usual routine. Rather than lie in bed waiting for her turn in the bathroom, she decided to go for a swim on her way to work. She could take a shower at the pool.

For years, Ava had been a bit of a fitness freak, but she'd lately begun to cut back on her unforgiving exercise regime. She still liked to run and swim but was less fanatical about the whole thing. She'd taken up yoga and dropped some of her gym sessions. And she'd never felt better.

After a brisk swim and a shower — even at the pool she'd had to wait as one of the showers was out of order — she arrived at work feeling energised. PJ greeted her with a smile, saying, "I've been to the gym this morning. Decided to get in shape and become more positive in my outlook."

"That's good news, Peej. I was starting to worry about you. It's good to have the old cheerful PJ back."

"I'd barely noticed she'd gone," Tom said, gallantly.

"Where's the boss?" Ava noticed that he wasn't in his office.

"With the big boss," Tom said, meaning George Lowe. "He wants the DI to do a press conference this morning. There's been a lot of interest in the murders. It's the Valentine's Day Massacre and Beast of Northfields labels that are firing everyone's imagination."

It was the morning after the fire and Soren Hunter was still missing. Tom had coordinated a search for Hunter but it was as though he'd vanished into thin air. "Probably back to London, where he can just disappear," Tom concluded. "Might be worth contacting that Pixie you spoke with at the hostel, Ava. She could give us a heads-up if he turns up on her patch."

"I suspect her loyalty lies with Hunter, not us," Ava said. But it was worth a try, even though she couldn't see Hunter making the mistake of showing up in a place where he was known.

"How have you been getting on?" she asked PJ, who had been tasked with finding out more information on Toby Swallow and with trawling through the interviews conducted with the guests and charity committee members, as well as anyone else who had been at Northfields on the fatal night. Swallow, Ava already knew, had no record. Though he appeared to be squeaky clean, he remained a suspect.

Going through the data from the interviews was a dull but necessary task; it was often in the detail that the key to a big break in a case was found. PJ had approached the task without complaint.

The members of the committee had been questioned in some depth. Most of them had arrived at Northfields in the afternoon to make the final preparations for the dance. All of them lived in the village, a ten-minute walk or a couple of minutes' drive from Northfields. They had all left the barn on one or more occasions to go across to the farmhouse to discuss arrangements with Bea Stratford, to fetch supplies from their cars or make phone calls if they couldn't get a signal in the barn.

The buffet had been supplied by a catering company based in Stromford. A mobile bar had been hired to take care of the drinks. They'd had to cover everyone who'd been involved on the day.

"Well, no one seems to have noticed anyone else behaving suspiciously," PJ said. "Hardly surprising, as everyone was there to have a good time, not to spy on the other guests." Ava had spoken to PJ about her own impressions of the evening and hadn't been surprised to learn that all PJ could remember was the enticing buffet, which hadn't even paid lip service to the concept of wartime rationing, and the dancing. And that was before she'd had her fourth lime daiquiri. She certainly didn't notice Ava slip outside. The first hint she'd had that something was wrong was when Ava took to the stage to make her announcement.

"I've spoken at last with Meredith Price, the committee member who left Northfields before the dance started," PJ said. "She's been away in Dorset staying with her sister. I'm not sure, but something Meredith said might be of interest to us."

Ava and Tom eyed PJ keenly. She looked a bit worried. Maybe she thought she'd raised their expectations too much. Ava gave her an encouraging nod.

"Okay. So, Meredith had been at Northfields in the afternoon helping out with the preparations for the evening, but she couldn't stay on for the dance. She was going off to Dorset the following day and her son was picking her up early to drive her down. She'd been so busy the last few days that she hadn't had time to pack. Anyway, when she was making her way back towards the farmyard where she'd parked her car, she passed the outbuildings where Aubrey has his workshops."

Ava raised an eyebrow. "What time was this?"

"Around 6:15. She saw a man approaching the larger of the workshops — the one Aubrey calls the garage, where Nick's body was found. She said he'd come across the field from the direction of the yurts."

"Did she give a description of him? Was it Nick?" PJ was going too slowly for Ava.

"It was dark at that time, remember, and he was a distance away, but she did make out what he was wearing because there was some light coming from the garage. She didn't see his face, but she was pretty sure he was dressed in a pinstriped suit and a trilby hat."

"He was dressed as a spiv, then?" Ava said. When PJ gave her a questioning look, she added, "You know, like Private Walker from *Dad's Army*? Thin moustache, slicked-back hair . . ."

"Duck's arse," Tom said.

Ava and PJ stared.

"The slicked-back hairstyle favoured by spivs was called a duck's arse."

"Right," said Ava. Tom was full of surprises. "That's what Nick was wearing when we found him in the ambulance. So, if it was him that Meredith saw, that means he was still alive at 6:15. Meaning we could be right that he was going over to the farmhouse to get something, possibly for Samantha, and intended to return to the yurt." She high-fived PJ. "Good work, Peej. That gives us a more accurate approximation of the time of Nick's death."

"It might also confirm our suspicion that Nick was killed first," said PJ.

"Not meaning to throw a spanner in the works," Tom said, "but Nick probably wasn't the only one dressed as a spiv, was he? There must have been other men in zoot suits and Fedora hats. But a lot of people hire costumes to wear to these things. I suppose we could check with local costume hire shops. Find out who else hired outfits like that the same weekend, question them all."

"We could do that," Ava said. "But given that the man was making his way over from the direction of the yurts, we can, if only tentatively, assume it was Nick."

At that moment, Neal walked into the room with a face like thunder. Ava noticed PJ grimace. But his expression lightened when he saw his team. No one asked about his meeting or the press conference. Ava briefed him on the information PJ had just supplied. Neal asked her to contact the costume hire shops and liaise with uniform. Then, he updated them on a few points.

"Forensics are taking their time, as ever, but I've had confirmation that the prints found on the tut recovered from the ambulance didn't match those of any of the Stratford family and they didn't show up in the database.

"For the time being, Toby Swallow, as jealous ex-fiancé, remains a suspect for the murders of Nick and Samantha. But we can't ignore the possibility that Nick might have been mixed up in something during his time in London that led to him becoming a target. The most likely scenario would be drugs." Neal surveyed the faces of his team. "Then there's Soren Hunter, aka Glen Bolton." It hadn't taken long to find evidence to confirm that Hunter was in fact Glen Bolton, but they still knew very little about the man.

"What if Nick discovered something about Hunter's past?" Tom suggested. "Hunter might have killed him to shut him up, then killed Samantha, too, in case Nick had let her in on his discovery."

"That's a possibility. Yet another scenario is that one or more members of the Stratford family committed the murders for who knows what reason." Neal turned to Tom. "Where are we with locating the man we knew formerly as Soren Hunter?"

Tom looked frustrated. "No further forward, sir. It seems likely that he's gone back to London."

"Hunter . . . Bolton is a credible suspect. His disappearance only strengthens the case against him." He looked at Tom. "Contact the Royal Military Police. Find out as much as you can about his past life as a soldier."

"Yes, boss."

* * *

The following day, the case for Toby Swallow being the killer gained an unexpected boost, thanks to some clever detective work from PJ.

"It was just a hunch, really," she began after requesting to speak with Neal, Tom and Ava.

"Ava, do you remember Arthur?"

Ava frowned. "Arthur? As in taxi driver Arthur?"

"Yes. He made a comment when we he drove us out to Northfields on the evening of the dance. Something about dropping another passenger off in the village earlier in the day. He remarked on it because he'd hardly ever taken anyone out that way, never mind twice in one day."

"So?" Ava sounded a bit impatient.

"Well, it's just that Arthur described his passenger as being a bit of a toff. It made me wonder . . ."

PJ looked at Neal. He gave her an encouraging nod. Sometimes she was inclined to be a bit hesitant in the company of two such dominant personalities as Ava and Tom, as though she was afraid of making a silly comment. He should encourage her to be more assertive. Somewhat to his irritation, Ava butted in.

"You wondered if he might have been Toby Swallow."

"Yeees. I wondered if it might be worth showing a picture of Swallow to Arthur — just to see if he recognised him."

"Go on, PJ," Neal said.

By now they had all clicked that PJ wouldn't be raising this unless she had made some sort of discovery. Ava and Tom were uncharacteristically quiet.

PJ described how she had arranged to meet Arthur and show him the picture over a cup of tea. They had chatted for a few minutes before PJ reached into her bag and brought out her phone. She showed Arthur a picture of Swallow taken from a brochure for his clinic.

"He recognised Swallow immediately." PJ struggled to contain her excitement. "Which means that Swallow was lying when he said he was at home with a migraine on the day of the murders. Arthur's evidence places him in the vicinity on the day in question."

"Good work," Neal said. "Let's bring him in under caution and see what he has to say for himself."

CHAPTER SEVENTEEN

Swallow sat opposite Ava and Neal in the interview room. Beside him sat his legal representative, Pauline Norwood, an attractive but somehow unnaturally perfect-looking woman, who could have been any age between thirty and fifty. Ava thought the upper age limit was closer to the truth. Norwood's goddess-like features probably owed a lot to Dr Toby's expertise with the knife.

Swallow was clearly incensed at finding himself in his present predicament. He had been brought in first thing in the morning. While being processed in the custody suite, he'd complained bitterly about having his fingerprints scanned and his mouth swabbed for DNA.

He had spent some time alone with Norwood since then, and now sat tight-lipped with nostrils flared. All he lacked was a ring through his nose to complete the raging bull effect. He needed to control his anger or he'd be tripping himself up all over the place. Ava got right to the point.

"Mr Swallow, did you kill Nick Winter?"

"No."

"Did you kill Samantha Benrose?"

"No. This is outrageous."

"Mr Swallow, we have a witness who can place you in the vicinity of Northfields Farm on the day that Samantha Benrose and Nick Winter were murdered. Previously, when asked where you were that day, you informed us that you were at work in the morning and at home all afternoon, incapacitated by a migraine. Care to tell us why you lied?"

Swallow shifted in his seat. He leaned forward slightly. "What witness?"

"A taxi driver who dropped you at Summerthorpe village, which, as you are presumably aware, is the closest village to Northfields Farm."

"A taxi driver?" Swallow sneered. "He's lying."

"He identified you from your profile photograph in the brochure for your clinic."

"He made a mistake."

Ava sighed. She showed Swallow a photograph of the charm from Samantha's bracelet. "Do you recognise the charm in this photograph?"

Swallow took his time to reply. "I've already answered that question. Why are you showing me this again? Your colleagues showed it to me that day at my clinic. I told them I gave her one *like* it. Samantha had rather unimaginative taste in jewellery. I would have bought her a more exclusive piece but she preferred that sort of thing. Those charms are very common." *As in vulgar.* Ava didn't miss the implied meaning.

"*As we informed you previously*, this charm was found near the yurt in which Samantha was murdered. The scans we took of your fingerprints will be checked for a match."

Her words elicited a bored shrug from Swallow. He covered his mouth, as if stifling a yawn. Time to rattle him a little. She slid another photograph across the table. Swallow looked at it. He glanced at his solicitor.

"I don't think the taxi driver made a mistake. When he told us he'd dropped you in Summerthorpe, we checked CCTV footage from cameras positioned in different locations around the village." Ava slowly drew another photograph from a brown envelope and slid it between Swallow and his lawyer. "It's not a particularly flattering likeness, but I think you'll agree that it's definitely you, Mr Swallow. I'd like you to pay particular attention to the date and time when the image was captured." She waited a moment before adding, "Are you absolutely certain that you were at home sick that day, because unless you have an identical twin brother or can teleport, I'd say that picture is pretty conclusive proof that you were near Northfields Farm. In fact, the camera that caught you there . . ." she tapped the picture with her middle finger ". . . is positioned on the side of a house next to a lane that leads only to Northfields. The owner runs an online business from his home. He takes security very seriously."

Swallow glanced at his solicitor. She raised an eyebrow. Ava noticed that Swallow's right hand was balled into a fist, the knuckles showing white. When he saw her looking, he flexed his fingers, as though to suggest he'd been merely relieving a cramp. Pauline Norwood requested a moment alone with her client.

"Nicely done, Ava," Neal said, as they waited for Norwood to brief Swallow.

"Well, it was a stroke of luck that the residents of Summerthorpe are big on CCTV. Made Tom's sleepless night worthwhile finding those pictures." If only Soren Hunter were as unaware as Swallow, they'd have him in custody now, she reflected. "Seriously, though, it's looking bad for Swallow, isn't it? He has motive, he lied about being anywhere near Northfields that night. Let's hope that when Tom and PJ search his home they find some sort of evidence to incriminate him further. And I'm pretty sure those prints on the charm will match his."

When the interview resumed, Pauline Norwood spoke first. "Dr Swallow would like to make some changes to his previous statement." She gave her client a nod.

"Okay," Swallow said, sullenly. "I was at Northfields that day. One of Sam's friends had posted on Facebook that Sam was going there for the weekend."

Silence ensued. Ava waited for Swallow to fill it. Sure enough, he cracked first.

"Look, I didn't kill Sam — or Nick. I lied about my alibi because I knew that as soon as you lot found out I was there that night you'd jump to the obvious, if misguided, conclusion that I was a jealous ex-lover bent on revenge. Why look any further? All you care about are quick results. You don't give a damn about whether you've arrested the right person."

Ava decided to let that one go. She hadn't met a detainee yet who failed to protest their innocence and have a go at the police. "Why exactly did you go to Northfields, Dr Swallow?"

"I just wanted to talk to Samantha. See if I could get her to change her mind."

"About what?"

"About our relationship."

"Why wait until she was in a different county to do so?"

"It was hard to get her on her own in Nottingham. She was always with Winter, or her friends, or her bloody interfering sister."

Natasha Benrose had told them that Swallow had been pestering Samantha to resume their relationship. It was likely he had been stalking her. Samantha had been afraid of him, that much Natasha had confirmed.

"Samantha wasn't alone that weekend," Ava pointed out. "She was with her boyfriend, Nick Winter."

Swallow did that thing with his fist again. It wasn't hard to imagine him exercising less restraint in more favourable circumstances. Inflicting harm. "I. Just. Wanted. To talk. With her." He bared his teeth as he spoke. Norwood touched his arm lightly, a reminder that he needed to stay calm. Swallow took a couple of breaths. "I thought I could get her on her own at some point. I didn't really think it through. I was still in love with Sam. You don't always act rationally when you're in love."

Or when you're angry. Ava imagined how furious Swallow must have been when he discovered that Samantha and Nick were planning a romantic getaway for Valentine's Day.

She'd checked, and Swallow had proposed to Samantha on Valentine's Day. Perhaps he feared that Nick was planning to do likewise. "And did you get a chance to talk to her?"

"I . . . No. I didn't actually enter Northfields until around 6:45. I was working up the nerve. I had no idea which of the yurts she was staying in. Or whether Winter would be there. The first one I looked in was empty. It was then that I heard a noise — like someone approaching. So, I slipped inside to wait until they'd gone past. I must have waited in there for about ten minutes."

Ava nodded. She remembered Hunter remarking on an odour lingering in one of the empty yurts. Had he detected the scent Swallow wore? She could detect it now, though she hadn't been aware of it in the yurt.

"Go on," she said.

"During the time I was in the yurt, I had a moment of . . . er . . . of clarity, I suppose. My plan to confront Sam suddenly seemed . . . ill thought out. I decided I should just give up, go home and forget all about her."

Right, Ava thought. "What happened next?"

Swallow glanced at his solicitor. She gave an encouraging nod.

"I left the yurt. I was going to leave Northfields there and then — I swear it. I wish I had. I would have been spared the terrible sight of . . . of Sam." He appeared to be overcome but recovered quickly. "I carried on until I reached the next yurt. The door was open slightly. I approached with the intention of listening to see if I could hear Sam and Winter talking inside, but when I drew near I couldn't hear a thing. So I risked a look inside." Another little display of emotional distress followed.

Ava cleared her throat, impatient to hear the rest.

"I saw Sam, sprawled across a four-poster bed. She . . . she was covered in blood."

Ava glanced at Neal, who was leaning forward in his seat, listening intently. "What happened next?" she asked.

"I . . . I'm a doctor. I'm used to the sight of blood. But there was something particularly shocking about seeing Sam, a woman I'd loved, lying there like that. Of course, I reacted immediately, crossed to the bed to see if there was anything I could do." He faltered. "But it was too late. Sam was beyond help."

"She was already dead?"

"Yes."

"Did you touch her?"

"I felt her neck for a pulse, even though I could see it was hopeless. She'd been stabbed multiple times. In the throat and in the heart." Swallow leaned forward, resting his elbows on his knees. He covered his face with his hands. Ava couldn't decide whether his emotion was genuine or forced.

"How long did you stay with Samantha? Did you remove the charm from her bracelet?"

"I . . . Not long. Five minutes? Yes, I took the charm." He looked down. "I wanted something to remember her by. I put it in my pocket."

Neal spoke again. "Was it you who ran out of the yurt when DS Merry and Soren Hunter turned up?"

Swallow hesitated a moment. Ava felt his eyes slide from Neal back to her. "Yes, that was me." He looked directly at her then. "My apologies if I injured you when I stumbled into you, Detective."

"I wouldn't call hurling yourself at me full pelt 'stumbling.'"

"That's probably when the charm fell out of my pocket."

"What were you wearing that evening?" Neal asked.

"Black jeans, a black sweater and jacket." He dropped his head and gazed at the table. "A black balaclava."

"A balaclava? Hardly appropriate headgear for a cosy chat with your ex-girlfriend, is it?"

"No comment," Swallow said.

"I'll be honest, Dr Swallow . . . the fact that you withheld this information from us previously does not incline us in your favour. It sounds very much as though you've just concocted this version of your story when you realised that you could no longer deceive us over your whereabouts on the day of the murders. Are we supposed to believe that this noise you heard was the killer?"

"I've already explained why I lied to you before. I knew I'd be the obvious scapegoat for the murders."

"I'm going to recommend that you be held in custody pending further investigation."

Swallow's face and neck flushed red. "That's outrageous! I'm innocent!" He turned angrily to his solicitor, who purred reassuring noises.

* * *

"So, what do you think, sir? Is he our killer?" Ava said, after a protesting Swallow had been led away and Norwood had gone off to arrange his bail.

"I'm quietly optimistic. Though let's wait for some supporting evidence to come through from forensics."

"What do you think of his story about hearing someone outside while he was in the yurt? It sounded like a lame attempt to suggest that person, not him, was the killer."

"I agree."

"It's just not credible that he went there to have a cosy chat with Samantha, knowing that she'd gone to Northfields to be alone with Nick. His story is full of holes. I reckon he went there with the intention of killing them both."

"So, was he thwarted in his attempt? Did someone else beat him to it? Until we have more evidence, we need to keep an open mind."

CHAPTER EIGHTEEN

Tom Knight had enjoyed an interesting morning. His conversation with Royal Military Police Officer Cassie Singleton had proved worth the long drive out to the army base in Northeast Stromfordshire. He'd contacted Sergeant Singleton in the hope of gaining some background information on Soren Hunter — or Glen Bolton, as he was known to the British Army.

"We suspected from the start that he might be ex-army because he appeared to demonstrate observational and other field skills that suggested he'd had some kind of specialist training," Tom had explained when he'd called to request the meeting.

Tom had felt slightly out of his comfort zone walking onto the army base, but Sergeant Singleton put him at his ease by greeting him in a familiar accent, reminding him of home. It turned out they'd both grown up within a few streets of one another.

After a bit of reminiscing, Tom showed her a picture of the dog tags.

"Thanks. Bear with me for a bit. Help yourself to a coffee. There's a machine in the corridor outside."

By the time Tom returned, two coffee cups in hand, Singleton had obtained the information he required. She slid a printout across her desk to him. In the top right-hand corner was a photograph of a clean-shaven young man who bore some resemblance to Hunter. The name next to the photograph identified him as Glen Bolton.

"This is an old photograph. Nearly eight years, in fact. It was taken when Bolton joined the Paras from his regular unit in 2007. Two years later he failed to report back to his unit after some authorised leave. We've heard nothing from him since."

"No disrespect," Tom said, "but, being honest, I'm struggling with being able to tell if it's definitely him."

"Well, he's had a few years to grow the dreadlocks he's sporting in your photograph. Remove them and the bushy beard, add a few years and some harrowing battle experiences, and I'd say there's no question your Soren Hunter is our Glen Bolton."

"Right." Tom thought he could see it. The blue, slightly almond-shaped twinkly eyes were a fit. But the man in the picture looked so fresh-faced and young. What had he experienced to transform him from eager new recruit to a man whose eyes had a haunted look behind their sparkle? "What can you tell me about Bolton?"

"He served with the Parachute Regiment, which as you probably know is an elite unit of the British Army."

Tom nodded. His knowledge of all things military was pretty sketchy, but even he had heard of the Paras. Mostly down the pub back home where everyone who'd ever served claimed to have been one.

"He had all the qualities you'd expect of an elite soldier . . . courage, mental resilience, self-discipline and self-reliance. He was also intelligent and, from what I've been able to ascertain, he was well-liked, loyal and empathic."

"I suppose the big question is . . . why do you think he deserted?"

"Bolton served with his battalion in Afghanistan in 2008. It was after his tour there that he failed to report back for duty. Those who were closest to him claimed that while over there he'd begun to have doubts about his role in the conflict. About whether he should be there at all."

Tom recalled stories he'd read about soldiers who'd become disillusioned over their role in Afghanistan. Some had questioned the legality of Britain's involvement in the conflict; others had been deeply affected by witnessing civilian casualties. Was Hunter — or Bolton, as Tom probably needed to think of him now — one of those? Six years was a long time to be on the run. What had he been doing all that time?

Sergeant Singleton explained that a deserter would need to live under the radar. Applying for a job that would necessitate giving information such as his National Insurance number would lead to him being arrested. Then again, she admitted that the army didn't have the resources to track down everyone who went AWOL. Apparently, it was the responsibility of someone from the soldier's own unit, the 'rat catcher,' to do the investigative work.

Before he left the base, Sergeant Singleton had reminded Tom of his duty to contact the Military Police should he become aware of Glen Bolton's whereabouts. It had made him feel uneasy.

Knowing Hunter's real identity wasn't going to make it any easier to find him. He had managed to evade the British Army, after all. All the qualities that had made him a good soldier, combined with his training, made him a formidable opponent. But did it make him capable of murder outside of conflict? Everything that Tom had learned about Soren Hunter — okay, he'd stick to the name he knew him by — disinclined him to believe he'd take a life without a very compelling reason.

What else had Sergeant Singleton said? He was loyal and empathic. Not the sort to let people down, then. Had he let the Stratford family down by disappearing from their lives at a critical time? In London, he'd proved that his instinct was to protect and help those in need. Tom reasoned that someone with a profile like Hunter's wouldn't readily turn his back on his friends.

Unless he was guilty of murdering Nick Winter and Samantha Benrose, which, try as he might, Tom just couldn't see. Nor could he accept that Hunter would simply abandon the Stratfords in their hour of need. All of which led him to the conclusion that Soren Hunter, AKA Glen Bolton, was probably hiding in plain sight.

* * *

Bea Stratford was struggling to do any work since the murders. She had been unable to think about the holiday lets. She'd wanted to cancel their existing bookings and put a message on the website saying that the yurts were not available to rent for the rest of the season, but Monty and Blue had dissuaded her. The kids were being great. It was Aubrey she worried about most. This was a terrible setback for him.

He'd been doing so well since their arrival at Northfields. Bea stopped herself right there. She had enough to worry about at the moment without reflecting on the reason for their leaving Brighton. She had to stay strong and keep the family together. Especially now her baby granddaughter had arrived.

Today had been a difficult day. Nick Winter's sister, Jenny, had contacted her for a second time yesterday to ask if she could come and see the place where her brother had died. Bea had had to put her off when she'd called previously. The police were still gathering evidence, she'd said, truthfully. How could she tell her that it would take days to get rid of the blood?

Jenny had arrived at ten. Much as she abhorred the thought of seeing the scene of the murder again, Bea had accompanied her to the garage. She'd winced at the sight of the khaki ambulance, which she'd previously regarded as quaint. Jenny had been overcome peering into its interior where, despite someone's best efforts to clean up — the smell of disinfectant still lingered — faint pink spots remained as a reminder of her brother's violent end. Bea had put her arm around Jenny to comfort her.

Over a cup of tea in the kitchen afterwards, Jenny told Bea a bit about her brother's life. Bea had been saddened to learn that Nick's parents had not loved him as they'd loved their other three children, as though he'd been the runt of the litter, the one left to fend for himself. She couldn't imagine loving one of her children more than the other. She'd heard it said that parents often had a favourite, even if they refused to admit it. That wasn't the case with her. Of course, she and Aubrey had stopped at two, but she was sure that her love would not lessen the farther it was stretched.

It was strange for Bea to hear Jenny speak about the man who had come to her brother's aid in London. Should she tell Jenny that she suspected she knew who he was, that he had rescued Monty, too? But then she would have to explain what Nick had clearly not told his sister: that he had kept in touch with his Good Samaritan and that it was because of him that Nick had booked a weekend break at Northfields. In the end, she decided not to mention Soren Hunter. Jenny might wish to thank Soren for helping Nick, and no one even knew his current whereabouts.

It was probably only a matter of time before one or all of Samantha Benrose's family got in touch. People seemed to think that it would offer them closure. Bea wondered, if Monty had died in that knife attack in London, whether she would have wanted to visit the spot, see the very place where he had bled out onto the pavement, breathed his last breath. She didn't think so, but who knew what she would have done, really? It wasn't until people were faced with a situation that they discovered how they would react.

Thinking of Monty in this way made her feel a sudden urge to see him. After checking on Blue and Esmé, both fast asleep in the rocking chair in Blue's bedroom, she made her way across to the brewery. She couldn't remember the last time she'd been in there. Monty had to work extra hard now that Soren wasn't around to help. Perhaps that was why he was eating enough for two. Half an apple pie had disappeared from the fridge today; Monty had taken it to eat in the brewery. They'd have to start looking for someone to help in Soren's absence; it was too much work for one person.

She was surprised to find the door locked. Maybe the murders had unnerved Monty, made him more security conscious. She knocked and waited. Eventually a smiling Monty opened the door. "Sorry, Mum. I was through the back."

Bea looked over Monty's shoulder to the back room. His gaze followed hers and he seemed nervous.

"Is Soren in there?" She surprised herself with her sudden intuition. Monty, bless him, was not an accomplished liar. His face reddened and he stammered when he spoke.

"S-Soren? In the back room? Why would he be?"

Bea shook her head and marched straight past him. She shoved the door open.

"Hello, Bea." Soren Hunter met her eye.

Bea's response was instinctive. She walked over to him and clasped his shoulders. "Thank goodness you're safe!" She was pleased to receive one of Soren's rare smiles. She turned to her son. "How long have you been keeping this a secret?"

Monty looked down.

"Please don't blame Monty, Bea," Soren said. "I asked him not to tell anyone."

"We've all been so worried about you. You could have been burnt alive in that caravan."

"Mum, you know the fire chief told us they didn't find a body," Monty reminded her.

Bea glared at him. "That's not the point."

"I'm sorry, Bea. The last thing I wanted to do was upset you or your family. I wouldn't have disappeared like that without good reason."

"Well, it had better be a *really* good one." She perched on an upturned beer cask and crossed her arms. "I'm waiting."

"Soren thought the police were going to arrest him for the murders because he didn't tell them he knew Nick Winter and had met Samantha Benrose before they came here," Monty blurted.

"No, there's something more to it than that. Something else you're not telling us, Soren." She stared at him. "Come on, you must know by now that you can trust all of us, not just Monty."

"It's a long story," Soren said.

"Well, you'd better come over to the farmhouse and join us for dinner this evening. You can tell us all then — save you having to repeat yourself." She looked at Monty and came to a decision. "And in return for sharing your secret with us, we'll tell you about something we've all been keeping from you."

Soren looked at them curiously.

Bea stood up. "See you at seven, then." As she turned to go, she added, "I hope you enjoyed the apple pie."

CHAPTER NINETEEN

Neal listened as Tom explained his theory. He noticed how intently Ava was staring at the photograph Tom had just shown them of Glen Bolton. Doubt was written all over her face at first, but the longer she stared, the more it seemed to fade. Finally, all concurred that the man in the picture was indeed Soren Hunter.

"So, you think he's still here, in Stromfordshire? Probably at Northfields?" Neal asked Tom. It was entirely possible. They simply hadn't been able to afford the manpower to carry out more than a desultory search for Hunter. It had been taken for granted that he would have made for London, where he could simply disappear.

"Yes, sir. It just doesn't fit his Good Samaritan profile to abandon people who need his help."

"Chronic hero syndrome," Ava commented.

Neal raised a quizzical eyebrow.

"Remember Pixie at the hostel saying Hunter was a bit of an urban legend because of his propensity for saving people?"

"I know what it means." Neal didn't add that he was surprised Ava had heard of the term. Then he remembered that her brother Ollie was a comic book fan. In the comic book realm, chronic hero sufferers, of whom Batman was a prime example, were unable to resist saving people. Tom, he noted, was nodding vigorously. "You said this Sergeant Singleton mentioned that Hunter — or Bolton — began to question the morality of what was going on in Afghanistan . . . Is it possible he's been trying to atone for something he did out there? By saving people?"

"Could be. He was deeply troubled over contributing to the deaths of innocent civilians."

"Yes. He wouldn't be the first to feel guilt over that." Neal told them about a soldier he'd read about who had faced a court martial after refusing to fight in Afghanistan.

"The question is . . . do we think any of the Stratfords know he's there?" Ava said. "I think it would be difficult for him to hide out there without at least one of them knowing. I know he's probably got survival skills, but even so . . . What about Blue? She'd definitely be on his side."

"I'd go for Monty," Tom said. "He believes he owes Hunter for saving his life. He wouldn't betray him."

"We need to search the place again," Neal said. "Let's go, Tom."

He had chosen Tom because they were acting on his hunch. Ava couldn't conceal the disappointment at not being offered a piece of the action as she uttered a flat, "Good luck."

* * *

As Tom drove, slightly above the speed limit, it occurred to Neal that he hadn't had much opportunity to get to know his other detective sergeant. Tom had been assigned to Neal's team when his old DI was arrested for murder in a case Neal and Ava had investigated the previous year. From what Ava had told him, Tom had been relieved at his reassignment. DI Reg Saunders had been a poor role model, to say the least. He was currently doing time for murder. Neal suspected that Tom might have put up with racist innuendo from Saunders. Saunders had been infamous for his thinly disguised sexist comments to female colleagues. It was unlikely he'd limited his prejudices to one section of the population.

"Watch your speed," Neal cautioned.

"Sorry, sir." He was clearly eager to get to Northfields as quickly as possible and seemed to find it hard not to let the dial creep up every so often. Neal focused on the road ahead, trying not to look like he was constantly monitoring their speed. Tom didn't seem like the reckless type. He needed to relax and trust him to handle the car safely.

Being honest, he preferred to drive himself but, as the superior officer, he was supposed to let his minions taxi him around. He had never felt entirely comfortable with the idea of outranking other people. In his appraisals, he'd been commended for his natural leadership abilities but that was different from putting yourself above other people, wasn't it? Leaders were enablers now, anyway, weren't they? Just another member of the team. They just got paid more. That was another thing with which he wasn't entirely comfortable.

Tearing himself away from his thoughts, Neal decided he should start some sort of conversation with Tom. He had no interest in cars, which he knew was one of Tom's passions. He wasn't sure what else he was interested in. As he mulled this over, Tom helped him out.

"Did you have a nice time at your sister's wedding, sir?"

"Er . . . yes. Thank you."

"Ava showed us some photos. Loved the kilt."

Neal flinched, thinking of Ava holding her phone out for everyone to have a laugh at the sight of the boss in a skirt. He could just imagine the comments: *What do you think he's wearing underneath?*

"I wore a kilt once." Tom surprised him.

"Oh? What was the occasion?"

"Mate's wedding. He was a Glaswegian. Joined the Hertfordshire Constabulary same time as me. His brother lent it to me. What sort of tartan was it now? Eternity, I think. Does that sound right?"

"Yes," Neal said. "Was the wedding held in Scotland?"

"No. St Albans. That's where the bride was from. Pity. I've never been to Scotland. Is it as cold as they say?"

Neal deliberated. He thought of what Maggie always said when confronted with that question: *You don't go to Scotland for the weather.* He said as much to Tom.

"Yeah, right. It's the scenery, isn't it? So where would you recommend visiting?"

Neal made some suggestions. Tom seemed to enjoy hearing about his hobby of 'Munro bagging' — climbing Scottish peaks over three thousand feet. The conversation flowed more fluently after that. Tom was an easy person to get along with.

"Here we go!" Tom slowed to take a right turn for the road leading to Northfields.

"Park a distance from the farmhouse."

"I like your thinking, sir. Element of surprise."

They parked about a quarter of a mile from the house. A brisk walk brought them to the wooded area where the yurts were spread out amongst the trees, none of them too close to any of the others. They trod quietly over fallen leaves and tufted mounds of grass. Neal signalled to Tom to check the shower block while he checked the first yurt. Both were clear.

They looked inside the other yurts, one by one. Surprisingly, all were unlocked. Perhaps because it would have been easy enough to cut a hole through the material if someone really was determined to get inside. Neal worried that if Hunter had been hiding out here, he would have detected their presence already and fled, but there was no sign that any of the yurts had been inhabited recently.

It seemed unlikely that Hunter would hide in either of Aubrey's workshops, but as they too, were unlocked, they checked them anyway, Neal bemoaning the family's lackadaisical approach to security. Then they made for the barn.

Inside, the dim interior looked much as it did the day after the murders when he and Ava had arrived to interview the Stratford family. The trestle tables stood undisturbed, still covered with gingham tablecloths, although the food had now been cleared away. The makeshift stage had not been dismantled but the microphones and musical equipment were gone. A string of bunting had come loose and trailed on the floor.

"Looks like they've hardly been in here since the night of the dance," said Tom. "Wonder what they use a big space like this for? Other than for storing stuff. And the occasional dance."

"It was probably used for storing farming equipment and vehicles in the days when this was a working farm. Let's check the brewery."

The door to the brewery was locked. "Want me to force it, boss?"

Neal thought for a moment then gave Tom the nod. A moment later and it was done, quietly and efficiently. They stepped inside. Tom shone a torch around the room and the light bounced off the giant stainless-steel casks, dazzling their eyes and casting hulking shadows on the whitewashed walls.

Neal tapped Tom's shoulder. He pointed at the ledged and braced door leading to the store and office. It was unlocked. Tom kicked it open with his foot and shone his torch around, finally directing it at the floor. By the side of some casks arranged against one wall of the room was a sleeping bag placed on top of an airbed on the floor. Beside it was a water bottle, some crumpled foil covered in crumbs and a small toilet bag, which on inspection turned out to contain a toothbrush and toothpaste.

"Seems you were right," Neal said. "Unless Monty likes this place so much, he's taken to camping out here."

"So, where is he now? Have we just missed him, do you reckon?" Tom showed no delight over his theory being proved right. Neal understood. To be so close, and to have just missed Hunter, was immensely frustrating.

"Let's check the farmhouse."

Tom closed the door as securely as he could. There was nothing he could do about the broken lock.

They approached the farmhouse from the rear. "Lucky for us they don't bother with security lighting," Tom said.

Neal agreed. When this was over, someone needed to give the Stratfords a talk on protecting their property. "The lights are on in the kitchen," he said, softly. "There are at least three doors to this property. If Hunter is here and he sees us he's going to bolt, and from what I've heard about this man, I don't feel confident that we'll be able to catch him." He cursed his oversight in not arranging for a couple of uniformed officers to meet them at the property.

Tom squinted at the kitchen window. "He's in there. Sitting at the kitchen table with the rest of them, cheeky sod." Neal was surprised to see that Tom was right. There was Blue, cradling the baby in one of those slings. She was sitting next to her brother on one side of the table. Hunter sat opposite them dressed in jeans and a black T-shirt. Bea and Aubrey were at either end of the table, presiding over the meal. They had certainly all made fools of the police.

Neal felt a stab of anger at the family's failure to report Hunter's whereabouts after he'd explicitly instructed them to do so. He had a good mind to nick them all for obstructing the course of justice. But his anger was momentary: the Stratfords trusted Hunter; he had saved Monty's life. On one level, he admired their loyalty. On another, he worried that it might be misplaced. Hunter was a man who could inspire loyalty. But he could well be playing them all.

Neal assessed the situation rapidly. The kitchen was large, running from the front of the house to the back. As was the custom these days, it had obviously been extended by knocking through a wall to another room. Neal whispered to Tom to cover the front entrance.

He waited a few moments for Tom to sneak around the side of the farmhouse before he approached the door. Then, just as he was about to rap on the door with his knuckles, Hunter looked directly at the window and caught his eye. Damn the man! He really did seem to have heightened senses. Hunter stood up, toppling his chair. Then, he bolted from the kitchen.

Hoping Tom would be quick enough to intercept him, Neal bolted too. He arrived at the front of the house in time to see Tom make a lunge at Hunter. Hunter fought him off and took off at a sprint across the farmyard, heading in the direction of the woods beyond. Tom was doubled over.

"I'm okay, I'm okay," Tom puffed as Neal slowed to assist him. "Fucker winded me!" He struggled to his feet.

Neal shot off in pursuit of Hunter, sensing that it was hopeless. Their quarry was already out of sight. Their best chance had been to catch him unawares. What the hell had made the man look up at that crucial moment? Whether aided by luck or superpowers, Hunter now had the advantage.

After a few moments, Neal slowed down, acknowledging the futility of the chase. Aided by his head start, the dark and his better knowledge of the meadows and woods surrounding Northfields, Hunter had vanished into the night, just like bloody Batman.

"Dammit!" It was Tom, puffing mightily. He came to a halt beside Neal and turned in a circle before bending to his knees, his breath coming in wheezy rasps.

"Sorry, boss," Tom said between pants.

"Nothing to apologise for. We lost our advantage. He looked up and saw me."

"Maybe the rumours are true and he has got superpowers," Tom said, without a trace of humour.

When both had recovered, they walked back to the farmhouse where the Stratford family had formed a reception party to greet them. Neal sensed their hostility from a long way off. Even the baby was grizzling disconsolately.

Monty took a step towards them. "Soren's done nothing wrong. He lied about knowing Nick because he knew you'd suspect him, a stranger who'd lived on the streets."

"His name is not Soren Hunter," Neal said. "It's Glen Bolton."

There was the briefest pause before Monty replied, "That's his business."

"It's also ours," Neal pointed out. "And the army's."

"What the devil has the army got to do with it?" Aubrey said.

"He's a deserter."

Blue gave a terse laugh. "Is that all?" Her tone was icy. "You should be trying to find the real killer instead of going after an innocent man." She stood beside her mother, clutching baby Esmé to her as though Neal and Tom intended on snatching her away.

Neal knew he couldn't win here. The whole family was stubbornly on Hunter's side. He singled Monty out. "We're going to need another look in your brewery." He silenced any objections by adding, "We've already seen that Hunter's been sleeping there."

"You can't do that without a warrant," Bea protested.

"Actually, we can if we have sufficient cause. And I should point out that I could arrest the lot of you for obstructing the course of justice."

"I thought it was *perverting* the course of justice?" Aubrey said, absently. "That's what they usually say on the telly. I could be wrong . . ."

Neal's patience was beginning to wear thin. It must have shown on his face because Monty stepped forward and offered to accompany them to the brewery without another word of protest.

CHAPTER TWENTY

An atmosphere of deep gloom had descended on the Stratford household following the police's attempt to arrest Soren.

"It's a shameful business," Aubrey declared to his friend, Charles Unwin, who had arrived the day after to give Monty a book on home-brewing that he'd picked up in a charity shop. Monty thanked him effusively for the tattered volume, which he suspected was years out of date. It was kind of Charles to think of him.

"So, he gave them the slip again, did he?" Charles said. "Think he'll be back this time?"

"I doubt it," Monty said. "He knows the police are on the lookout for him."

"So they say," Bea said. "But we all know they don't have the money to launch a big manhunt."

"How did they discover he was holed up here?"

"We don't really know," Monty said. "I'm guessing it was a hunch." He glanced nervously at his mother.

"Ah!" Charles exclaimed. "So, do they think he's their man for the murders, then?"

"I don't know if they have any other suspects but they seem very interested in Soren — which we all know is ludicrous. Soren's not a killer."

"He might have killed people." It was Blue. She had been more upset than the rest of them at Soren's disappearance so soon after his return. "If he was in the army, he could have killed people."

Aubrey filled Charles in on the police's story that Soren was a deserter from the British Army.

"Had to be something like that," Charles said. "Such a resourceful fellow. They used to shoot them, you know. Deserters."

"Yes, well. Thank goodness we're not living in the dark ages, anymore," Bea said. She thought it was a rather crass remark in the circumstances. Charles often made strange comments. He was a bit like Aubrey in that respect. Both eccentrics, but at least Aubrey would have read the situation better in this instance. Or so she hoped. You never really knew with Aubrey.

Sometimes she grew a bit weary of Charles forever hanging around, devouring her home baking and behaving as though he was everyone's favourite uncle. Still, he'd been just what Aubrey had needed when they moved here: a friend who shared his interests; someone to help take him out of himself.

Perhaps it was mutual. Aubrey had told her Charles had been widowed several years before. He had family somewhere down south but didn't see much of them. He was quite a bit older than Aubrey but was in great shape. She'd often seen him striding across the fields with his dog, Winston, looking like a person half his age.

"He could face a court martial at the very least," Charles went on. "Life imprisonment."

Blue gave a sniff.

Monty said, "Yeah, well I'd like to see them try and catch him first. He's been evading capture for years."

"Did he tell you why he ran?" Charles asked.

"No."

"He was probably suffering from PTSD," Blue said. "That happens to a lot of soldiers."

"Or a bad case of cowardice," Charles said. No one smiled. He held up his hands. "Sorry, sorry. I know you all liked the fellow, but I didn't know him that well."

"No. You didn't," Monty said pointedly. Charles didn't say much more after that. Aubrey, sensing that his friend's lack of tact was becoming irritating, asked if he'd like to join him in his workshop. He had acquired a new engine part that he might be interested in. The two went off together.

"It doesn't look good for Soren, you have to admit," Bea said when they had gone.

"Mum! You're as bad as Charles. And the police." Blue stomped out of the room, leaving Bea and Monty behind.

"She's just upset, Mum," Monty said. His eyes narrowed as if a thought had just occurred to him. "You didn't tip the police off, did you?"

"No! Monty, how can you think that?"

Monty stared at his mother for a moment, his eyes alight. Then, he apologised. "Sorry, I'm just so angry about all of this."

"We all are," Bea said, gently. "It's just as well we can all vouch for being in the barn most of the evening or we'd be on their radar, too."

"We can't assume we're not," Monty said, gloomily. "I'm off to the brewery. Got to turn the hot liquor tank on and sterilise some equipment." He kissed his mother on the cheek. It was already eight o'clock. "I'll be at least a couple of hours."

* * *

As soon as he got to the brewery, Monty crossed to the back room and looked inside. The sight of Soren's sleeping bag and his meagre possessions caused him a moment's anguish. Would Soren think that he or another member of the family had betrayed him? One thing was certain: this time he wouldn't be back. Not if he had any sense.

While he waited for the hot liquor tank to heat to the optimum temperature, Monty weighed up the malt and sterilised the mash tun ready for the morning. Without Soren around, he'd have to consider asking his dad to help him with the mashing — Blue was in no fit condition yet. It was a two-person job, though he had on occasion had to do it unaided. Ideally, one person would add the malt gradually while the other stirred it with a big plastic paddle, as hot liquor poured into the mash tun from the liquor tank. The process always reminded him of making a giant vat of porridge.

When he checked the time later, he was surprised to see that it was gone ten. Time to call it a night. He was a little reluctant to leave the brewing shed. Sometimes, he felt more comfortable here than anywhere, surrounded by the familiar trappings of his trade. He looked forward to tomorrow when the whole shed would be filled with a delicious malty aroma from the mash. Later, after the hops were added, the aroma would become more complex and enticing.

There wasn't a single aspect of the brewing process that Monty didn't love. He knew how lucky he was to be making a living from his passion. For most people, brewing was only ever likely to be a hobby to be fitted in around the day job. He'd come a long way since he'd bought his first home-brewing kit on eBay.

He hoped that the family would be able to survive this latest setback so that he could stay at Northfields and continue to live his dream. Guilt set in immediately. Thinking of the horror of two young people losing their lives as a setback made the tragedy sound like nothing more than an inconvenience.

It was hard to get his head around all that had happened recently. Nick and Samantha had been murdered, an attempt had been made on Soren's life, and now he'd disappeared again.

Never down for long, Monty brightened at the thought that something wonderful had happened, too. He'd become an uncle. Baby Esmé had brought joy into their lives. He liked to think that she represented hope for the future.

He rubbed his tired eyes and remembered then that he'd promised to look over some marketing blurb that Blue had forwarded to him earlier. She'd wanted to get his opinion on the content before producing the final copy. He went into the adjoining office and turned on his laptop. For the next twenty minutes, he stared at the screen, trying to concentrate. But he was so tired that it was hard to focus. His eyelids began to droop and his head dropped to his chest. Moments later, he woke with a start — he must have dozed off.

But something had disturbed him, a noise of some sort. He remembered a sound intruding into his dream, a sound that didn't belong in a dream of a woman he'd met on holiday in Crete the previous year.

He was now wide awake. The noise he'd heard was the door to the outhouse dragging over the concrete floor as it opened inwards. Someone was in the brewery. It was a bit late for any of the family to be coming out here. It was probably his mother. He'd be extra nice to her. He needed to make up for asking her if she'd been the one to betray Soren. He'd never really believed she would do that.

She'd probably come to see why he was working so late. Sometimes, she texted him when he stayed in the brewery until the early hours of the morning, asking when he was going to bed, as if he were still a child. A glance at his phone confirmed that she hadn't left a message.

"Is that you, Mum?" he called.

There was no answer.

He closed the lid of his laptop, feeling a prickle of unease — not surprising given what had been going on around here lately.

He wondered if Soren had returned after all. But, deep down, Monty sensed that it wasn't his mother, or Soren. A tingle crept up his spine. Not fear exactly, but something approaching it.

He looked around the room, wondering if there was something he could use as a weapon. Just in case, he told himself. He didn't really believe he was likely to need one, did he? Suddenly, he wasn't so sure. He thought of Nick Winter and Samantha Benrose. They probably hadn't believed they were in any danger either, moments before they were murdered. His thoughts were making him jittery.

The door to the office opened a crack. A hand reached in and flicked the light switch, pitching the room into darkness. Monty let out a gasp. He groped for his phone and found it but he fumbled in his haste and it clattered to the floor.

"Who's there?" he called. "Soren, is that you?"

He knelt on the floor, hands sweeping a wide arc on the cold stone. He found his phone and activated the torch, but it was swept abruptly from his hand. It landed on the floor, the light shining upwards. A face, masked by night-vision goggles, loomed over him. Monty gasped in recognition.

The man's hand shot forward and Monty felt a sharp, scaring pain. Looking down, he saw the handle of a knife jutting through a gap in the clenched fist pressing against his stomach.

Only the handle. The blade was buried deep in Monty's innards. He could feel it twisting cruelly inside him, as it was guided towards its target.

Pain exploded in his chest and he tasted blood, salty and metallic in his mouth. He'd cheated death once, thanks to Soren. But Soren wasn't here to save him now.

CHAPTER TWENTY-ONE

Neal got the call first thing in the morning. His initial emo-
tion was one of profound sadness, rapidly followed by anger.
He called Trish and asked if she could come around, give
Archie some breakfast and then drop him off at school.
While he waited for her to arrive, he rang Ava and gave her
the news.

"Monty Stratford is dead?"

She sounded breathless. Probably out for a morning run.
"How?"

"Murdered. Stabbed in the heart. His mother found his
body about an hour ago. She'd got up because she heard the
baby crying and was puzzled to see Monty's bedroom door
open. When she saw his bed hadn't been slept in, she went
out to the brewery."

There was silence.

"Ava?"

"I'm here. I just . . . needed a moment to process. I kind
of liked Monty. And I feel for his family."

"Yes, well. Best thing we can do is our job." Neal meant
to sound understanding but was still feeling angry. The
words came out a little snappy.

"I know," Ava said. He suspected that Ava's regret, like his, would soon turn to anger. He encouraged her to get to work as soon as possible.

Tom and PJ also fell silent when Neal broke the news of Monty's death. Tom seemed particularly affected. Seeing him turn away, Neal waited a few moments before asking if he was okay.

"I feel . . . responsible," Tom explained. "If I hadn't clocked that Hunter was likely to be hiding out at Northfields, he'd still be there. He could have protected Monty."

"It's not your fault. We did what we had to do. And you seem to forget that Soren Hunter is still a suspect." He sensed his words had fallen on deaf ears. Apart from himself, it was clear no one in the team really accepted that Soren was the killer. PJ pressed Tom's arm, but he shrugged her off and asked to be excused.

"He shouldn't blame himself." PJ looked concerned. "We can't take these things to heart. If we blamed ourselves every time we made a bad judgement—"

"It wasn't a bad judgement, Detective Constable," Neal corrected her. "We were doing our job."

PJ nodded, but she looked unhappy.

Ava arrived, hair still damp from what must have been a hasty shower. Neal instantly suppressed the image that flashed into his mind.

"Tom's taking it badly," he told her as they pulled out of the station. "He's convinced it's somehow his fault for going after Hunter."

"He'll get over it." Ava tooted the horn impatiently at the driver in front who had made a left without signalling. "I don't mean to sound unsympathetic or anything, but we can't afford to start questioning our every decision." She wavered. "Then again, Tom has a point. Hunter wouldn't have let anyone get at Monty."

The drive seemed to take forever. As was usually the case on these quiet country roads, they found themselves stuck behind slow-moving farm vehicles more than once. That was the worst thing about not being in a patrol car. You couldn't just stick on the flashing lights and blaring sirens whenever you were in a rush to overtake.

Two local patrol cars were parked outside the farmhouse when they arrived at Northfields. Neal nodded at the uniformed officer guarding the entrance to the house. He thought he recognised him from a previous case.

An atmosphere of grief permeated the farmhouse kitchen. The Stratford family, now diminished by one member, sat around the kitchen table in sad imitation of the last time Neal had seen them when he and Tom had come to arrest Soren Hunter. Aubrey had his arm around Bea, whose eyes were red and swollen. She looked as though she was there only in body. Her mind, like her gaze, was no doubt somewhere else entirely. Blue was cradling the baby.

Neal cleared his throat. He wasn't expecting this to be easy. "I am so sorry for your loss . . ." he began.

No one reacted. Bea continued to stare into the near distance, moving her upper body in a rocking rhythm. As the silence lengthened, Neal began to wonder if they'd heard. He'd been expecting anger, criticism, accusations of blame. Somehow, this failure to react seemed more difficult to bear. He cleared his throat again.

"We heard you," said Bea Stratford. "I don't know what you want us to say. Thank you, I suppose, is the polite response, though manners aren't really that important when it comes right down to it, are they? I don't care one bit about hearing you express your condolences. You have no idea what Monty meant to us. How can you be sorry?"

I have a son. Neal didn't give voice to the thought. True, he was a father, but his son was alive. He couldn't begin to imagine what it would feel like to lose Archie. Bea was right. Grief was private and not for outsiders to intrude upon. Still, he had a job to do.

"I'd like to speak with you all later," he said. "But first, DS Merry and I need to see the . . ." He had been about to say *body* but corrected himself. "We'd like to see the brewery."

The word brewery was enough to tip Bea over the edge. She sobbed loudly, burying her face in her husband's shirt. Aubrey patted her hair.

"That was awkward," Ava said, when they were back outside. "I couldn't think of a thing to say that wouldn't upset them more."

"I know what you mean. We're strangers to these people. What right do we have to disturb them in their grief?"

"Well, we wouldn't if Monty had died of natural causes," Ava reminded him. "We're only here because a murder has been committed."

Sometimes Ava's pragmatic outlook on things took Neal by surprise. There was no arguing with her reasoning, though.

They had arrived at the brewery. The other local police officer had secured the scene. Neal and Ava put on the protective clothing they'd brought from the car.

"He's in the back room, sir," the officer said.

Monty lay on the floor near a row of casks. Neal glanced at Ava. This was the third victim she had seen in under a week. He knew she'd reacted physically to the sight of Samantha Benrose's mutilated corpse. It was a relief to see that her expression was one of professional curiosity when she crouched beside Monty's body.

"It was early morning when his mother found him," the officer informed them. "She said the light wasn't on. The poor lad was lying in the dark."

It wouldn't have made much difference to him, Neal thought, though he could relate to the PC's comment. "Did his mother say anything else? Did she touch the body or anything else in the room?"

"No. She remarked that his eyes were open. That's how she knew he was dead. There was no 'spark of life in them,'

177

as she put it. But she had the presence of mind to feel for a pulse." He shook his head. "Nothing."

"Did she call an ambulance?"

"Yes, sir. A paramedic confirmed that the lad was gone. She thought it likely that he'd been dead for some hours."

"Thank, you, Constable."

"Well, one thing's certain," Ava said. "Swallow couldn't have done this. So, are we looking at two separate killers? Possibly Swallow for Nick and Samantha and someone else for Monty? Either that or Swallow's innocent and someone else killed all three victims." She looked gloomy.

Neal wondered if she was considering that Soren Hunter might be that person. He was also worrying about other possible permutations, such as one or two killers they had not yet identified as potential suspects.

"Monty believed that his London attacker wanted to kill him," Ava said, "but he also believed that he was a random victim. What if he wasn't? What if his attacker really did set out to kill him then, and because Hunter got in his way, he came here to finish the job? He waited until Hunter was out of the way again so he'd be less likely to fail."

Neal nodded. "We need to keep an open mind. Swallow is still our primary suspect for the first two murders." He rubbed his chin. "But let's consider for a moment that we are looking at a single killer. What motive would he have had for killing Nick and Samantha?"

Ava had no answer to his question and, for the time being, neither did Neal. It was slightly depressing to think that, of all scenarios, the one involving two separate killers was the least awful option, for then they could at least hope that they might already have one of them in custody.

CHAPTER TWENTY-TWO

Neal called his core team into his office to update them.

PJ evidently felt the need to be clear on what he had just related to her and Tom about the possibility of there being either one or two killers.

"So, what you're saying is that *either* Nick and Samantha were murdered by Swallow and someone else was responsible for killing Monty . . ."

"Correct."

"*Or* the same person killed all three of them?"

"If we'd taken the attack on Monty in London to be attempted murder," Tom said, "we would have been focusing our investigation on him as well as on Nick and Samantha."

"It would have been a stretch to make a connection between a seemingly random mugging in London and the murder of two people in the Stromfordshire Wolds," Ava pointed out.

"Hunter's a connection, though, isn't he?" PJ said. "He met both Nick and Monty in London."

"A link, but not necessarily a causal one," Neal said. "Soren already knew Nick when Monty turned up on his territory."

"Yep," Ava said. "We can't assume there's reason to attach any more significance to it than that." PJ looked unconvinced.

"So, we now have to pose the question . . . who wanted Monty dead?" Neal reclaimed their attention. There followed a silence which he perfectly understood.

Tom was the first to offer a suggestion. "What if Monty was killed because of something he'd discovered about Nick and Samantha's killer? The killer needed to silence him."

"Yes," Neal agreed. "That's a decent theory."

Ava spoke next. "Well, Monty did lie to us before, and we know of one other secret in the family, at least."

"You mean the identity of Esmé's father?" PJ said.

"There's no room for secrets in a murder investigation," Neal said, briskly. "Ava, PJ, drive out to Northfields tomorrow morning and question Blue Stratford again. I think we'd better avoid descending on her twice in one day."

"Yes, sir," Ava answered.

"And speak with Aubrey and Bea too, if they're available. See if you can uncover a bit more about their lives in Brighton and why they made the decision to move. If this is all about Monty, we need to know more about him and his family." After a moment, he added, "It would also help if we could locate the elusive Mr Hunter or whatever his bloody name is."

"Glen Bolton," PJ said immediately. Tom and Ava grinned at each other. "What?" PJ asked. "Did I get his name wrong?"

"I don't think the boss really forgot what it was, Peej," Ava's tone was slightly condescending. Tom was still grinning.

"Actually, I did," Neal said. "Thank you for refreshing my memory, DC Jenkins." It was worth the white lie to see Tom and Ava's expressions.

* * *

Ava and PJ drove out to Northfields the next morning. It was raining, so visibility on the roads was poor and the journey took longer than usual. Despite the sadness underpinning the mission, PJ chattered most of the way and Ava learned a lot of gossip about her colleagues that she'd have preferred not to. Who knew, for instance, that shy Andy Coates from IT had been spotted with his girlfriend at a notorious dogging spot? Everyone but Ava, it appeared. PJ's comment that DI Neal wouldn't have known about it either wasn't exactly reassuring.

"Park as near to the farmhouse as you can," PJ said, as Ava pulled into the farmyard. "I don't want to get a soaking."

"I've got a giant brolly in the boot," Ava said, "but I don't know why you didn't wear a coat."

PJ made a face. She was wearing a smart navy suit that looked a bit thin for the time of year. Ava had recently invested in one of those waxed jackets so beloved of the country set. She was wearing it now with her customary jeans. No more being soaked to the skin when she was on an outdoors job in bad weather.

Out of consideration for her friend, she parked practically outside the farmhouse's kitchen door. Bea Stratford, watching from the window, opened the door before they could knock.

A pink baby girl balloon bobbed against the kitchen ceiling, its trailing ribbon grazing the worktop. Ava had seen Bea since the baby's birth but it hadn't seemed appropriate to offer congratulations, given what had happened to Monty. It still didn't.

Bea looked worse than she had the day before and, although she was able to communicate this time, her eyes lacked animation.

"We haven't heard from Soren, if that's what you're here about. I thought he might have sent us a message, just to say he was okay." Though Bea's voice was heavy with disappointment, at least it expressed some emotion. "We were all so fond of him. Especially Blue."

It struck Ava as odd that Bea didn't mention Monty.

"How are you coping?" she asked.

Bea shrugged. "As well as can be expected. Why have you come here today?"

"Actually, it's Blue we've come to see. Is she here?"

"Yes, she's just feeding Esmé. Would you mind waiting a bit? She's not finding breast feeding easy." Who would? Ava thought. "I can make you a cup of tea or coffee while you wait."

A drink was welcome after the longish drive. Ava and PJ accepted immediately.

"It doesn't feel right to congratulate her on becoming a grandma under the circumstances, does it?" Ava whispered to PJ. "But it doesn't seem right not to, either."

PJ nodded, her eyes on the pink balloon.

Tea arrived, along with an offer of homemade lemon drizzle cake, which Ava refused. PJ considered for a few moments, then declined with a sad shake of her head. Bea joined them with a cup of tea.

"What brought you all to Stromfordshire?" Ava asked. She thought Bea recoiled slightly at the question.

"Er . . . Aubrey had always planned to retire early. He'd had a busy and successful career as an engineer. He worked on projects all over the world, but it meant that he was away from home quite a lot. He actually retired even earlier than planned."

"Why was that?" Ava asked.

"Er . . . there was an accident."

"What kind of accident? Was Aubrey injured?"

"No, Aubrey wasn't injured." She gave a deep sigh, cradled her tea in both hands and took a sip. Ava waited.

"Aubrey was involved with a project in Sussex. The construction of a pedestrian bridge. The bridge collapsed while under construction. It . . . it was something to do with a truss splitting and causing some girders to collapse. Two men fell to the ground. One sustained minor injuries, and the other was fatally injured."

"Was Aubrey held responsible for the accident?"

"The conclusion of the investigation was that the accident was caused by a structural design fault. It was Aubrey's design, but there was an investigation that concluded that others involved in the project contributed by not consulting him about some of the construction materials being used. If he'd been made aware, he would have pointed out that they were inadequate."

Ava nodded. She guessed that a project like that would involve a lot of different professionals and contractors. Assigning blame might not be as straightforward as would first appear. Still, Aubrey did share a portion of that blame.

"Aubrey was devastated. He'd been working as an engineer for twenty-five years. The safety of the workers was always a priority for him. He couldn't go back to work after that. It nearly broke him."

"I'm sorry," Ava said.

"That's why we moved to Stromfordshire. A fresh start. Where nobody knew us." Bea paused. Ava sensed she had more to say.

"There's something else." Bea looked around a little nervously. "The worker who died. He . . . he was a young man with a sort of connection to us." She took a breath and continued. "His name was Nate Crow. He was the younger brother of one of Monty's friends. He was planning on studying engineering at university. Aubrey persuaded the firm that he was working for at the time to take Nate on as an intern for the months between sixth form and university, to give him a bit of work experience." Bea took a gulp of tea before continuing. "While he was on site with Aubrey, one of the contractors offered him a few days' paid work, helping the men pouring the concrete. That's how he came to be on the bridge when it collapsed."

There was silence for a few moments. Why had no one thought to mention any of this before? Was it because they believed that it could have nothing to do with the current investigation or because it might have shown Aubrey Stratford in an unfavourable light? Surely not the latter. It was a bit of a leap from causing a death accidentally through a faulty design to brutally stabbing a young couple.

"The move has been good for Aubrey. He'll never forgive himself for playing a part in that young man's death, but he's gradually coming to terms with it."

PJ, who had been quiet throughout, leaned across the table and pressed Bea's arm. "It was a terrible thing to happen."

"Mrs Stratford, did Nate Crow's family bring a case against your husband or any of the other professionals involved?" Ava was surprised when Bea shook her head.

"They weren't interested in suing. They said it wouldn't bring Nate back. They are exceptionally forgiving people. Deeply religious. Nate's father even came to see Aubrey personally to tell him he forgave him for his part in the tragedy. The company Aubrey worked for was fined. It obviously suffered some damage to its reputation."

"What was the name of the company Aubrey worked for?"

"Scarlett & Son Engineering," Bea said, her face flushing.

Ava nodded. So much for Blue not liking the colour red. "How were relations between Aubrey and his employer when he retired?"

"Not the best. Aubrey hadn't worked for them for that long. It was made pretty clear to him that he wasn't welcome to stay. Aubrey was depressed for a while afterwards. Then, I got the idea about moving and buying a bit of land where we could run some sort of business. Monty . . ." Bea's eyes became glassy with tears and she sniffed loudly. "Monty had always fancied micro-brewing, so he came on board too, then Blue. I would manage the holiday lets and Aubrey could work on his cars. He hires them out for events, did you know? I call what he does *tinkering*, but it's actually bringing in a small income.

"It was the best thing we could have done at first, but now it's a living nightmare." PJ pressed Bea's arm again.

"Where is Aubrey this morning?" Ava asked.

"He's with his friend in the village, Charles Unwin. You met him at the dance but I don't suppose you'll remember with all that was going on."

"I do remember him."

"Aubrey and Charles have become such good friends. They have exactly the same interests — vintage vehicles and an obsession with all things 1940s."

"How lovely, your husband moving to a small village in the middle of nowhere and finding a kindred spirit," PJ said.

"Yes," Bea said. "Almost as if it was meant to be. It was nice for Charles too. He was new to the village himself. He moved here a month or two after us, actually. He bought two houses and merged them to accommodate his collection of wartime memorabilia, would you believe."

"Yes." Ava remembered hearing that snippet of information before.

They were interrupted by the arrival of Blue, with the baby asleep snuggled against her chest in a sling. After the usual congratulations and some complimentary comments about the baby's appearance — mostly from PJ, who had a bewildering number of nieces, nephews and young cousins — Ava asked Blue if they could speak with her alone.

Bea was immediately tense. "Why do you need to speak with Blue without me here?"

Blue had already guessed. "They want to ask me who Esmé's father is, I expect."

"Oh." Bea hovered at the table, no doubt hoping that Blue would invite her to stay, but her daughter was stubbornly silent. Finally, she said, "I'll just be in the sitting room."

"Why do you need to know?" Blue asked fiercely. "Why can't everyone just accept that I don't want to talk about him?"

"Did the father know that you were pregnant?" Ava asked.

"No. Believe me, he wouldn't have been interested. Still wouldn't be — not that I have any intention of ever telling him."

"Blue, I'm sorry, but we do need to ask you for his name and contact details."

Blue stiffened. "It's none of your business. I don't see what the identity of my baby's father has to do with your investigation."

"I know it probably seems irrelevant, but in a murder investigation it's important that we know as much as possible about the people surrounding the victims. Believe me, the most unlikely details can be significant. It's all about making connections, seeing the big picture."

Blue stared sullenly at the table. Then she mumbled, "Aidan Crow."

Ava raised an eyebrow. "Is he by any chance related to Nate Crow?"

"How do you know about that?" Red splodges had appeared on Blue's neck. "Oh! You've been speaking with my mum, haven't you? Nate was Aidan's brother. What else did she tell you?"

"About the accident that your father was involved with."

"Right." Her tone was scornful. "We came here to get away from all that." She stroked Esmé's velvety scalp. "Seems like the past follows you wherever you go."

"You're afraid that it would upset your family to know that you'd had a relationship with Nate's brother. Were you worried that the baby would be a constant reminder to your father of Nate's death?"

"Something like that," Blue said. "But that wasn't the only reason."

"A baby can help heal . . ." PJ faltered at Blue's hostile glare.

"Not in this case. When I got together with Aidan, I knew who he was, but he didn't know me. I'd seen pictures of him with Monty on Facebook. I sought him out with the intention of just talking to him, but . . . well, I'm sure you can work the rest out for yourself. When he found out who I was, he was furious. He said he never wanted to see me again."

Blue didn't look stricken at the thought. It was all a bit of a mess. Ava could almost appreciate why Blue was reluctant to reveal the identity of Esmé's father. Unfortunately, in her experience, secrets like that had a way of worming their way to the surface.

"Did Monty and Aidan remain friends after Nate's death?" Ava asked.

"No. That's why I made contact with Aidan in the first place. To see if I could persuade him to renew his friendship with my brother. Monty was so upset about it all. The accident wasn't his fault, but Aidan blamed him for introducing Nate to Dad." Blue bit her lip. "It wasn't wholly Dad's fault either, but as far as Aidan was concerned, the whole family was tainted."

"Did Aidan ever threaten you or any of the rest of the family?"

"He came around to our house once. I wasn't there, but Monty told me it got quite nasty. He assaulted Dad on the doorstep."

"Assaulted him how?"

"Punched him in the face. Monty had to pull him off."

"Was the incident reported to the police?"

"No. Dad said he deserved it. And that Aidan was mad with grief."

So, Aidan Crow wasn't as forgiving as his parents. Ava exchanged a look with PJ. "Thanks for speaking with us, Ms Stratford. We'll be as discreet as possible about the baby's father."

Blue looked sceptical, then asked, in a hesitant voice, "I don't suppose there's any news about Soren?"

"I'm sorry, no," Ava replied. "We've been unable to track him down so far."

"What about Monty? Have you made any progress on finding out who . . . killed him?"

"I'm sorry, there's nothing I can tell you yet. We are doing everything we can to investigate your brother's murder."

"Right. I'll just fetch Mum. She'll be annoyed if I let you leave without letting her know."

Upon her return, Bea's eyes searched Ava's, but she must have realised that she would not betray Blue's confidence.

But she did ask how the investigation into the murders was going. Ava considered sharing with her that they were now considering Monty might have been the killer's target from the beginning, but she decided against it, for now.

"None of it makes any sense," Bea said. She was showing signs of breaking down again.

Ava had no answers for her. Poor Bea. PJ got up and gave Bea a hug. She assured her that they would do everything in their power to ensure that Monty's killer was brought to justice. Bea didn't react, only stared at the baby balloon, her eyes glazing over as she seemed to retreat further into herself.

It worried Ava slightly. She'd seen that look before and it was never a good sign. "Thanks for speaking with us, Mrs Stratford. We'll see ourselves out." Bea gave a vague nod and continued to stare at the balloon.

"I hope she'll be okay," PJ sounded concerned. They were crossing the cobbled farmyard to the car. "She's losing the plot a bit, don't you think? Turning in on herself."

Ava didn't comment.

PJ gave a loud sigh. "Another suspect." She referred no doubt to Aidan Crow.

"Yep," Ava answered. "If only we'd learned about all this sooner. Why do people always keep secrets? Not that we have a reason to think this Aidan Crow is linked to the murders of Nick and Sam, at least not yet. It will be very interesting to find out whether he has an alibi for the night of Monty's murder, though. It sounds like he's harbouring a giant grudge over Nate's death, which gives him a possible motive . . . revenge. You'd think he'd go after Aubrey, though, not Monty, wouldn't you? Unless he hoped to inflict the same kind of pain he's suffered over losing his brother on Aubrey. It must be a terrible thing to lose a child."

"Powerful emotions." PJ tapped the side of her nose, knowingly. "If you think about it, that's what our job's all about, isn't it? Dealing with the fallout from extremes of human emotion."

"I suppose so."

"As my great aunt Joan used to say . . . when you're in the grip of a powerful passion, common sense goes right out the window. She was talking about love, of course. Psychologists say that love is a kind of madness. But I expect it's the same with strong emotions of any description."

Ava nodded. She thought of the victims, the terrible wounds that had been inflicted on their bodies. She couldn't help thinking of the moniker the papers had given to the killer: *the Beast of Northfields*. What had Soren said after seeing Samantha's mutilated body in the yurt? *No beast so fierce but knows some touch of pity* . . . It seemed particularly apt. Pity could be a strong emotion, but the killer had shown his victims none.

CHAPTER TWENTY-THREE

Archie was in bed reading for half an hour before lights out. Neal appreciated having more time to himself in the evening now that his son no longer wanted him to read to him at bedtime, but he did miss their old routine, particularly as he had not always been around to put Archie to bed due to the demands of his job. For once, he didn't wallow in guilt. On balance, he'd probably read to Archie more often than not and his son didn't seem to resent the absences. He seemed proud that his dad was a police officer and appreciated that sometimes family life was disrupted.

Before sitting down to go over the recent developments in the murders at Northfields Farm, Neal flicked through the latest collection of photographs posted by Maggie, as he'd promised when he'd spoken to her a few days before. She'd called to ask if he'd seen the pictures she'd posted of Uluru, which she and Jock had just visited. No, he hadn't. He avoided social media, finding the outpourings of emotion he encountered there disquieting. As a deeply private person, he couldn't relate to the concept of baring his innermost thoughts and feelings in public. He supposed he was an old-fashioned, buttoned-up male, out of touch with his emotions. Still, he'd promised Maggie he'd take a look.

He'd listened as Maggie enthused about sampling bush tucker, riding over the sand dunes on the back of a camel and viewing the vast Australian Outback from the air. It all sounded exotic and far away, which, of course, it was.

Archie had been excited when Neal showed him the pictures. He wanted to go to Australia and see the camels and eat bush tucker and sleep under the stars. "Can we go there, Dad?" Neal told him it cost a lot to travel such a long way but that maybe one day they could go. For now, he could look at Maggie's pictures and experience Australia via Google Earth, which seemed to satisfy Archie, who had never travelled farther than Scotland.

It took about ten minutes to view the latest lot of pictures. He'd need to remember to show them to Archie in the morning, if there was time. It looked as though his brother-in-law and his sister were still having an action-packed honeymoon. He viewed some short films of them cycling, kayaking, kiteboarding, surfing — didn't they know there were sharks in Australia? And one heart-stopping minute of Maggie throwing herself off a bridge into an abyss. And she'd promised him she wouldn't do a bungee jump. She must have had her fingers crossed behind her back. Neal derived a certain sense of satisfaction from her blood-curdling screams. She should have listened to her big brother.

He smiled to himself. He was happy for them.

"Now we just need to get you sorted, Jimmy," Maggie had said to him tipsily at the wedding reception. She'd meant with Ava Merry, of course. Maggie had been dropping hints for some time that he and Ava were meant to be together.

Neal didn't reveal to her that on the afternoon two days before the wedding, when she, Jock and Archie had been at a rugby match at Murrayfield, he had slept with a woman called Aileen, with whom he'd had a brief affair years before when he was still living in Edinburgh.

They'd run into each other on Princes Street and gone for a drink, then to her flat in Corstorphine. Afterwards, they'd both been embarrassed, at pains to point out that they weren't in the habit of one-night stands.

He had sensed that she was married and she'd confirmed his suspicion, saying that her husband was away a lot. She sounded quite bitter, and Neal guessed that the husband had been unfaithful first. It seemed unlikely the marriage would last.

There was no question of them seeing each other again; they hadn't even exchanged contact details. Aileen had kissed him on the cheek when they parted. She'd told him to have no regrets. It didn't stop him feeling a certain sadness about the whole affair. He did not want the rest of his life to be punctuated with meaningless one-night stands. Nor, he acknowledged, did he want a future without love and the comfort and security of a long-term relationship.

He clicked the mouse and the pictures disappeared. It was time to get down to some work.

The following morning, he and Ava drove to Norfolk to pay the Crow family a visit. They lived in a pretty flint cottage deep in the countryside.

"Beautiful place to live." Ava parked by the low stone wall surrounding the front garden.

Neal thought it was a bit isolated but nodded his agreement.

"We've only got an hour," Martha Crow told them after inviting them in and offering them tea. She'd already explained when they had arranged the visit by phone that she and her husband were expecting some guests who were coming for a religious retreat and would be arriving at noon.

She was a tall woman who exuded confidence. By contrast, her husband, Bob Crow, who prepared the tea, was shorter than his wife and had a cowed look about him. Martha worked as a nursery nurse in Holt. Bob worked in student support at the University of East Anglia. Nate had been the youngest of their four children.

"This shouldn't take long," Neal assured them. He began by apologising for needing to ask them about what he acknowledged must be a painful subject for them. The

Crows nodded, both appearing stoical in their acceptance of the tragedy in their lives. Always drawn to books, Neal had already noted the rows of religious titles on the bookcase.

He asked the Crows to tell them about Nate. Martha crossed to the windowsill. She took down a photograph of a smiling, sandy-haired boy in a rugby shirt. "This was taken when he was seventeen," she said. Nate hadn't made his eighteenth birthday.

"He was a handsome lad," Neal said. "My condolences for your loss."

To his astonishment, Bob said, "It was probably for the best." To his even greater astonishment, Martha nodded, wiping away a tear. Neal looked at Ava, whose frown reflected his own puzzlement.

"Our son was a homosexual," Martha said, as if this explained their attitude. Neal felt his sympathy for the Crows evaporate. He knew that they were religious, but he had not appreciated that their views were fundamentalist.

"What's that got to do with anything? He was still your son!" Ava blurted.

The Crows didn't react.

For once, Neal didn't wince at his sergeant's forthrightness. All he wanted was to extract the information they needed and get out as quickly as possible. "I understand that Nate's brother, Aidan, was a friend of Monty Stratford. Monty's father, Aubrey Stratford, offered Nate the opportunity to shadow him for a few weeks when he learned that Nate was interested in studying engineering at university. Is that right?"

"Yes, it was a very kind offer," Martha said. "Nathan jumped at the chance to get some real-life experience to put on his personal statement."

"Did you ever meet Aubrey Stratford?"

"No. At least not until after Nathan's death. We did speak with him on the phone after he'd offered to take Nathan on. He explained what Nathan would be doing. We were perfectly happy with the arrangement."

"Did he mention that Nate — sorry, Nathan — might be offered the chance of earning some money by taking on some practical work on the project?"

"Yes, but he emphasized that health and safety was paramount, and that Nathan would never be asked to do anything dangerous. Or be left unsupervised."

"Aubrey Stratford has told us that you didn't blame him for the accident. Is that correct?"

The Crows exchanged a glance. Then, Martha said, "My husband and I accepted that more than one person was at fault. We forgave them all. To err is human, Inspector." Neal knew the rest of the quotation, but Martha reminded them. "To forgive is divine."

But not when it came to Nathan's sexuality, it seemed.

"Nothing we could do to 'get even,'" Bob made air quotes, "would bring our son back. It was God's will. Hard to bear, but He has His reasons, which we can't aspire to comprehend."

Neal nodded. He didn't subscribe to that *through a glass darkly* stuff. He wondered if the Crows believed they were being punished for rearing a gay son. He felt a profound sadness for Nate, reaching puberty in a household where his sexuality was regarded as sinful.

"You have three other children, don't you? How did they react to Nathan's death?" he asked.

"The girls, Frieda and Lottie, were devastated." She looked down at her lap. "And angry." She lifted her eyes to her husband, who gave her an encouraging nod. "But we prayed with them, and they accepted that what had happened was God's will."

"And Nathan's older brother — Aidan, isn't it?" Neal asked. He watched them closely.

"Aidan has not yet found it in his heart to accept or forgive," Martha said, stiffly. "We continue to pray for him."

"Who did Aidan feel bore the most responsibility for his brother's death?"

Martha sighed. "He blamed himself because his friendship with Monty Stratford was what led to Nathan meeting

Aubrey Stratford. But he blamed Aubrey most of all because it was his design that was flawed. He said Aubrey should have specified in his design plans what materials should be used — or avoided."

Perhaps, Neal considered. But Aubrey had made assumptions that other people involved in the project would do their job, act professionally, carry out the appropriate checks. Not cut corners to save money. He wasn't the sole person at fault.

"Did Aidan ever act on his anger towards Aubrey?"

"What do you mean?" Bob spoke up at last.

"He stopped being friends with Monty Stratford," Martha said. "They'd been such good friends. They'd even talked about going into brewing together." She made a disapproving face.

"Did you know that Aidan assaulted Aubrey?"

"No!" Martha and Bob said in unison.

"Where can we find Aidan?" Neal asked. The Crows looked alarmed. Neal had explained the reason for their visit when he'd phoned to arrange the interview. The Crows were aware of the murders that had taken place on the Stratfords' land. They had to be wondering why the death of their son on a project Aubrey Stratford was involved with was of interest.

"You can't think Aidan had anything to do with those murders? That's monstrous!" Martha exclaimed.

Neal tried to reassure her. "We'd just like to ask him some questions." They could easily find out where Aidan was without the Crows' input, but an address now would save a bit of time.

"He lives in Norwich," Martha said. Ava wrote down both his home and work address and mobile number.

"Thank you both for your time. And, once again, please accept my condolences for your loss," Neal said.

As soon as they were out of earshot, Ava gave vent to her feelings. "Can you believe a father would say such a thing? He as good as said 'better dead than gay.' It's outrageous. And his wife was in total agreement, wasn't she?"

Neal thought of Archie. "No, I can't believe it."

Ava ranted on for a few moments more, then just shook her head. "Are we going to Norwich?" She put the clutch into first.

"Yes. Might as well speak with Aidan Crow while we're in the county."

Ava tapped the postcode of Aidan's workplace into the satnav.

This time, they didn't call ahead to announce their arrival. It would be useful to see how Aidan reacted to their visit. He was currently employed as a research assistant for a pharmaceutical company. It was based in a business park on the outskirts of the city.

"Bit of a far cry from brewing beer, isn't it?" Ava remarked as they pulled into the car park. "His mum said that he and Aidan had considered going into the brewing business together, didn't she?"

"There's a space coming up over there." Neal pointed to a Vauxhall Corsa reversing out of a parking space.

"Already on it," Ava grinned. "Don't even think about it," she mouthed to a driver approaching from the opposite direction.

Neal gazed out of the side window, embarrassed.

The receptionist asked them to wait while he contacted Aidan Crow. He was obviously curious about the purpose of their visit but was too professional to pry. After five minutes or so, a medium-built young man in a white lab coat walked towards them. He shot them a quizzical look.

Neal introduced himself and Ava. He asked if there was somewhere they could talk in private. After a bit more frowning and rubbing his chin, Aidan Crow led them down some stairs and along a corridor to his office. "I share this room with a colleague, but she's probably at lunch," he explained. "You've come all the way from Stromfordshire? I can't begin to guess what on earth you want to talk to me about."

That was unlikely. His mother or father had probably phoned to alert him to their visit.

His eyes widened as Neal explained that they were investigating the murders of Nick Winter, Samantha Benrose and Monty Stratford.

"I saw the story about that couple on the news," Aidan said. "But I didn't put two and two together. Or maybe I just didn't hear the name of the family involved. I . . . I didn't know about Monty. But what has all that got to do with me? I haven't seen any of the Stratford family recently."

He'd seen Blue Stratford more recently than any of the others. Nine months ago to be exact. Admittedly, he hadn't known who she was at first. But Neal doubted he'd forgotten.

"You had a relationship with Monty Stratford's sister."

"Is that what she told you?" Aidan's lip curled. "She deceived me. She knew I wanted nothing to do with Monty or any member of his family after what happened to Nate. She looked me up to try to persuade me to speak with Monty because he was oh so upset about losing my friendship, but she failed to mention that until we'd slept together a couple of times. As soon as I found out who she was, I broke up with her. She even gave me a false name. Monty told me his sister's name was Scarlett, not Blue, otherwise I might have guessed." He paused, "I take it you already know about Nate?"

"Yes, and I'm sorry for your loss," Neal said.

Aidan laced his fingers and placed his hands on his head. He leaned back in his chair, sighed deeply. Then he leaned forward again, looked Neal in the eye, and said, in a steady voice, "Aubrey Stratford is a murderer."

He'd had plenty of time to reflect on the accident. It was unlikely he'd ever shift from his point of view. But Neal wasn't there to persuade him to change his mind. Should he tell Aidan that he was now a father? He sensed the knowledge would bring him no joy. He was glad it wasn't his decision to make. He got straight to the point.

"Mr Crow, I'm afraid I need to ask you what you were doing on Saturday 14 February 2015."

"Are you serious?" He looked from Neal to Ava, as though she might reveal that Neal was having him on. "Unbelievable," he said, drawing out every syllable.

"Given that you went to the Stratfords' home and assaulted Aubrey Stratford, we need to ask the question," Neal said. "If only to eliminate you from our enquiries."

"Why? Nobody's killed Aubrey Stratford, have they? I can just about get my head around you thinking I might do away with him, but why the hell would I kill an innocent couple? Or . . . or Monty?"

He was convincing this time, but it could be an act. "Please answer the question, Mr Crow."

"I was at home the weekend the couple were murdered. I had the flu."

"Was anyone with you?"

"No. I told my girlfriend to stay away. I didn't want to infect her. I had to take a few days off work. You can check with HR."

"We will. And the other date? The date of Monty's murder?"

"I was here, at work. Again, check with HR."

"Would you be willing to give a sample of DNA, Mr Crow?"

Aidan looked like he'd explode. "Absolutely no way! I've done nothing wrong. Arrest me if you want to treat me like a criminal."

Neal nodded. Aidan knew his rights.

At that moment they were interrupted by a young woman who glanced at Ava and Neal then at Aidan.

"Sorry, am I interrupting?"

"We were just about to leave," Neal said with a smile. "Thank you for your time, Mr Crow. We'll be in touch, if it proves necessary."

The young woman held the door for them. Neal thought she looked nervous. He didn't doubt that the receptionist they'd encountered earlier had spread the news that Aidan Crow was being interviewed by the police.

"What did you think?" Neal asked, as they walked across the carpark.

"I think I can relate better to Aidan's anger than the rest of the family's forgiveness. It seems more human somehow." Ava sighed. "I'll contact the girlfriend, but he's probably calling her now, asking her to verify his story. He did sort of have a point when he said that he couldn't see why we'd question him about two complete strangers when Aubrey Stratford is the person he holds accountable for his brother's death."

"What do we know about the other man who was injured when that bridge collapsed?" Neal said.

"PJ checked him out. He escaped with very minor injuries. Made a claim on the grounds that he'd been traumatized by his ordeal and accepted an offer of compensation from Scarlett & Son Engineering. He's been travelling the world on his windfall. He's currently in Thailand. We can definitely eliminate him."

"The company must have taken a hit to their reputation over the affair."

"Not enough to put them out of business. The accident wasn't widely reported — probably because there was only one fatality."

They had reached the car. Neal glanced at his watch. "Are you hungry?"

"Famished."

"Let's look out for a place to grab some lunch. A country pub would be nice. Must be plenty of those in Norfolk."

They drove several miles before stopping in a quiet country village. The local pub was surprisingly busy. Heads turned in their direction as they approached the bar. Maybe they didn't get too many non-locals here. They both ordered a ploughman's, which arrived promptly, on rectangular wooden platters.

Ava unfolded her napkin. "How are the newly-weds enjoying their honeymoon?"

"They're having a wonderful time by all accounts. Packing in plenty of adventures. Bushwalking, skydiving, snorkelling on the Great Barrier Reef." Exactly the sort of activities that would appeal to Ava, Neal thought. He'd be happier visiting galleries or reading a book — or walking in the mountains, of course. He wondered briefly what it would be like walking in the mountains with Ava. He wasn't likely to find out any time soon.

"Wow, sounds amazing. It's so great that they got together at last."

Neal bit down on his hunk of sourdough bread. "Yes, though it's going to take a bit of getting used to having my best friend as my brother-in-law." He often wondered how much Maggie had told Ava about his past. When his sister had become friends with Ava, he'd feared that the privacy of his personal life would be endangered, but that hadn't proven to be the case. Maybe Ava was just very good at keeping Maggie's confidences.

"Maggie told me that you went to stay with Jock's family after you lost your parents and that she went to stay with your aunt. So, you and Jock were sort of brothers already in a way."

It was true. He and Maggie had lost their parents when they were teenagers. The arrangements for their care had been a bit unconventional, but as Jock's parents lived near his and Maggie's aunt, he had never felt that he and his sister were ever far from each other. Maggie had been in and out of Jock's house all the time.

He was aware that Ava also knew about Archie's mother, Myrna, who had gone off to pursue her singing career immediately after giving birth. It had been an arrangement that suited them both. Only a couple of months before, Myrna had got in touch with him for the first time in years. He'd feared she planned to be a part of her son's life again, perhaps take Archie away from him. But she was engaged to be married, and planning to move to the US. She'd only wanted to confirm that she had no lingering feelings for Neal.

Neal knew scraps of information about Ava's past. He knew that she'd dropped out of university. A friend of hers had been abused and subsequently taken her own life. Ava had been deeply affected by the tragedy. It had caused her to rethink her own future. It had also influenced her decision to become a police officer.

He also knew that her parents were divorced and that her father was currently living abroad somewhere. Was he in the US? Ava's brother, Ollie, had come to live with her just over a year ago. Neal had gleaned that neither Ava nor Ollie got on particularly well with their mother, which was why Ollie was now living with Ava. That both he and Ava were close to their siblings was one thing that they had in common.

"Yes. I suppose we were like brothers," he said, replying to Ava's observation.

"I wish I could have made the wedding. I watched the live stream, of course. Maggie looked radiant, and you and Jock looked really cool in your kilts." Ava grinned. "Archie too."

Neal grimaced at the thought that the whole ceremony had been live. He'd been unable to object, particularly as Maggie had told him that one of her best friends couldn't make it up to Edinburgh and was consoled by the thought of still being able to see the ceremony in real time. "Yes. To tell the truth I was glad to get the ceremony out of the way. I can confirm that the role of best man is far more stressful than that of detective inspector."

"You did look a bit nervous, I have to say."

Neal steered the conversation away from himself. "Is your brother recuperating well?"

"He's doing great. His biggest worry was about losing school time, with A levels only a few months away."

"He did well in the AS levels, didn't he?"

"Very well. I'm not concerned. School's been good about keeping him up to date on the work."

"I hear he's applied for Cambridge."

"Yes," Ava said, hesitantly. "He should hear by the end of the month whether he's got a conditional offer of a place."

"That's excellent."

"Yep. It would be fantastic for him to study there. He works so hard he deserves it." She spread some butter over her hunk of bread. "We'll both be glad when our mother goes home. It was good of her to come and help out, but . . . well, even on this visit, she's more interested in herself than in Ollie and me. All she talks to Ollie about is his Cambridge application and how proud she'll be if he gets in. I honestly think she just wants to crow about it to her friends."

Sometimes when people confided in him it made Neal feel awkward. While he was wondering how best to respond, Ava saved him the trouble.

"It's weird, this case. It's full of parents who either don't get their kids, or outright reject them. Look at the Benroses — they'd almost rather see their daughter in an abusive relationship with a wealthy man than in a loving relationship with someone who's been homeless. And the Winters — loving parents to three kids but rejecting the fourth. As for the Crows, the less said about them the better. Hope if I ever have kids, I make a better job of it."

Neal wanted to ask if Ava wanted children. He couldn't, of course. Instead, he said, "It's not always easy being a parent."

"You're doing a great job with Archie. How are you coping while Maggie's away?"

"I have an excellent childminder."

"Be great if Maggie and Jock decide to stay in Stromford."

"Yes." Neal took a swig of his Diet Coke. He was aware of a feeling of tension in the muscles at the back of his neck. Ava was tucking into her bread and cheese, apparently relaxed. He wished that he could feel more at ease in her company.

"Perhaps you could come around for dinner one evening when she and Jock get back," he said. Where had that come from? Neal could feel his palms begin to sweat. There was a long pause while Ava chewed her food. He wished he could take back his words. Instead, he added, "Maggie would like that."

"Sure, that would be great." Ava flashed him a smile.

"Good. I'll speak with her."

His phone buzzed and he was grateful for the distraction. It was an unknown number. "Hello?"

"Detective Inspector Neal?" A woman's voice. There was the merest hint of a Scandinavian accent that sounded vaguely familiar.

"Speaking."

"My name is Pernille Jespersen. I saw you and your colleague at the lab this morning." She had to be the woman who'd entered the room as they were leaving. She'd looked a bit worried. How had she got hold of his number?

"Aidan lied to you," she said in a hushed voice. "I am his girlfriend. He was not sick on the weekend of the murders at Northfields Farm. He was away that weekend. Visiting his grandfather, he told me." There was a pause. "I was listening at the door when you spoke with him."

No wonder she'd appeared anxious. He thanked Pernille for the information and asked if she would meet him and Ava in Norwich. Pernille named a pub and gave him directions.

"Come on," he said, urgency creeping into his voice. "We're going back to Norwich."

CHAPTER TWENTY-FOUR

Soren knew that he couldn't return to Northfields a second time. It was far too risky. The police must have found his dog tags, worked out why he was living under a false name. They would be looking out for him now, perhaps more rigorously than before. He also knew that their resolve to find him would be restrained by lack of resources. There was, after all, something positive to be said for ever-dwindling police budgets — from the point of view of the hounded, at any rate.

It had been a close shave. If he hadn't happened to look up at just that precise moment when DI Neal looked in the farmhouse window . . . Sometimes he wondered if rumours about his superpowers really were exaggerated. Perhaps it was simply that his intuition, as well as his senses, had been sharpened by his training and his time living as an outlier — or maybe he'd just been lucky.

He had been expecting someone to be waiting for him at the front of the farmhouse. The surprise was that there was only one copper and not a carload of them. Surely they'd realised by now that he was a resourceful individual and not one likely to be easily taken. Once, his unit of five had held off three times their number until help arrived. He was more than capable of seeing off a couple of policemen.

After leaving Northfields behind, he'd made for the road and hitched a ride to Stromford. There, he'd bought a razor and a pair of scissors from an all-night shop. In no time at all his appearance had been substantially altered. Gone were the dreadlocks and the beard he'd been growing for years. He peered at his newly shaven face in the mirror of the gent's toilet and was surprised to see how much younger he looked. Since moving to Northfields, his hollowed cheeks had filled out and his skin looked less sallow. The haunted look in his eyes remained; as long as his memory of the horrors he'd witnessed stayed intact, it would never truly disappear.

He considered his options. Taking a bus or train would be far too risky. Hitching wasn't a great idea either, but it was less dicey than public transport. In the end, he acted on a stroke of good luck when he saw an open-topped truck parked at the roadside, its driver shamelessly relieving himself in some hedges. Soren slipped unnoticed under the sheeting covering a load of builder's rubble. Not luxury transport, but it would do.

It was too cold and too uncomfortable to sleep. He reflected on the conversation he had had with the Stratfords before they were interrupted by the police, when they'd shared their secrets. Bea had revealed the real reason why they had moved from Brighton to Stromfordshire.

Since then, the assault on Monty in London had been playing on his mind. Soren had never believed that it had been a mugging. He'd witnessed and intervened in enough muggings to know that an attempt had been made on Monty's life.

He'd intended to warn Monty that he might be in danger, but then Monty had offered him the job at Northfields. Soren had seized the opportunity as a means of both temporarily alleviating his own predicament and of keeping an eye on Monty — just in case. After hearing the story about the bridge collapse and the tragic death of Nate Crow, his brain had started to tick over possibilities.

Bea had assured him that the fanatically religious Crow family had borne Aubrey no ill will over the tragedy. It was only when pushed that she had revealed that not every member of the family had been equally forgiving. Nate's brother, Aidan, who had once been Monty's best friend, had severed all links with Monty following the death of his brother.

In many ways it was a natural reaction after losing a loved one. It was human both to apportion blame and to seek retribution. The justice system was supposed to balance the scales, stop people taking the law into their own hands. In a case like this, where more than one person was at fault, accountability was complex, even elusive. Had Aidan's grief over his brother twisted a desire for justice into a quest for bloody vengeance?

If Aidan Crow had become obsessed with avenging the death of his brother, he might have reached the conclusion that the best way to punish Aubrey would be to take away someone he loved. Only then could Aubrey be made to feel the anguish Aidan had felt in losing his brother.

Soren had no idea if his theory had any basis in reality. It might just be that Aidan had shunned Monty because he reminded him of the tragedy.

He wondered how long it would take the police to uncover the story of the bridge collapse. They needed to check out the Crow family, particularly Aidan. He'd been telling the Stratford family this just before he'd seen DI Neal's face at their kitchen window. He had no way of knowing if they'd taken his advice. He sighed. For once, he was going to have to suppress this need of his to save people and trust that the police knew what they were doing.

Two hours later the truck slowed. A couple more minutes and it juddered to a halt. He guessed they were at a motorway service station. He waited until he heard the driver's door slam and his footsteps recede before raising the sheeting slightly and checking for security cameras and watchful eyes. Satisfied that there was no immediate threat of being detected, he emerged from the trailer, feeling stiff and sore from the ride. His bones had felt every bump and rattle. He pulled his hoodie around his face and walked towards the service station.

It was still dark and bitterly cold. A white frost crunched under his feet as he made his way towards the entrance. He bought a bacon sandwich and a coffee from one of the outlets in the food court. He decided to sit at a table to eat. Even if he was captured on camera, he would be long gone before the police checked any footage.

No one gave him a second glance. People were more interested in interacting with their mobile phones than with the real people around them. It had been freezing in the back of the truck. The wind had snaked in under the loose tarpaulin, chilling him to the marrow. He was still shivering, even in the overheated concourse.

A single bacon butty didn't even take the edge off his hunger, so he ordered another, along with a side of fries. As he ate, he caught sight of his driver tucking into a giant burger a few tables away. He was staring at his phone, which was propped against the condiments rack. Whatever he was watching was making him chuckle. After a while the driver got up and walked off in the direction of the exit. Soren regretted that he couldn't thank him for the ride.

He was reluctant to go back out into the cold and dark. He looked around the busy food court to see if anyone had left a coat on a chair that he could steal, but most people were either still wearing theirs or had it draped safely over the back of their chair — not much chance of picking one up unnoticed. The last thing he wanted to do was draw attention to himself by being pulled up for theft by some bored security guard. He would just have to put up with the freezing temperature. He'd endured much worse.

Outside in the car park, he asked a driver standing smoking by his lorry for a lift. The driver nodded. They struck up a conversation while he smoked his cigarette down to the stub. His name was Pete. He was transporting a lorryload of chickens. Soren decided he would ask Pete to drop him off after an hour or so. He could easily pick up another lift at the nearest junction. No need to reveal his final destination to Pete.

After a while, their conversation dried up. Soren dozed as the lorry sped southwards through the freezing night. Pete turned on the radio. On the hour, the news came on. He turned up the volume.

And that was how Soren heard the news that Monty Stratford had been murdered.

"Drop me as soon as you can find a place to stop," he said to the driver, using a tone of voice he hadn't used in years.

The driver looked at him out of the corner of his eye. "Aye, aye, Captain," he mocked.

Soren hardly noticed. The driver would do as he asked, just as people always had when he used that tone of voice.

As soon as he got out of the lorry, he would cross the motorway somehow. He needed to hitch a lift in the opposite direction. He was going back to Northfields.

CHAPTER TWENTY-FIVE

Ava had barely had time to ask Neal about his phone call before they left the pub and were back on the road to Norwich. She, too, had noted that the young woman who had entered the office seemed nervous. "I didn't clock her as his girlfriend. They didn't give out any signals that they were anything more than colleagues."

"Perhaps they aren't broadcasting their relationship in the workplace," Neal suggested.

"That's possible, I suppose. There are a lot of reasons why people wouldn't want their colleagues to know they're an item."

"Yes," Neal agreed.

Pernille was waiting for them when they arrived at the pub she'd directed them to in the Lanes. She was drinking some sort of fruit cocktail and an unopened packet of cheese and onion crisps lay on the table in front of her. She looked up at their approach and slid over on the banquette, as if expecting one of them to sit beside her. They sat opposite.

"How did you get my number?" Neal asked.

"You gave Aidan a card. You asked him to get in touch if he had any information for you. He threw the card in the wastepaper bin after you left. I took it out."

"How long have you known Aidan?" Ava asked.

"About a year. We've only been seeing each other for about four months."

"You live together?"

"No. Sometimes I stay over at Aidan's place. He rents an apartment in the Pottergate area of town. I have housemates, so he doesn't tend to stay at my place. I have been staying over at weekends since Christmas, but on the weekend of the murders, he told me he was going to visit his grandfather. I have the key to his flat. I went around to get something I left there. Aidan was not there. His bed had not been slept in. I had no reason to think anything was different to what he told me until I heard you speaking with him." Pernille fingered her crisp packet, made as if to open it, then just covered it with the palm of her hand, crumpling it slightly. "Do you think he might have killed that poor young couple?"

Ava had no answer to that. "Aidan lost his younger brother. Has he spoken of it ever?"

"Nate? Yes, he speaks of Nate often. He was very affected by his death."

"Has he ever seemed angry or resentful about the way his brother died?"

Pernille looked surprised. "Of course. Why wouldn't he be angry? His brother was murdered."

"Is that the word he uses?" Ava asked.

"Yes. He's angry because no one has ever been brought to justice for Nate's murder." She looked at Ava. "What is it? Did Aidan lie to me about this?"

"Aidan's brother died in a tragic accident. A bridge collapse."

"Oh. This he did not tell me." Pernille sipped her mocktail.

"What about the other date we asked Aidan about? The date of Monty Stratford's murder?"

"He was at work that day. We both were. I stayed overnight with him."

Ava looked at Neal. It didn't make sense. Aidan had no apparent motive for killing Nick and Samantha, yet if

Pernille was to be believed, he had lied about his alibi for that weekend and not for the night Monty was murdered.

"I think I will not see Aidan again," Pernille said flatly. "I do not wish to be in a relationship with a man who is perhaps guilty of murder." She looked to Ava, as if seeking approval for her decision. Unsure of how to answer, Ava gave a slight nod.

They left Pernille tearing open her crisp packet, a gloomy look on her face.

As they walked back to the car, she said to Neal, "Are we going to talk with Aidan again?"

"Yes." Neal sounded weary. Ava knew he hated wasting time. Problem was, hardly anyone ever told the truth. And lies were time thieves.

* * *

Aidan was at home when they turned up at his apartment, which was on the second floor of a Georgian conversion. He seemed startled to see them again, particularly at his home. "Don't mind if we come in, do you?" Ava said, giving him no opportunity to refuse entry before pushing past him into the entrance hall.

Neal signalled for Aidan to follow Ava then brought up the rear, giving Aidan no chance to bolt.

"I'll come straight to the point," Ava said. "You lied about where you were on the fourteenth of February this year. Aidan Crow, I am arresting you on suspicion of—"

"Excuse me? I didn't lie."

"Your girlfriend told us differently."

"She's lying."

"If that can be ascertained, you've got nothing to worry about. In the meantime . . ."

Ava began cautioning him again. This time, he didn't interrupt.

* * *

Bea Stratford was feeling unlike herself. It was as though she had drifted a beat away from the real world and was hovering in a state of disassociation on some unfamiliar plane.

She had seen what no mother should ever see. Her great-great-grandmother had lost her youngest son in the First World War, but she had been spared the horror of watching him bleed out on that muddy tract of land between the trenches known as no man's land. He'd met a wall of machine gun fire shortly after going over the top at the Battle of the Somme. Great-Great-Grandma Lacey could only have imagined how her boy might have suffered. Bea had witnessed it at close hand. It was an image that she would never get out of her head. The lifeblood of her only son spread out in a wide pool on the floor where he lay, like beer spilt from a cask of one of his prize-winning ales.

She was trying her best to function, for the sake of her remaining family. It was amazing how they didn't seem to notice the mental turmoil that she was suffering behind her coping façade. The routines of everyday life helped. She prepared meals, helped care for Esmé. The baby had been fractious for the past few days. It was as though, even at only a week old, she knew how many years of love had been stolen from her with the death of her uncle Monty.

Aubrey had found his own way of coping. He retreated to his shed to fix things: the broken radio she'd asked him to look at weeks before; the toaster that only toasted one side of the bread; a whole boxful of electrical appliances that no longer needed repairing because Bea had long since bought replacements. He couldn't fix the things that really mattered, of course: their broken hearts; his son's torn body.

Charles Unwin was trying to be supportive, but ineptly. Yesterday afternoon, he'd sat in the kitchen, drinking tea and eating leftover Christmas cake. Bea kept hinting that he should go out to the shed, keep Aubrey company for a bit. But he had lingered in the kitchen, saying things like, "I don't know how you can bear your loss," and, "It would be bad enough coming to terms with a normal death, but a murder . . ."

His lack of tact irritated Bea. She appreciated that he was trying to be sympathetic in his own clumsy way, but being constantly reminded of the family's misfortune wasn't particularly helpful. If it had been anyone else but Charles, she'd almost have thought he was indulging in schadenfreude.

The previous morning, he had turned up first thing and joined them for breakfast. She'd made the full English because none of them had eaten much for the past couple of days. While she, Aubrey and Blue picked at their food, Charles had wolfed his down and asked for an extra sausage, if it was going to waste. "I suppose none of you feel much like eating," he said. "It'll be a long time before you feel much like doing anything, I suppose. That's what grief does to you. It sucks out your life force." He spoke from experience, Bea knew. He was a widower.

"Can't you tell him to stop coming around, Mum?" Blue said after Charles had gone out to the shed with Aubrey. "I don't need reminding every five minutes how awful it is to lose my brother."

"Don't be too harsh on him. He means well. I'm afraid Charles is like your dad — a bit compromised when it comes to dealing with other people and their feelings. All this is probably reminding him of his own grief. His wife died not that long before he moved here. That's why he moved. Just like us, to make a fresh start. And he's been such a good friend to your dad since we arrived here."

"I'm going out to the brewery. There's a lot to do. Can you look after Esmé? She's had her feed. She should sleep for a couple of hours."

Bea wasn't convinced of that. Esmé was still grizzly, but she did look drowsy. Or maybe that was wishful thinking. She didn't feel up to dealing with a crying baby all morning. Still, she was glad that Blue was throwing herself into the brewery, keeping busy. It was the only way to get through this.

"I'm going to name a beer after him," Blue said. "The Full Monty or Monty's Magnificent Malt. He'd like that, I think . . . to be immortalised as a brew."

Bea smiled for her daughter's sake. The idea made her feel slightly nauseous, conjuring up the image of Monty on the floor of the brewery all over again.

Blue was right. Esmé was asleep in Bea's arms within minutes. She laid the baby down in her pram and wheeled it into the kitchen so that she could keep an eye on her. She tucked her satin quilt around her and gazed tenderly at the face of the sleeping child. Bea felt a stab of despair. Monty had once been tiny and helpless like this. She'd tucked this same quilt around him. To keep him warm. To keep him safe. What had been the point?

Her thoughts then turned to the bridge collapse and the tragic death of Nate Crow. Her heart stirred for the young man's parents in a way it had not done in the aftermath of the tragedy, when all her sympathy had been for Aubrey and what he was going through.

The emotions arising from her thoughts were too overwhelming to bear. She felt that strange feeling of detachment washing over her again.

CHAPTER TWENTY-SIX

"Do you know what this is, Mr Crow?" Neal placed a clear plastic evidence bag on the table before Aidan Crow.

Aidan shrugged. "Yes. It's called a tut — or a peg. It seals the hole in a shive, which is used to seal the bung hole in a cask of beer."

"You once considered going into a brewing partnership with Monty Stratford, didn't you, Mr Crow? Is home-brewing still a hobby of yours?"

"I don't have much time for hobbies these days."

"Answer the question, please."

"Yes, I still brew at home, as a hobby." He glanced at the blue peg.

"We've matched your prints to the ones found on the tut in that bag," Neal said. "Would you care to know where we found it?" Aidan showed no sign of answering, so Neal enlightened him. "Our CSIs removed it from the folds of Nick Winter's clothing. Only thing we're slightly puzzled about is how it got there." Neal leaned forward in his seat, not quite in Aidan's space, because of the table between them, but close enough. "Any chance you can help us with that?"

"No comment," Aidan said, but he glanced nervously at his legal representative.

"You haven't been in touch with Monty Stratford since the time of your brother, Nate's, death, have you, Aidan? Okay if I call you Aidan?"

No reply. Silence gave assent, so Neal proceeded. "Aidan, you claim that you've never been to Northfields. That's why we're puzzled about that tut. Monty Stratford's sister has confirmed that it's not the same colour as the ones they use at the Northfields brewery. They use red. This one is blue. So, you can appreciate our confusion."

"Is that all you've got? Monty could have kept some from before, from when we used to brew together. And everyone knows fingerprint evidence is notoriously unreliable. I'm surprised you're even bringing this up."

Neal ignored the comment. "Do you still use blue tuts, Aidan?"

"Yes. What of it? Loads of people do."

"But this particular one has your prints on it, remember?"

Aidan's face flushed with sudden anger. "Look, what possible motive could I have for killing this Nick Winter? I've never even met him. Or his girlfriend, for that matter."

"Were you in London last July?" The sudden change of tack threw him, as Neal hoped it would.

"I'm . . . not sure. I think I was there at some point last summer. I'd have to check the date." He gave another nervous glance at his legal representative.

"Please do. We'll check too. It won't be too difficult. Like most people, I'm sure you use a credit card. If not, there are plenty of other ways we can find out." He wanted Aidan to know that they had the power to scrutinise his private life and finances in detail. No harm in making him feel vulnerable.

"I'm asking because Monty Stratford was assaulted in the Bloomsbury area of London in July last year. His attacker wounded him with a knife. Forensics think that the weapon used was likely to have been of the same type used to kill Nick Winter and Samantha Benrose."

Neal was aware that unless they tracked down the actual murder weapon, this was not a concrete piece of evidence.

He didn't mention that the indications were that a different sort of knife had been used on Monty Stratford.

"No comment," Aidan said. He was becoming agitated, struggling to keep a lid on his anger.

"You told us before that you hold Monty Stratford's father, Aubrey Stratford, responsible for your brother's death. That you believe him to be — quote — *a murderer*."

"I don't deny saying that. It's true. A fact."

Neal stared down at the recording machine. It didn't add up. Aidan had something of a motive for killing Monty, but he had no apparent reason for killing Nick and Samantha. Swallow was a far more credible candidate for their deaths.

The duty solicitor interrupted to ask if they were intending to charge Aidan Crow. Neal feared that they had insufficient evidence to proceed. What they did have was circumstantial. Still, he was reluctant to let Aidan walk before they had a chance to gather more evidence. He had to make a decision. He informed Aidan that he would be held in custody.

Aidan growled, "It's Monty you think I killed, really, isn't it? But you don't have a scrap of evidence, so you're trying to pin this Nick Winter's murder on me instead." Between clenched teeth, he added, "Just to be clear . . . I didn't kill Monty Stratford. You'll never be able to prove that I did that. God knows I'm innocent."

Well, fortunately they didn't have to persuade any supernatural agent of his guilt, Neal thought, just the CPS and a jury of twelve mortals.

After the interview, he sought Ava's opinion.

She shook her head. "Swallow has confessed to being at Northfields that day. The reason he gave for being there was lame." She mimicked Swallow's plummy accent. "*I wanted to talk to Sam.* He could easily have found a way to speak with her in Nottingham without her being surrounded by friends and family. He even admitted that he took the charm from her bracelet then lost it. He has motive. He was abusive towards Samantha when they were in a relationship and we know that he resented her for choosing Nick over him. Everything points to him . . . and yet it's Aidan's prints that are all over that tut."

"And Monty's killer?"

"Aidan's the one with the motive, but he has an alibi."

"Let's consider that it was Aidan Crow who attacked Monty in London," Neal said. "Say his failure on that occasion stoked his anger and brought him to Northfields on the day of the forties dance — which also happened to be Hunter's day off. With Hunter out of the way, he clearly had a better chance of success this time around."

"Did he know about the dance, do you think? It would provide him with cover, wouldn't it? The fact that there would be so many people around. And in costume. Even better — he could disguise himself and blend in. All of which would suggest that he would've needed to plan in advance." Ava looked thoughtful, then seemed suddenly to grasp where he was headed.

Neal nodded. "His plan went wrong. That was why he ended up killing Nick and Samantha instead. He has no alibi for that day. He came to Northfields with the intention of killing Monty and something went wrong."

There was an obvious assumption to be made here and Ava made it. "One, or both of them discovered what he was up to?" She looked at Neal. "They got in his way?"

It was plausible. "The question is . . . would someone on a mission of vengeance for the death of his brother be prepared to kill two innocent people who had nothing to do with his death?"

"Collateral damage," Ava said. "Remember Tom said that it was likely Soren Hunter deserted because he couldn't stomach the civilian deaths resulting from what he was doing in Afghanistan? Maybe Aidan's conscience bothered him less. He would have been fired up. His adrenalin would have been racing. He needed an outlet. He killed Nick and Samantha because he was thwarted in his attempt to kill Monty. All the more so because it was his second attempt. That would have pushed up his level of frustration a few bars."

But collateral damage was meant to be accidental, wasn't it? Or was that consequential — foreseen but unavoidable consequences for the 'greater good'? There was nothing accidental about the way that Nick and Samantha had been butchered and, as far as Neal could see, no one had benefitted.

"Maybe he even convinced himself afterwards that he was justified in killing Nick and Samantha because their deaths would have a terrible impact on the Stratford family," Ava said.

"Hmm . . . We need to consider how it could have played out in practice. If Meredith Price was correct in saying that she saw a man dressed as a spiv walking over from the direction of the yurts, then we can speculate that Nick was killed around 6:15. Monty Stratford would have been in the barn at that time. He left the brewery at four and went across to help with the last-minute preparations." Neal rubbed his chin. "Is it possible that Aidan mistook Nick for Monty? That he then had to kill Samantha to stop her coming to look for Nick when he failed to return to the yurt?"

"That's unlikely. He knew what Monty looked like."

"It was dark. Nick and Monty were of similar height and build. What if they were wearing similar costumes? Aidan could have mistaken Nick for Monty."

Ava shook her head. "I saw Monty at the dance. He was dressed as an American GI. Anyway, how would Aidan have known what Monty was going to be wearing? And how would he even know about Samantha?" She frowned. "*Unless* someone had told him what Monty was going to be wearing and that Nick and Samantha were staying at Northfields. Hate to say it, but Blue Stratford would be the obvious choice of informant. She could have lied about not being in contact with her baby's father." Then Ava shook her head. "I just don't see it, though. She adored Monty, and it's pretty obvious she's in love with Soren Hunter, not Aidan Crow."

Neal suspected that Ava was still more convinced of the argument for Swallow being Nick and Samantha's killer. He worried that he was too keen for Aidan to be guilty of all three murders, that he was stretching credibility to fit his theory. "What about Hunter?" he said.

"Doesn't make sense. He came to Monty's rescue when he was attacked in London."

"Because he didn't want to be denied the opportunity of killing Monty himself?" Neal thought he'd just put the idea out there.

Ava pursed her lips. She was unconvinced, Neal could tell. He knew she hoped Hunter was innocent of any blame for the murders at Northfields. Being honest, he'd come around to hoping the same thing.

* * *

It took Soren three hours and four lifts to get back to Stromfordshire, then a further hour to get to Northfields. He had spent the time thinking about the murders, particularly the latest: poor, sweet-natured Monty. He wondered how Blue, Bea and Aubrey were faring. They had to be devastated.

The night the police had come for him, Soren and the Stratfords had shared their secrets. Soren had revealed that, six years before, he had deserted from the British Army. To his surprise, no one had asked him to explain his reasons for doing so. Monty had actually patted him on the back and said, "Well done."

He'd been concerned about what Blue might think of him, but she'd merely shrugged and said that no one should ever sign up for a job that they couldn't just walk away from after giving a month's notice. Aubrey agreed wholeheartedly. Bea, wonderful woman that she was, had given him a hug, declaring, "I thought you were going to say you'd done something really awful." Which was ironic, because out in Afghanistan, Soren really had done some awful things, including killing two men with his bare hands. At the time he'd believed that what he was doing was defensible. He'd come a long way since then.

And then, Bea had told him about the family secret: the bridge collapse and the death of Nate Crow. Aubrey had stared at the table all the time she was speaking. It was obvious that he was also convinced that he had done something truly awful.

Soren had long wondered at Aubrey's unworldly personality, his reluctance to engage fully with the people around him. Only a few days after he'd arrived at Northfields, Bea had taken him aside and said, "Don't mind Aubrey. He's always been a bit odd, but now that he's retired, he's become more so. I think he managed to function as a normal human being because he had to go out and earn a living. Now that he doesn't need to do that anymore, he's become a full-blown eccentric."

Soren had suspected that there was more to it than that. He thought he'd detected something in Aubrey that he also identified in himself. They were both men who carried a heavy burden of regret and guilt. In his own case, perhaps even a hint of darkness. The difference between them was that Aubrey had taken refuge in his rather odd personality, whereas Soren had reinvented himself.

His final ride dropped him at the junction leading to Northfields. "You sure this is where you want me to drop you, mate?" the driver asked. "It's the middle of nowhere. There's a village about a mile and a half up the road."

"Yes, thanks. This is exactly where I need to be."

He had been watchful on his approach; the police could still be looking for him. Although surely no one would expect him to make the mistake of returning to Northfields a second time.

He saw Bea through the kitchen window, Esmé close by, asleep in her pram by the side of the table. Bea was staring into space. Soren's heart lurched at the sight of her. There was a glazed look about her eyes that worried him. He didn't want to startle her, so he tapped softly on the window. Bea looked up and saw him. The glazed look disappeared, but Soren suspected it would return. He would need to keep an eye on her.

She stood up immediately and came to the door.

"I'm so, so sorry, Bea." He wrapped her in an embrace.

Bea wept and shuddered in his arms. "You shouldn't have come back. The police probably think you killed Monty." She looked him in the eye. "None of us believes that."

"I know. Thanks, Bea. How are Aubrey and Blue?"

"Blue's devastated. She and Monty were always close. At least she and I have our work and little Esmé to distract us. Aubrey spends nearly all his time in the garage or his shed trying to fix things. He's out there now. Charles is with him. Though I'm not sure he's much help at a time like this." She looked at Soren, her eyes welling up again. "Oh, Soren, why would anyone want to harm Monty? He was such a gentle soul."

"What have the police said?"

"Oh, they don't know, do they?"

Soren thought for a bit then said as gently as he could, "I think that when Monty was attacked in London last year, it might have been an attempt on his life."

Bea covered her mouth with the palm of her right hand. "But you said it was just a mugging. You even managed to convince Monty of that when he thought otherwise."

"I didn't want him to worry."

Bea responded with a flare of anger. "Maybe he should have been worried! Maybe he would have been more on his guard if he'd known!"

Soren accepted the criticism but Bea apologised immediately. "You took the job here to look out for him, didn't you?"

"Yes. I failed. I'm so sorry."

"Don't go talking like that. Monty's safety wasn't your responsibility."

"I wasn't here for him."

"If you'd been here, the police would have arrested you." Bea glanced nervously towards the window. "You need to stay indoors and out of sight."

"I'm going to find out who did this," he said.

Bea looked worried. "That's a job for the police, Soren. Though I have to admit they've not done much of a job so far."

"What you told me the other night, Bea . . . about the accident — the death of Nate Crow. Nate's brother Aidan apart, do you think his family were as forgiving as they made out?"

"Yes. They're devout Christians. I didn't give it a lot of thought at the time, but now I've lost my son I understand the pain they must have felt. I know the circumstances were very different, but I . . . I find their capacity for forgiveness truly astonishing." Her face hardened. "I will never forgive the man who killed Monty. Never. I hope he rots in hell. I hope I can be the one to put him there." Anger and tears flashed in her eyes. She looked away.

He pressed her arm. "It's natural to have feelings like that, Bea. It's the hurt speaking."

"I don't know how to deal with my anger. I've never felt this way before. I keep seeing Monty lying in the brewery, blood everywhere . . ." She gasped. "I feel as though I could kill with no remorse. Does that make me as bad as the man who killed Nick and Samantha, and . . . and Monty?"

"You're grieving," he soothed. "You're not thinking rationally at the moment, Bea. Give yourself time. And no, I don't think you're a monster. But I do think you may be suffering a bit from the trauma of finding Monty like that."

"You said you've come back to find the killer. What will you do to him if you do?"

"I'll turn him over to the police."

Bea nodded. He sensed her disappointment. It saddened him to see her like this. To be honest, he was struggling with his own anger over Monty's death. If he did track down Monty's killer, it wasn't going to be easy to rein it in. He'd focus on Blue, he decided, the love he felt for her and the future they might have together. The love he might also come to feel for her child, asleep just a few feet away from him.

"Regarding Aidan Crow . . ." Bea said. He had almost forgotten that he'd asked her about the Crows. He raised an inquiring eyebrow.

Bea seemed hesitant, as if there was something she was reluctant to tell him. He waited.

"Aidan Crow is Esmé's father."

It shouldn't have mattered to Soren who the father of Blue's baby was, but somehow it did. He would have preferred not to know. He listened without comment as Bea told him about Blue's attempt to repair the friendship between Aidan and her brother. How she'd ended up going to bed with Aidan without revealing to him that she was Monty's sister — the resulting pregnancy.

"She didn't tell Aidan about the baby. I only found out yesterday, when she finally confided in me. Before then, I had no idea who Esmé's father was. Aubrey doesn't know. We agreed that it would be best if he didn't find out, for now."

"Will she tell the Crows? They're Esmé's grandparents."

Bea shook her head. "At the moment, she doesn't want to. I don't know if she'll change her mind. It will be her decision."

Soren's gaze slid to the pram and the slumbering baby blissfully unaware of any controversy over her origins. Would she wish to know her biological father's identity one day? Would the love that he could bestow upon her, given the opportunity, be enough to stop her wanting to find out?

Bea was looking at him with concern. "You look like you haven't washed in days. Why don't you take a shower? I'll fix you some breakfast."

"Thanks." He removed his backpack from his shoulder. "Would you mind sticking this in the washing machine? It reeks of fish. My last ride was in a van loaded with seafood." Bea took the backpack. She tipped the contents out over the table. The lid of the tin containing the scrap of material that Soren had torn from the sleeve of Monty's assailant in London had come off in the bag. The piece of cloth lay on the table. Catching sight of it, he wished, as always, that he could make a psychic connection with its wearer.

It turned out he didn't need to.

"Where did you get that?" Bea looked puzzled. Soren hoped it wouldn't upset her too much to learn.

"I ripped it off the shirt sleeve of the man who attacked Monty in London. I kept it because I wasn't wholly convinced that the attack had been a random one. Why? Do you recognise it?" It seemed unlikely.

"Yes," Bea said. "It looks just like the material I used to make a 1940s-style vintage shirt for Aubrey a few years ago. He only wore it on special occasions. Eventually, it got too tight for him, so he gave it to Monty. Monty didn't like it, so he gave it to . . ." She looked at Soren, her face ashen. "He gave it to Aidan Crow."

Both were quiet for a few moments, then Bea said, "It must be a coincidence. But . . ."

"Bea?"

"The material was very old. It belonged to my mother. She'd had it since the forties. That's why Aubrey liked it. It was authentic. I can't believe there are many other shirts around these days made out of that exact same material, that particular pattern." She stared at the piece of cloth for a few moments, her gaze becoming ever more distant.

He pressed her arm gently. "Did you tell the police about the bridge collapse?"

"Yes."

He picked up the scrap of material. "The police need to know about this. Let them determine whether it's a significant piece of evidence. They can have it tested. There might be traces of DNA on it." He hoped she hadn't noticed the speck of brown that was probably Monty's dried blood.

Bea seemed to recover. Her words came out in a rush. "I'll explain where you got it from. I'll tell them we all forgot about it with everything that came after. No need to let them know you're here."

Soren nodded, "Thanks, Bea."

"Go take your shower. I'll get you something of . . . of Monty's to wear. Then I'll make the call."

"Bea," he said, as she was about to leave the kitchen. "I can't keep running for ever. As soon as the police have established that I didn't kill anyone here, I'm going to give myself up to the Military Police and face the consequences. I want my life back. I want . . ." He looked over to the pram. Words failed him.

Bea crossed to him and stroked the side of his face. "I know," she said. "This is where you belong now, Soren. You've been a part of this family since the moment you saved Monty's life in London."

"He saved me too, Bea," Soren said, quietly.

Bea smiled. She busied about for a few minutes, her eyes returning time and again to the scrap of material. The next time she glanced up, Soren noticed that the glazed look had returned to her eyes. Maybe she had seen the speck of brown on the torn cloth after all. He needed to speak to Aubrey and Blue about her state of mind, and soon.

CHAPTER TWENTY-SEVEN

"She wanted to speak with you, or the DI," PJ informed Ava. "I explained that Inspector Neal was in a meeting and that you weren't available."

"Typical!" Ava exclaimed. "Arrive a bit late 'cos I stopped off at the patisserie to get a treat for everyone and I miss an important call." She plonked a box of pastries down on her desk. "Couldn't she have left a message?"

"I offered to put Tom on in case she thought a DC too lowly a creature to waste her time on, but she insisted it had to be one of you two." PJ leaned across her desk. She helped herself to a toffee pecan Danish.

"Hey, that's my favourite," Tom said.

"Tough." PJ bit down.

"Thought you were meant to be dieting," Tom grumbled.

Ava took advantage of PJ's full mouth to pre-empt further bickering. "Oh, for pity's sake. There's another of those in the box. No need to squabble."

Tom came over and picked out an almond croissant. "Didn't realise you'd got some of these as well," he said.

PJ rolled her eyes. "Do you even know what the word *favourite* means, Tom?"

Ava called Northfields Farm and Bea Stratford answered immediately. Ava listened to what she had to say, aware of PJ and Tom straining to hear. When she finished, Tom got in first.

"So, was it something that will crack the case wide open?" He spoke in a phoney American accent. Who knew why?

"Maybe," Ava said. She gave them the gist of what Bea had just told her. "I'm not completely convinced of her story about how she came to have this piece of material. And if Hunter had it from the night Monty was attacked in London, why on earth didn't he give it to us when we interviewed him? He must have realised it might be significant. I guess he thought that Nick and Samantha's deaths were unrelated to the attack on Monty."

"They were, weren't they?" PJ said. "Toby Swallow's still the lead suspect for their murders, isn't he?"

Ava explained the tentative theories that she and Neal had formulated the day before.

PJ reacted with characteristic excitement. "If we could prove Aidan was wearing the shirt when he attacked Monty in London, that would strengthen the case for him making another attempt to kill him on the night of the dance and finally succeeding on his third attempt— alibi or no alibi. Is it too much to hope that there might be DNA evidence on that torn sleeve?"

Despite also feeling a frisson of excitement, Ava decided to play it down. "Probably shouldn't get our hopes up too much. We don't know anything about this mysterious piece of cloth yet. Might be a waste of time rushing out to Northfields to collect it." PJ's face fell then brightened when Ava said, "Would the lowly DC like to accompany me to collect the evidence?" She turned to Tom. "Can you let the boss know where we've gone?"

* * *

Neal was in his usual growly mood when he returned from his meeting with George Lowe. "Don't ask," he said to Tom when he looked up with a raised brow. "Usual bollocks."

"Have a pastry, sir." Tom proffered the box. "I think there's a cinnamon swirl left over."

"No thanks," Neal said, curtly. He looked around. "Where is everyone?"

Tom filled him in on Bea Stratford's phone call.

"Right," Neal said. "Good excuse to put a bit of pressure on Aidan Crow. Come on."

They had to wait for Aidan's legal representative to arrive. Neal explained that they may have some new evidence. They needed to question their suspect again.

The solicitor was unimpressed when he explained about the scrap of material. "Bit premature to confront him about it, isn't it? You haven't got hold of this piece of cloth yet, never mind submitted it for forensic testing. If there is DNA or blood on the remnant, that could simply be because it once belonged to Monty Stratford. And hasn't it occurred to you that Mr Crow might have passed the shirt on? To a charity shop, for example?"

"Of course. A lot of things occur to me all the time," Neal said, rather defensively.

The solicitor, whose name was Rose Plunkett, gave him a sceptical look.

Aidan Crow seemed subdued when he was led into the interview room. He'd had some time to ponder his predicament. Depending on how you looked at it, he'd also had time to tweak his story.

"Why am I back here?" he asked, as soon as he sat down. Neal ignored him until the preliminaries had been dispensed with, including starting the tape.

"Some evidence has come into our possession that potentially ties you to the assault on Monty Stratford in Bloomsbury last July."

"You don't know if I was in London that day. I don't even know. I told you, I'd have to check." His tone was defiant, but Neal could tell that he was curious about the evidence. He waited for Aidan to fill the ensuing silence. "What evidence?" he blurted after less than twenty seconds.

"You know it's mind-blowing, the advances in forensic science in recent years," Neal said. "From a single scrap of material, a forensics team can extract the most detailed information about its origins. The fibres it's made from will give clues to where and when it was manufactured. They can work out what sort of garment it came from, even match it to the very roll of cloth from which the garment was made. All that before they even look for DNA."

"What are you talking about?" Aidan took off his glasses, rubbed his eyes and blinked a few times as if the lights were too bright.

"Seeing better now?" Neal asked, once Aidan had returned his glasses to his nose. "I hope so. To answer your question, I'm talking about a scrap of material torn from the shirt you were wearing the day you attacked Monty Stratford in London. Unfortunately for you, the person who came to Monty's rescue kept the material, once part of a shirt cuff. The shirt was hand stitched by Monty Stratford's mother as a gift for his father. Monty's father gave it to him. Monty passed it on to you."

There was a brief silence. Aidan sighed. "That thing? I gave it to the Oxfam shop. I only accepted it because I thought Monty might be offended if I didn't." Sweat trickled down his face. He removed his glasses again, this time to give them a wipe.

"Big coincidence, wouldn't you agree? A piece of material torn from a shirt given to you, turning up on a complete stranger in London who just happens to assault its former owner?"

Aidan shrugged. He rubbed his shoulders and rolled his neck.

Neal continued. "You had a very religious upbringing, didn't you, Aidan?"

"What's that got to do with anything?" Aidan uncrossed his arms and fiddled with his glasses again.

"Your brother's death must have been a great challenge to your faith."

"I don't have any faith."

"Yet, when we last spoke, you said, 'God knows I'm innocent.'"

"You must have mistaken my meaning. It was only a turn of phrase — I could just as easily have said, 'Goodness knows I'm innocent.'"

Neal wasn't buying it for a second. "Did you find it baffling that your parents could forgive the people whose negligence led to Nate's death, but couldn't forgive Nate for coming out?"

No answer.

"I know you loved your little brother. I bet you had a very strict upbringing. *Spare the rod and spoil the child* — was that your parents' motto? Did they apply it to Nate when they found out he was gay? Did you become his protector? You fought hard to protect Nate from your parents' intolerance. So much the worse, then, for your little brother's life to end through the carelessness of others. It's perfectly understandable that you'd have a desire for revenge."

He gave Aidan a moment to think this over, before adding, "Did it never occur to you to blame your parents for Nate's death? One of the reasons you pushed Monty to ask his father about taking your brother on for the summer was to get Nate away from them, wasn't it? Because they were inflicting psychological damage on him by telling him that being gay was a sin."

Neal had intended to provoke. He was prepared for an angry outburst. So, he was all the more astonished when Aidan Crow burst into tears.

* * *

231

Bea left Blue in the kitchen with Esmé after telling her that Soren was upstairs taking a shower. The news had brought a smile to Blue's lips for the first time since she'd learned of her brother's murder. "I've left one of Monty's black tee shirts and a pair of his jeans out for him." Everyone wore black tees and jeans. She'd been careful not to choose clothes that would remind them too much of Monty. "I've told him to stay upstairs. The police will be here in under an hour."

"Where are you going?" Blue asked.

"Out to the shed. I thought I'd let your dad know about Soren. I'll ask him to come over. The police will probably want to question him about the shirt."

"I don't understand. Does this mean Aidan Crow killed Monty?" Blue's voice trembled. She glanced at the pram where Esmé was just beginning to stir.

"We don't know that for sure, love. Let's just wait and see what the police think."

As she made her way to the shed, Bea wondered if she should have offered Blue more reassurance. Her daughter was no doubt weighing up Esmé's chances of growing up to be a murderer. Nature versus nurture. A loving environment versus evil genes.

Aubrey and Charles were standing side by side at the workbench, bent over the replica tank. Charles was holding a spanner. When neither of them looked up, Bea said, "Soren's back." That got their attention. "He thinks he has something that will help the police find out who murdered Monty."

Aubrey put down his tools and moved from the other side of the workbench to join her. "What is it?"

Bea explained about the torn-off material, but Aubrey looked blank. He evidently hadn't grasped the significance of what she had just told him. Perhaps he didn't know that Monty had passed the shirt on to Aidan Crow. She explained, and was rewarded by a faint spark of hope in her husband's eyes, the first since their son's shocking murder.

* * *

Neal pushed a box of tissues across the table to Aidan, who didn't even bother to remove his glasses to wipe away his tears. He merely pushed them halfway up his forehead out of the way.

"Is there something you want to tell me, Aidan?" Neal asked quietly.

Aidan blew his nose. The sound jarred with the silence in the room following his emotional outburst. "They were planning on making him see someone in the church. For therapy."

"Conversion therapy?" Neal was incredulous. Had the Crows really believed that it was possible to reorient their son's sexuality? And by such monstrous means?

"Yes. I read up on it. There was no way I was going to let those people torture Nate. You know what they do, right?"

Neal nodded. He did. Conversion therapy was practised by some Christian fundamentalists. The cases he was familiar with had all taken place in the USA, but it was naïve to believe that it didn't go on elsewhere. The 'treatments' he'd read about included aversion therapy and electric shock. It was barbaric. He looked at Tom and saw that he, too, was disturbed by Aidan's claim.

Aidan gave Rose Plunkett an apologetic shrug. "Sorry," he said. Then, he turned to Neal. "I didn't kill Monty. I tried, but I made a mess of it. Twice. I'm not going down for a murder I didn't commit."

"The first time was in London?" Neal asked.

"Yes. That man, Soren Hunter, got in the way."

"And the second time?"

"I did everything I was supposed to do. I arrived at Northfields in costume so that I wouldn't stand out from all the other guests. I was supposed to wait for Monty to come out of the barn, but then I thought I saw him walking across the field. I wasn't sure what to do. I know now that I should have waited . . . but the place and timing were both perfect. It was already dark. There was no one else around. I jumped on him from the shadows. It was surprisingly easy.

He wasn't very strong. I dragged him into the outbuilding and slit his throat. I tried to do it quickly because I didn't really want him to suffer too much. Aubrey was the one who needed to suffer."

"When did you realise that you'd killed the wrong person?"

"After I'd put him in the ambulance. I hadn't really looked him in the face before then."

"Was Nick Winter already dead at that point?" Neal asked.

"Yes."

"Then why the overkill?" said Tom, who'd seen first-hand the multiple wounds that had been inflicted on Nick.

"When I saw that it wasn't Monty, I was filled with a terrible rage. A sort of explosive anger. I stabbed him over and over."

"You felt better then, did you?" Tom didn't mask his disgust. "*Cathartic* for you, was it?"

"No! Don't you understand anything? I'd killed the wrong person. Mutilating that man's body wasn't any sort of release. I'd messed up. Again. I'd killed an innocent person."

"Your parents forgave everyone involved in Nate's death. Why didn't you?" Neal asked.

Aidan met his eye. "Because I knew that if they were wrong about not being able to forgive Nate over his sexuality, they could be wrong about a lot of other things too. I'm not like them. I told you, I don't believe in anything. I'm like my grandfather. He can't stand all that religious crap. But he does believe in justice, and so do I. People should pay for the wrong they do. But nobody paid for poor Nate's murder."

Two things were bothering Neal. Aidan had said, *I did everything I was supposed to do.* Why not, *I did everything I'd planned to do?* Moreover, his tone had sounded petulant when he said it, like a small child trying to escape the blame. Maybe he thought fate or circumstance or the fact that Monty — who turned out to be Nick — had turned up early and from an unexpected direction was the real reason for his failure.

The other thing that bothered Neal involved that word *supposed* again. Monty Stratford was *supposed* to come out of the barn.

He was about to put both questions to Aidan, when he had a sudden flash of insight. *Someone else was involved.* The planner, the one who had told Aidan what he was *supposed* to do. How things were *supposed* to happen that night. This was someone who had known and loved Nate as much as Aidan and who shared his belief in vengeance, someone who knew that Soren would not be at Northfields on the day of the forties dance.

"You didn't act alone, did you, Aidan? There was someone else. Was it your grandfather?"

Aidan's face crumpled as he fought back his tears. Finally, he nodded.

"Yes."

"We're going to need his name," said Neal, although he'd already guessed.

"You already know it. His name is Charles. Charles Unwin. Grandpa Charles killed Monty."

CHAPTER TWENTY-EIGHT

"We'd better go over to the house," Bea said. "The police are already on their way. Charles, I don't expect they'll need to speak with you." She hoped he'd grasp that she was asking him politely to leave. Her phone rang. "Police," she mouthed to them both.

Bea listened for a few moments. "Oh!" A small exclamation escaped her lips. "Oh!" she said again. Then she made a big mistake. She looked directly at Charles.

Still grasping the spanner, Charles leapt across the workbench like a man half his age. Bea screamed as he stepped behind Aubrey and pressed the spanner against his throat.

"End the call!" he barked at Bea.

Bea obeyed. "You murdered our son," she said, with sudden insight. There hadn't been time to hear much more than a warning from DI Neal. He had said something about Charles being a very dangerous man. She'd been about to tell the inspector that he was being absurd. Then, Charles had performed his miraculous leap.

Aubrey's eyes widened as he grasped what she was saying. He tore at Charles's hands, trying to pull them away. Charles responded by tightening his grip, pressing until his knuckles showed white. He was older than Aubrey, but stronger and fitter. He had killed already. Bea didn't doubt he was ready to do so again. Aubrey's eyes bulged in their sockets and his face began to turn purple.

"Don't struggle, Aubrey!" cried Bea. "You'll only make things worse!"

"She's right, old chap," Charles mocked. His usually hesitant voice sounded different, more strident.

In fact, Charles's whole demeanour had altered. Gone was the slightly bumbling replica of Aubrey, the shy, amiable man who'd been co-opted into the family, the one who had sat at Bea's kitchen table devouring her home baking, declaring that her lemon drizzle cake was the best he'd ever eaten. He'd been a tonic for Aubrey, sharing his interests with enthusiasm. They'd all thought it a serendipitous coincidence that two such kindred spirits had arrived at the same village at a similar point in time. Bea saw now that it must all have been part of a plan.

A total stranger was holding a spanner to her husband's throat. A monster who had murdered her son. A wolf in sheep's clothing. But Charles was no wolf. He was a man who'd deceived them and repaid their trust and friendship by taking their beautiful son.

Why? Why would anyone do such a thing? Unless . . . The truth hit her. Bea understood. Charles had also lost someone he loved. It took only a beat for her to work out the rest. He was too old to be Nate's father. "You're Nate Crow's grandfather!" she gasped.

Her next thought was that her husband was unlikely to leave this shed alive. She was aware of her heart pummelling inside her chest, of her mouth going dry. She began to sweat. *Glow*, her grandmother had called it. *Men sweat, women glow,* she'd said. How ludicrous to remember such an absurd fact at a moment like this.

Charles nodded. "Nate was a great lad. He and I were close. I had to stop working for a couple of years when he was a toddler. Contracted ME after a bout of flu. It meant I got to spend more time with him than I did with the other grandchildren. My daughter used to drop him with my wife and me in the mornings. We bonded, I suppose.

"I knew what he was before his parents caught on. I knew they'd give him a hard time over it. Sure enough, they told him it was a sin to be *that way inclined*. Pressured him to *suppress his degenerate urges*. The ironic thing is, I was happy when he got that summer job. It meant he'd be out of their way. He was going to come and stay with us when he went to university."

"I'm sorry for your loss," Bea said. Surely the police were nearly here? If she could try to show some empathy with Charles, keep him talking, maybe there was still some hope of a favourable outcome. Charles was a father, a grandfather. But he had suffered great pain over the loss of his grandson and he wanted revenge. Suddenly all the insensitive comments he'd uttered over the past few days made perfect sense.

"You blamed Aubrey for Nate's death. You wanted him to feel what you've been feeling since his death . . ."

"Murder," Charles corrected her. "My grandson was murdered."

A strangulated growl rose from deep within Aubrey's throat. "Shut up," Charles said. "It's the truth. You got away with murder. All that crap about no one person being to blame. It was the flaw in your design that killed Nate."

Despite the current danger she and Aubrey faced, Bea was fascinated by Charles's transformation. Hatred had contorted his features, changed him into something not quite human. *The Beast of Northfields*. The thought made her sick to her stomach.

"I wanted your suffering to last for longer," Charles said, addressing Aubrey. "Just like mine. I've felt the pain of losing my grandson every single day since you murdered him. Pretending to be your friend has been the hardest thing I've ever done. Every time I looked at you, I felt like vomiting. I would have waited months after killing Monty before killing you. I would have savoured every tear you shed for your precious son."

He moved to the side slightly, so that he could look Aubrey in the eye as he spoke, still keeping the spanner in place over his throat. "Now I suppose I'll have to settle for the days I've had."

"It's not the same," Bea said. "Your grandson's death was an accident. No one set out with the intention of harming him. But you planned Monty's death. You and Aidan."

It was the wrong thing to say. Only minutes before, Charles had reiterated that Nate's death had been murder. Nothing she could say would persuade him otherwise. All she'd done was make things worse. Bea caught her breath as she realised her mistake. She sought out her husband's eyes. She held his gaze, her lips forming the words "I love you." She was absolutely convinced that Aubrey had only seconds to live.

* * *

"Yes, sir. I believe so, sir. Will do, sir."

"What is it, Ava?" PJ asked.

Ava had just taken a call from DI Neal. In front of Blue Stratford, she tried not to react to what he'd told her, but PJ was uncannily good at interpreting minute changes of emotion or expression.

"Is something wrong?" Blue Stratford asked. They were standing in the kitchen at Northfields. Ava and PJ had arrived only a few minutes earlier, and Blue had told them her mother had gone to fetch Aubrey, who was in one of the workshops with his friend Charles.

Shortly afterwards, the call had come through.

"Ava?" PJ pressed.

"No problem," Ava said. She looked at Blue. The young woman had seemed jumpy and ill at ease since she'd let them in — probably suffering from anxiety. She had a right to after all that had happened in the past few weeks.

She gave Blue a reassuring smile. "Just work stuff. Look, could you excuse us for a few minutes? I need to discuss something with my colleague."

"Okay," Blue agreed, uncertainly. "I'll just be in the living room." She looked up at the ceiling as though the living room had moved upstairs, then left the room, clutching Esmé tightly in her arms.

"Something's wrong," PJ said as soon as Blue was out of earshot.

"You could say."

"That was the chief on the phone, wasn't it?"

"Yes. Aidan Crow has just told him that Charles Unwin is his grandfather. Grandpa Charles killed Monty."

"Shit! We better get over there *now*."

"Listen, Peej, I'm going alone. You need to stay here."

"That's not—"

"There's a woman and a baby here. They need protection."

"Ava . . ."

"That's an order, DC Jenkins. Neal's called for backup from the local force. Make sure they know where to go when they get here." It was hard to know what would injure PJ more: being left out of the action or Ava pulling rank on her. It couldn't be helped. She gave PJ an apologetic smile as she headed for the door.

"Be careful," her friend and colleague called after her.

Ava went over it in her mind as she made her way swiftly to the workshop. Best-case scenario: Bea nagging Aubrey and Charles to put their tools down and accompany her back to the farmhouse. Worst-case scenario: a bloodbath.

It wasn't always easy to gauge what was required in a situation like this. Stealth or an element of surprise? Slide silently through the door or kick it in?

The door was ajar. Ava could hear voices but couldn't make out what they were saying; Bea — then Charles — then Bea again. It worried her that she could hear nothing from Aubrey. If only Soren were here, with his goddamn super powers. She could do with him covering her back right now.

Hoping the door wouldn't creak, she gave it a gentle push, just enough to make out more of the conversation. Charles was saying something about wanting to make someone suffer for a long time. Ava's heart beat a little faster. She risked a look and was alarmed at what she saw: Charles, holding a heavy-duty spanner to Aubrey's throat; Bea looking on in anguish.

Charles's back was to the door, giving her the advantage, but only if she could get up behind him without Bea reacting. That was unlikely. Between Bea catching sight of her and Charles catching on, there would be only seconds for her to act. She would need to be fast.

Her eyes darted around the workroom — tools everywhere, but none within reach. She looked up. In general, people forgot to look up. Pity; a lot was missed when you failed to see a whole dimension.

The nearest timber roof truss was a couple of feet away and about eight feet off the floor, a short skip and a jump — just like in after-school gym club.

Ava summoned a mental image of her body as a tightly coiled spring about to release. Holding it in her mind, she took in a deep breath, sprinted forwards, skipped and leapt into the air, straining for the truss.

Splinters tore into her palms as they grasped the rough wood. Ignoring the pain, she swung backwards, forwards, back again, gathering more momentum with every swing. Everything she had went into one final thrust forward. Then, she pulled upwards with all her strength and let go, launching her body into the air.

As she catapulted forwards, she was aware of a sudden hot pain searing through her right shoulder, a whoosh of air and a brief feeling of exhilaration before she crashed, feet first, into Charles Unwin's back, sending him sprawling across the floor of the barn.

Released from his grip, the spanner skittered away from him to end up at Bea's feet. Ava came to rest on top of Charles. She was relieved to see that Aubrey, who had been to the side of Charles, had escaped the worst of the impact. Wincing in pain, she stood up and twisted Charles's arm behind his back in a classic wristlock. Then she began to recite between gasping breaths: "Charles Unwin . . . I am arresting you . . . for the murder of Monty Stratford . . . You do not have to say anything . . . but it may harm your defence if you do not . . . mention when questioned something which you later rely on in court . . . Anything you do say may be given in evidence."

CHAPTER TWENTY-NINE

Charles swore at her and struggled to turn over. Ava restrained him with a flick of his wrist. He cried out in pain.

"Keep still if you know what's good for you," she cautioned.

Once Bea had recovered from her astonishment at Ava's daring rescue, she ran to her husband, who was spluttering and rasping, unable to speak. They clung to each other for a few moments, then Bea called for an ambulance, ignoring Aubrey's protestations that he didn't need one.

After that, she approached Ava and thanked her. "No problem," Ava said. "Though I don't think I fancy doing that again in a hurry. I was never as good at gymnastics as I was at other sports."

"What are you going to do with him?" Bea seemed hardly able to look at Charles. "The Beast of Northfields."

A growl emanated from Charles's mouth.

"You even sound like an animal," she said in disgust.

Ava was reminded yet again of Soren Hunter's quote from Shakespeare on the night of Nick and Samantha's murders. It didn't say a lot for *Homo sapiens*. She decided that the quote applied only to a certain sub-category of the species, of which Charles Unwin was a member. The one reserved for devils.

She asked Bea to take her phone from her back pocket and call PJ. "Ask her to bring some handcuffs from the car. Oh, and tell her we're all okay."

It wasn't strictly true for her, at least. Now that the adrenalin rush was receding, her shoulder was killing her.

By the time PJ arrived, she was in serious discomfort. It was a relief to straighten up when Charles had been safely restrained by the handcuffs.

Between them, Ava and PJ dragged him, protesting and spitting oaths, to his feet. One side of his face was bleeding from grazes sustained when he hit the stone floor. He claimed to have other, more serious injuries.

"The paramedics can check him out when they get here. He doesn't look like he's suffering that much to me." Ava pulled splinters from her hands and wiped the blood on her sleeve.

PJ eyed her with concern. "You'd better let them give you the once-over, too."

"I think I've pulled a muscle or a ligament or something. Hurts like holy hell. That'll teach me to ease up on my exercise regime."

"I didn't realise swinging from the rafters was ever part of your standard workout."

"I'm taking Aubrey back to the farmhouse," Bea said. Aubrey looked ashen and a necklace of purple bruises ringed his throat. He was leaning heavily on Bea, near to collapse.

"Let's put Unwin in the car," PJ said to Ava. "Then you can go and get cleaned up too." Ava opened her mouth to protest but PJ silenced her with a look. "That's an order, Sergeant Merry."

* * *

Soren watched from Blue's bedroom window as a procession of people made its way across the cobbled farmyard. Blue had warned him that two detectives had arrived to collect the evidence. He'd watched DS Merry walk off in the direction of the outbuildings. As the minutes ticked by and no one appeared, he began to feel a prickling sense of unease. Should he go downstairs and find out why it was taking so long? But he could hear Blue talking to the other officer, a woman whose voice he didn't recognise. He'd meant what he'd said to Bea about turning himself over to the police, but now wasn't the time to reveal himself. He needed to wait until he was no longer under suspicion. Even so, he would not be able to resist becoming involved if someone needed his help.

So, he waited and watched. Eventually, he heard the door bang and saw a young woman, presumably the other detective, running over to the unmarked police car parked outside. She opened the boot and rummaged inside, before producing a pair of handcuffs. What was going on?

"I don't know. No one's told me anything," Blue said when he hurried downstairs to join her. "DC Jenkins got a call from her colleague. She said she was needed in Dad's workshop. She said not to worry, that everyone was safe. But then I saw her taking some handcuffs out of the boot of the car."

"I saw that, too."

"Why did she need handcuffs? It's only Mum and Dad and Charles out there. Surely they can't be arresting any of them?"

Soren had met Charles Unwin on several occasions. He and Aubrey were superficially alike, but where Aubrey's eccentricity was genuine, Soren had found Charles's to be more of an artifice. It hadn't worried him particularly, but it did make him slightly wary.

He was deciding whether he should go over there and check if everyone was indeed safe when Aubrey and Bea appeared in the farmyard. Aubrey, head bowed, was leaning on his wife looking fragile. Close behind them were the two detectives, and Unwin sporting the cuffs.

Blue gasped at the sight of her father. Soren touched her shoulder. She tensed, but not with fear. Something seemed to pass between them. It was the first time he had touched her. He didn't want it to be the last. "He's okay, Blue. He's walking. That's got to be a good sign."

Blue laid her cheek on his hand, tilted her face and brushed his knuckles softly with her lips. Soren caught his breath.

"I'm going to find out what's been going on. Back soon. You need to go back upstairs." She smiled and left him.

Back upstairs, Soren sat on her bed, overcome with emotion. He should be happy; his instinct had been proven right. Blue wanted him. But to be with her, he would first have to go to prison. Did she want him enough to wait?

After a moment or two, he returned to the window. The detective he didn't recognise was standing outside the police car. Charles Unwin was in the back seat.

There were voices on the stairs. He heard Bea telling Aubrey to lie down until the ambulance arrived. Then she said, "Show DS Merry to the bathroom, Blue, and help her clean up those cuts on her hands. There's some antiseptic ointment in the cabinet above the sink." A few minutes lapsed then, before he heard Bea on the landing, saying she was going to make everyone some tea. He hoped she'd come into Blue's bedroom first, let him know what was going on, but he heard her going downstairs. It sounded like she was in a hurry.

He resumed looking out the window. A few minutes passed. Initially, he wasn't surprised when he saw Bea crossing the yard to join the young detective by the car. Probably going to ask her if she'd like a cup of tea. Then, with a start, he spotted the shotgun she was holding close by her right side. It was usually kept safely under lock and key.

"Oh no! Bea . . . *no!*" he murmured.

His feet touched only two or three steps as he hurtled down the stairs. He reached the farmyard in time to see Bea raise the shotgun to shoulder level.

The young detective immediately placed her body against the rear door of the car, arms outstretched, effectively turning herself into a human shield. She was brave, he'd give her that. And astute. She must have seen him but she gave no sign. Not that Bea would have noticed in the state she was in.

"Step aside," Bea instructed the woman. Her voice was shaking. The gun was shaking. Not a good situation.

"No." The young woman shook her head in defiance but looked terrified.

"I don't want to hurt you. It's him I want. My son's murderer."

"I can't let you do that."

Soren's thoughts raced. Bea was in the grip of powerful emotions: overwhelming feelings of love, grief and anger had triggered this reaction in her. He had to find a way to talk her down.

Earlier, Bea had told him that she didn't know how to deal with her anger, that she felt she could kill Monty's murderer without remorse. Soren didn't believe that she would when it came to the crunch but the gun was shaking violently in her hands, her finger hovering over the trigger. She could easily shoot someone by accident. He'd suspected on his return that she was psychologically unstable. She was probably not fully aware of what she was doing. He had seen people act like this in response to trauma before. And Bea had had her fair share of trauma lately.

It was risky to call out to her. If she jerked the gun in fright, it might go off. She would hear him if he crept up behind her. Either way, the outcome could be disastrous for the young policewoman.

"Bea . . ." He spoke as softly as he could. Bea swivelled her head, still keeping the gun on the white-faced detective. Charles, Soren noted, was nowhere in sight. He must have ducked down in the back of the car at the first sign of danger.

"Go away."

He wasn't sure if she recognised him. "Bea . . . listen to me."

"I don't want to listen!" Bea yelled at him. "I'm going to kill him."

"You're not like him, Bea. You're not a killer."

"We're not so different. I understand how he feels. He lost a grandson . . . I lost a son. He's had his revenge. Now it's my turn."

"Mrs Stratford . . ." It was the detective, her voice surprisingly calm. "Please don't do this. From what I've heard of your son, it's not what he would have wanted."

Soren nodded at her. Her instincts were good. She'd correctly intuited the way to reach Bea.

"She's right, Bea. Monty wouldn't want you to do this. He especially wouldn't want you to hurt an innocent young woman."

Bea seemed to be listening, but he could see in her eyes that she was still not herself. He had to reach her. "How would you live with yourself afterwards, Bea? You have a conscience. As soon as you fired that gun, you'd start to realise the enormity of what you'd done. You think it's justifiable at the moment, but taking a life . . . it changes you. It changed me, Bea. I've spent six years trying to atone for what I did out in Afghanistan. The guilt never goes away. I was telling the truth when I said Monty saved me as much as I saved him. Every time I help someone, I get some peace from my past." He heard his own voice break and his cheeks were hot and wet. He realised he was crying.

Bea was shaking even more violently now. The shotgun was like an extension of her arm, subject to any involuntary spasm, an accident waiting to happen.

She stared at him, frowning. The glazed look in her eyes was slowly clearing, to reveal confusion. She was pulling back from the brink of her temporary insanity. She began to lower the gun, but her muscles had been held taut for so long that they jerked wildly at the movement.

A shot rang out and Bea screamed. Soren rushed forwards. The young police officer, a look of sheer astonishment on her face, slid slowly down the rear door of the car to the ground. Blood blossomed over the crisp white material of her blouse, like the petals of a rose opening under time-lapse photography.

* * *

Ava was in the bathroom when she heard the shot. A moment before she had been trying not to wince as Blue dabbed ointment on her cuts.

"That was gunfire," she said, moving to the doorway. "Do you keep a gun in the house?"

"Yes. In the study downstairs. It's in a safe that's kept locked."

"Not anymore by the sound of it." Ava rubbed her hands on her jeans as she rushed from the room.

A chaotic scene awaited her in the farmyard. Backup had arrived at last, two uniformed officers in a police patrol car. Later, she learned they had been held up by a clumsily felled tree that had toppled the wrong way, blocking the road.

An ambulance had also drawn up and two green-suited paramedics were stepping down from the cabin.

But it was the scene in front of the police car that Ava locked onto: Bea Stratford, a horrified expression on her face, standing a few feet away from the vehicle; Charles Unwin peering uncertainly out of the rear door window; Soren Hunter kneeling on the ground beside PJ, who was slumped awkwardly against the car door.

"PJ! Oh no!" Ava sprinted to her. "How bad is it?" she demanded of Soren, who was pressing his rolled-up jumper against PJ's chest.

"These guys will know." He stood up to make way for the paramedics. Taking Ava gently by the arm, he pulled her aside.

"Wh-where's the gun?" she asked.

"I kicked it under the car. Look, I'm going to see if I can find one of those foil blankets in the ambulance for Bea. She's in shock." He eyed her closely. Ava nodded. She was too consumed with worry to care whether he might use this as an excuse to disappear again.

She stood by with mounting anxiety as the paramedics knelt beside her friend. Her chest felt heavy, her head light. She didn't hear when another car pulled into the farmyard, hardly registered Neal's presence beside her or Tom's gasp of dismay on catching sight of PJ.

Not until one of the paramedics got to his feet and gave a thumbs up did the tension holding her whole body hostage begin to release its grip.

The first thing she was aware of was the pressure of Neal's hand on her arm. "Ava? She's going to be okay. Why don't you come and sit in the car for a bit? You're shaking."

"I'm okay," she said. She pointed at Charles, who was sitting upright in the car again, now that the danger was over. "Did he kill Nick and Samantha as well?"

Before Neal could answer, one of the paramedics signalled that they were ready to go. Ava jumped aboard. She felt a sense of déjà vu, of things coming full circle. The case had begun and ended in the back of an ambulance.

CHAPTER THIRTY

Ava sat at PJ's bedside, peeling a banana from the bowl of fruit she'd brought with her. "All I could think of was Samantha Benrose lying on that four-poster bed in the yurt, stabbed in the heart. It was like I thought the same thing had happened to you, only I'd heard the gun going off and must have known on some level that you'd been shot. Weird."

"Hmm," said PJ. She ignored the fruit and reached instead for a giant box of chocolates on the table over her bed. As she popped one in her mouth, Ava pointed out that it was a strawberry heart.

"Will you stop it? I wasn't shot in the heart, only the shoulder. And the surgeon assures me there'll be no lasting damage."

"You looked like you'd been shot in the heart. Flipping blood all over the place."

"I've looked worse after a paintballing session. Though I must admit I'm getting a bit tired of people pointing real guns at me." PJ referred to their previous case when she had been in a hostage situation in a hospital room with an armed man.

They were both silent for a moment or two. Then PJ popped another chocolate in her mouth.

"Strange job we've got isn't it?" Ava said. "If you'd known when you woke up yesterday morning that a woman, traumatised by grief, would be pointing a shotgun at you in the afternoon, what would you have done?"

PJ didn't need to think. "Same as you, of course. Got out of bed and come to work."

Ava smiled. "When it goes right, it's the best job in the world, isn't it?" She took a bite of banana, kissed PJ on the cheek and left her to her box of chocolates.

* * *

Charles Unwin's anger seemed to have burnt itself out by the time Ava and Tom sat down with him to hear his account of the murder of Monty Stratford. He was eager to speak. Not because he was desperate to cooperate, Neal suspected, but because he had finally obtained what he described as 'justice' for the death of his grandson, Nate Crow, and he didn't care what happened to him next.

He had already confessed to killing Monty, but there were some details that still demanded an explanation. It was also important to hear his account of the extent of the collaboration that had taken place between him and his grandson. Neal had elected to watch the interview on CCTV.

"Aidan Crow has confessed to killing Nick Winter on the fourteenth of February this year," Ava said. "He has given us his version of the events of the evening leading up to their murders. We know that the two of you worked together. It's time for you to give us your version of what occurred that night."

"Might as well start from the beginning," Charles said.

"The bridge accident?"

Charles grimaced at the word *accident* but he nodded.

"You held Aubrey Stratford responsible for the bridge collapse that led to the death of your grandson, Nate Crow."

"Absolutely. There's no doubt in my mind that the man committed murder." Neal noted that Charles consistently avoided other terms such as *killing* or *manslaughter*, as though he believed that Aubrey had set out with the deliberate intention of causing his grandson's death. Ava frowned but didn't bother to correct Charles.

"When did you first decide that you wanted Aubrey to pay for what you believed he had done?"

"As soon as the report came out exonerating him of any blame."

"And, to be clear, you decided right from the start that killing Aubrey's son, Monty, was the best way of punishing Aubrey?"

Charles's reply was chilling. "I always intended to kill Aubrey at some point. A life for a life, so to speak — though, as you know, unlike my daughter and her idiot of a husband, I have no religious beliefs."

You can still have a conscience. Neal was struggling with understanding what kind of personality they were dealing with here. Charles Unwin was unlike anyone he'd met before.

"When I considered my options, I decided it would help my healing process more if I saw Aubrey suffer first. I wanted him to feel what I'd felt when my grandson was murdered."

Ava and Tom exchanged a look that wasn't difficult to interpret. They were probably thinking the same as Neal. Was Charles seriously suggesting that killing Monty to make Aubrey suffer was a form of *therapy*?

"When did your grandson, Aidan, come on board?" Ava asked.

"It wasn't long after the report — I was at my daughter's house for dinner. I was looking at Aidan while his parents were going on about the need to forgive. I could tell by his face that he didn't agree. So, I took him aside and asked him if he wanted to do something about the injustice to his brother."

"Just to be clear . . . was Aidan fully aware of what you were suggesting when you asked if he 'wanted to do something' about the injustice to his brother?"

"Oh yes." Charles leaned back in his chair and clasped his hands behind his head. "Aidan was never in any doubt that I meant to kill Monty, then Aubrey." There was a brief silence. Neal realised he was holding his breath.

"Did Aidan need much persuading?" Ava asked. "He didn't . . ." She cleared her throat. "He didn't try to dissuade you, or persuade you to seek some other way of . . . er . . . managing your feelings about Nate's death?"

"No. I was pleased that all the years of being indoctrinated by his parents hadn't turned him into an idiot, too." Charles gave a short laugh. "I got that wrong. The idiot bit, I mean."

"Why do you say that, Mr Unwin?"

"I'd have thought that was obvious. Aidan made two bungled attempts at killing Monty. In the end, I had to do it myself to make sure the job got done."

"Right. The first time was in Bloomsbury in London, wasn't it?"

"Yes. I'd told Aidan where Monty was going to be staying during his time in London. We researched the area together, worked out where the best place to strike would be. All Aidan had to do was watch and wait for the right moment." He threw his hands in the air. "I suppose on that occasion it wasn't entirely his fault. We didn't factor in Soren Hunter and his considerable gifts. Then, when Hunter followed Monty back to Northfields, I knew it was going to be more of a challenge to achieve our goal."

"Tell us about Aidan's second attempt on Monty Stratford's life."

"Well that took considerable planning. But eventually, the stars aligned in our favour. During one of my cosy chats over tea and cake with Bea, I learned about the forties dance, and that Soren Hunter was going to be away on the proposed date. Circumstances couldn't have been more favourable." His expression hardened. "All the more reason why I was furious enough with Aidan when it all went tits up to go off and kill that Benrose girl. God knows, I needed the release."

Neal leaned forward, studying Charles's face, looking for the merest trace of remorse, for Samantha's death, at least. Charles claimed to have been motivated by grief and a desire for justice. All Neal could see was a man who had lost touch with his humanity. A desire for justice had become an insatiable desire for vengeance. Almost a bloodlust. The Beast of Northfields was too good a name for him.

Ava's eyes flicked to the camera positioned high on the wall in the top left-hand corner of the room. She looked away quickly, but not before Neal caught the look of disgust and disbelief in her eyes. It mirrored his own. "Go on," she said.

Charles wiped his lips after taking a sip of water. "The plan was simple. I would take Monty aside at a pre-arranged time and ask him to go across to the farmhouse to see if I'd left my e-cigarette on the kitchen table. As soon as he left the barn, I would text Aidan and let him know. Monty would pass by the garage on his way. All Aidan had to do was wait for him there."

"And the plan went wrong?"

"There was nothing wrong with the plan. Aidan messed things up. He arrived early, before I'd even spoken to Monty. When he saw Winter walking across the field to the barn, Aidan assumed it was him. Rather than wait for my text, he decided to get on with it, the young idiot."

"Tell me why Aidan mistook Nick for Monty," Ava said. It was a piece of the puzzle that remained missing.

Charles shifted in his chair, a sign that he was becoming agitated. He seemed to want the interview finished quickly.

"Mr Unwin?"

"It was the costumes."

"What about the costumes?" Ava exchanged a look with Tom.

"Monty was supposed to be dressed like that spiv in *Dad's Army*, but he must have changed his mind — given his outfit to Winter. I would have told Aidan if he'd only waited for my text."

Ava nodded. "What happened next?"

"I received a text from Aidan asking me to come to the barn. When I got there, he was in a state. At least he'd had the presence of mind to drag the body into the ambulance, where it was less likely to be discovered. I helped him clear up a bit.

Then, I told him to get away from Northfields. It was only after I'd sent him off that I remembered Winter's girlfriend. I knew she'd come looking for him and raise the alarm."

"So, you went out to the yurt and killed her?"

"Yes. Bit of a risk, the time it took. I just had to hope that either no one missed me or they assumed that I'd gone out to vape." Ava remembered his dishevelled appearance when she'd first met him. No wonder he'd seemed harried.

"Why? Nick's body was going to be discovered anyway." Ava's voice shook with suppressed anger and Neal willed her to hold it together. Then he noticed something more alarming: Tom's right hand was clenched in a fist.

"I didn't want the Benrose girl raising the alarm before Aidan had time to get clear. If it hadn't been for those bloody kids, Winter's body wouldn't have been found until at least the following morning."

Tom jolted out of his chair. "You stabbed that woman fourteen times, you bastard!" He glared at Charles across the narrow table.

Ava pulled on the sleeve of Tom's jacket. "Sit down, Tom," she said quietly.

Tom sat down and remained rigid in his seat, his taut posture keeping the lid on his simmering anger. Neal forgave his momentary outburst.

Charles shrugged. "I was frustrated. And, as I mentioned before, I needed a release for my heightened emotions. Aidan and I had made a pact. He would kill Monty . . . I would kill Aubrey. I knew then that I would have to take care of both myself."

He paused as if for thought. "I regret the deaths of those young people. They just got in the way. I would have killed the girl quickly but I had to make it look like the same person had killed both victims. Aidan had lost control with Winter and stabbed him over and over, so I had to do the same." He looked directly at Tom. "Make you lot think you had some sort of crazy serial killer on your hands."

"Turns out we did," Tom said.

CHAPTER THIRTY-ONE

It had snowed in the night, a light fall that barely made a showing on the streets of Stromford. Out in the surrounding countryside, it was a different story. Field after field was dusted with white. Snow nestled in the deep furrows, untouched by the weak winter sunshine. A prolonged heavy frost was predicted, guaranteeing that it would be around for a while.

Ava and Neal pulled into the cobbled yard in front of the Stratfords' house. The whole place seemed unnaturally quiet after the recent turmoil.

At sixty-seven and facing a charge of double murder, Charles Unwin was unlikely to be freed from prison in his lifetime. Aidan Crow, who had at least shown some remorse — though, it seemed, only because he had killed the wrong person — would one day be released into the bosom of his family, who were committed in the meantime to praying for the salvation of his eternal soul.

Dr Toby Swallow was in the clear. He was expected to sue. None of the team felt good about his release. In Neal's opinion, it remained unclear exactly what his intentions had been towards Samantha and possibly Nick when he turned up at Northfields that night. The explanation he had provided had fallen far short of convincing. If Charles hadn't beaten Swallow to it, they might have been looking at a third murderer in the Northfields investigation.

Bea Stratford met them at the door and welcomed them into the cosy farmhouse kitchen. Aubrey was there, sitting at the table with his granddaughter cradled in the crook of his arm. If it troubled him that Esmé's father and great-grandfather were now convicted criminals, he showed no sign. Blue sat across from him, laptop open in front of her. She looked up and smiled at them.

Monty's body had finally been released by the coroner. They had buried him three days before. Neal attended the funeral with Ava, Tom and PJ, who had been released from hospital after two days, her arm in a sling. She was on sick leave for a few weeks. The first thing she had done on catching sight of Bea outside the church was to walk up and give her a hug.

There had been no question of Bea being charged. She had been diagnosed with a form of post-traumatic stress. She had not been fully aware of her actions between going down to make tea and being conscious of Soren's and PJ's voices. She had been shocked to discover that she was holding a shotgun.

One other person sat at the table: Soren Hunter, barely recognisable as the man they had met at the beginning of the investigation. Gone were the tangled blonde dreadlocks and the untamed beard. The new look suited him. He still had a slightly haunted look in his eyes, which Neal suspected would never fully disappear. Soren was not the sort of person to lay the ghosts of his past to rest completely.

Just after Unwin's arrest, Soren had voluntarily given himself up. Neal had driven him to the nearest army base, where, with reluctance, he had handed him over to the Military Police.

On the way, Soren had told him about his experiences as a soldier in Afghanistan. It was as they had guessed. Soren had joined up as a young man because he wanted to help people, but had gradually become disillusioned as he learned more about the background to the conflict there. He had witnessed an appalling amount of suffering among the civilian population, for which he felt personally responsible. In the end, he'd listened to his conscience.

"When the time came for me to report back for my next tour, I decided to disappear. I moved from Lancashire to the streets of London. No one looks at the homeless except people like Pixie. And people like Pixie aren't interested in how you ended up there, only how you can be helped."

Neal smiled, thinking of the quirky hostel manager with her dislike of clutter and hot-desking. He hoped she'd have a desk of her own one day.

"So, you found another way of protecting people — by becoming a hero of the streets, looking out for the homeless and the vulnerable?"

"I was never a hero." The light in Soren's eyes that was sometimes a twinkle and sometimes a glint flashed dangerously. "Never call me that."

Neal couldn't help wondering if Hunter's decision not to turn himself in and face trial for desertion years ago had been motivated by his desire to atone for his time in Afghanistan. "I did things out there that I'm not proud of," he'd said. Despite Soren's admission, Neal felt certain that he had never knowingly acted against his conscience. He seemed to have emerged from his experiences with his basic humanity intact.

Soren would face a court martial, but it was unlikely that he would receive a prison sentence. In the meantime, he had been released on bail. After the court martial, he would be discharged from the army.

The purpose of Neal and Ava's visit that morning was to return Monty's personal effects. It had not been easy for the family to reconcile the Charles they'd known as their friend and neighbour with the monster who had murdered their son and Samantha Benrose. Aubrey had been particularly distressed.

"Who could have guessed Charles was Nate's grandfather?" Bea said.

"I'm afraid Unwin began planning his revenge soon after Nate's death," Neal said. "He moved here so that he could inveigle his way into your lives — particularly Aubrey's. His interest in World War Two memorabilia was the only genuine thing about him. It made it easier for him to become Aubrey's friend."

Bea patted Aubrey's hand. "He was always here, accepting our friendship and hospitality. We treated him like a member of the family. He certainly took us for fools."

"Hearts and minds," Soren said.

"What will you do now?" Neal asked him.

Soren looked at Blue shyly. "Blue's asked me to be her partner in the brewing business."

"And I've asked him to be part of the glamping business," Bea added.

"He knows his way around an engine," Aubrey said. "Be a help to me with the vintage motors."

"Tinkering." Bea gave her husband a fond look.

Blue smiled at Soren. "You're going to be busy."

* * *

"It'll be good to have a weekend off," Ava said, later that day. They were leaving work, making for their respective cars. "It's so much more relaxed now it's just me and Ollie, without my mother fussing around."

"Yes. Long time since I've had a weekend off, too." Neal's hand paused on the door handle of his car.

"Ava . . . about that dinner I mentioned when we were in Norfolk that time." He cleared his throat. "Are you free tomorrow evening?"

"Tomorrow? I thought Maggie and Jock weren't due back until Monday."

"They're not," he said. "And Jock's parents are taking Archie to Legoland this weekend. I'm free until Sunday afternoon."

"Well . . ." Ava met his gaze. "In that case . . ."

THE END

ALSO BY JANICE FROST

DS MERRY & DI NEAL SERIES
Book 1: DEAD SECRET
Book 2: DARK SECRET
Book 3: HER HUSBAND'S SECRET
Book 4: THEIR FATAL SECRETS
Book 5: DIRTY SECRETS
Book 6: MURDEROUS SECRETS

FREE KINDLE BOOKS

Manufactured by Amazon.ca
Bolton, ON